DISCOVERY

CONTENTS

1 INVENTORS

49 SCIENTISTS

97 EXPLORERS

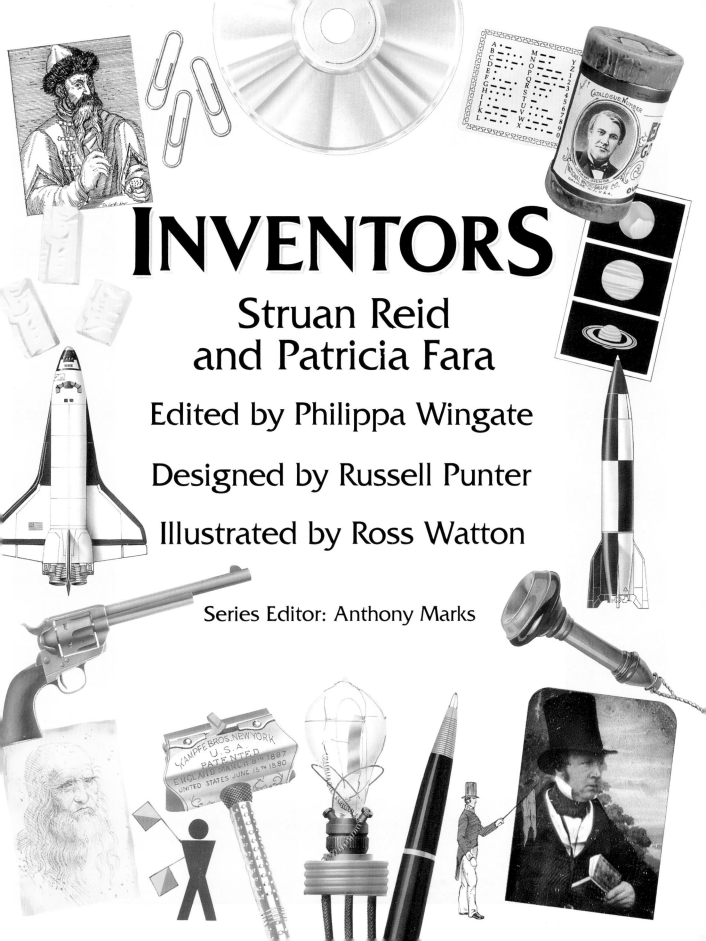

INVENTORS

Struan Reid
and Patricia Fara

Edited by Philippa Wingate

Designed by Russell Punter

Illustrated by Ross Watton

Series Editor: Anthony Marks

Contents

Introduction

Inventors and inventions

An inventor is someone who discovers or produces a useful object or process that did not exist before. This section of the book is about the lives and work of the people who invented many of the things we take for granted today.

Many inventions enable people to do things they could not do before; others help them to work more efficiently. Some inventions, like the telephone or television, have had a dramatic effect on the way people live. But while others may seem less revolutionary, they have had equally important consequences. For example, the invention of the harness for horses changed the course

A "Candlestick" telephone (1905)

of history, because it allowed people to use horses for long journeys and to pull heavy loads.

A stone carving showing a chariot pulled by horses in harness (7th century BC)

Modern invention

Modern inventions are rarely the product of a single inventor's efforts. For example, no single individual can claim that he or she alone invented the silicon chip. Thousands of people have played a useful role in its development and manufacture, and many thousands more have improved its design.

A silicon chip

Many companies employ teams of people to work on new ideas. For example, the managing director of the Japanese company Sony wanted a device which would allow him to listen to music while he played golf. As a result, a team of company technicians developed the Sony Walkman, the first personal stereo.

A personal stereo

Continuous invention

Many inventions have taken several centuries to develop into their modern forms, so it is impossible to give a precise date for their creation. The history of the invention of the piano, for example, lasts more than 2,000 years. Experts have calculated that more than 2,000 separate inventions and developments have contributed to the construction of modern pianos.

A dulcimer, one of the forerunners of the piano, shown in a 16th-century tapestry

Patenting inventions

When an inventor produces a new device, he or she usually applies for a patent. This is a document which gives the inventor the exclusive right to make and sell the invention.

Some people died rich and famous having made a fortune from selling their inventions, others died in poverty, unrecognized for their achievements. In this section of the book, you can read about the lives of both the successful and the unsuccessful inventors.

Whitcomb Judson's 1893 patent for the zip fastener

Dates

Some of the dates in this book are from the period before the birth of Christ. They are indicated by the letters BC. Early dates in the period after Christ's birth are indicated by the letters AD. Some dates are preceded by the abbreviation *c*, which stands for "*circa*", the Latin for "about". It is used by historians to show they are unsure exactly when a particular event took place.

About *Inventors*

Each chapter in this section of the book is a history of inventors and inventions in a particular field, such as medicine, communications and transport. On pages 46-47 a chart outlines the main developments described in the book.

Beside the title of every chapter, you will find a small picture or cartoon relating to an invention on those pages. You could try guessing what they are. There is a list of the answers on page 148.

Early inventions

As soon as the first people appeared on the Earth, about half a million years ago, they started to use materials like stone and wood to make their lives more comfortable. These people were the first inventors.

It is difficult to find information about early inventors. We can often only guess at how early people accomplished many of the things they did. For example, we are still unsure exactly how the Ancient Egyptians built their pyramids so accurately.

Some historians think that workers must have pulled huge stone blocks up ramps to make the Great Pyramid.

A sloping ramp leading to the top of the pyramid

Isolated inventions

Before roads and ocean-going ships were built, many communities were isolated. Individual inventors devised their own solutions to common problems, such as how to build solid houses, kill animals or prepare food.

Certain solutions appeared independently in different places around the world, like China, South America and Egypt. But some inventions used by one group of people simply did not exist anywhere else. For centuries the use of gunpowder and the manufacture of silk were only known in China. Inventions only became more universal when people began to travel, trading goods and exchanging ideas.

Early building

The earliest stone buildings were constructed with flat roofs supported by stone beams on upright posts. Roman builders, using new inventions like arches and concrete, were able to build larger, stronger buildings like the one shown here. Many of these buildings still survive today.

Building a Roman villa

Pillars

An arch under construction

The wheel

No one knows exactly when or where the wheel first appeared. Most scholars believe that it was first used by potters in about 3500BC, either in Mesopotamia (modern Iraq) or in the central or eastern parts of Europe. The first known transport wheel appears in a Mesopotamian picture dated to c.3200BC. The picture shows a cart with solid wheels held together by metal brackets.

Wheeled transport was not used in America before the arrival of European explorers at the end of the 15th century. This may have been because there was a lack of suitable domesticated animals for pulling carts.

The development of the wheel

Mosaic of 3200BC showing wheels held together by brackets

Wheel in three sections, fixed by brackets	Lighter spoked wheel from Egypt, 1500BC	Greek eight-spoked wheel, c.400BC	A Roman wheel of c.AD100	Wheel designed by Leonardo da Vinci, late 15th century	An early motor car wheel

The arch

An arch is made of wedge-shaped stones, held together by pressure. Arches which date from c.3000BC have been found at Ur, in Iraq. The Assyrians and Babylonians also used arches. The 6th-century Ishtar Gate of Babylon is made of sun-dried bricks. The Romans used arches to construct tall buildings like amphitheatres or aqueducts.

Constructing an arch

A wooden frame in the shape of an arch was constructed between stone columns.

Wedge-shaped stones were then built on the frame. The weight of the stones held them in place.

Arches were very heavy, so supports called buttresses were used to take the strain.

Strong walls were formed from two brick walls filled with concrete.

Once the concrete had dried, another wall could be built on top in the same way.

Tiles and gutters of baked clay were stamped with the name of the factory at which they were produced.

Central heating

The Romans were masters of home comforts and devised a central heating system in the 1st century AD. It was called the hypocaust and was mainly used to heat public baths, but in cold climates it was also used to heat houses. This Roman invention was forgotten in the West when the Roman Empire collapsed in the 5th century.

A Roman hypocaust

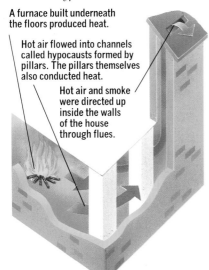

A furnace built underneath the floors produced heat.

Hot air flowed into channels called hypocausts formed by pillars. The pillars themselves also conducted heat.

Hot air and smoke were directed up inside the walls of the house through flues.

Writing

In about 3200BC, the Sumerians of Mesopotamia were the first people to write. Their script used pictures to represent words and is known as "pictographic writing".

Some early pictographic symbols and their meanings.

Bird   Fish   Ox   Grain   To stand or go

A stone tablet carved with pictographic writing (c.3000BC)

Five hundred years later, nearby people, like the Babylonians, Persians and Assyrians, had adapted this kind of writing into a type known as cuneiform (meaning "wedge-shaped"). They used a reed with a triangular-shaped end to make inscriptions in clay.

How to make clay tablets with cuneiform inscriptions

The cuneiform symbols for ox and grain

Ox

Roll a piece of clay into a pancake and then cut it into small squares.

Using sandpaper, shape the end of a stick into a triangular point.

Press the reed into the surface of the clay to form the symbols.

Grain

By about 1300BC, at Ugarit in Syria, the first alphabet had evolved from cuneiform. It contained 32 letters, each representing a single sound, which could be joined together to form a word. The Greeks adopted this system, which is the ancestor of the European alphabet.

In Egypt, in 3000BC, a writing system known as hieroglyphs was introduced. This used symbols to represent words, sounds or letters.

These Egyptian hieroglyphs spell out the name of the Egyptian queen Cleopatra

C   L   E   O   P   A   T   R   A

Money

Throughout history, many different things have been used for barter and exchange, such as copper bars, precious stones, shells and cattle. But as trade between nations increased, a standard, easy form of exchange was needed. The invention of money enabled deals to be carried out quickly using coins of an agreed value.

The first proper coinage was introduced in 700BC by King Gyges of Lydia (now in Turkey). The Lydian coins were made of a metal called electrum (a natural mixture of gold and silver) and were stamped with the king's emblem.

The king's emblem was a lion and a bull.

A mark was imprinted on the coin.

Two sides of a coin issued in about 550BC by King Croesus of Lydia

Measuring instruments

People have always attempted to measure quantities such as length, weight and time. Countless inventors, many of them now unknown or forgotten, have gradually improved the design of measuring instruments. Today, there are even devices that can measure things which are not visible to the naked eye, such as subatomic particles.

Early clocks

Sundials were the first method of charting the passing of time. In ancient times, water clocks and candles were employed, but they were never very accurate.

A 13th-century water clock, built for an Arab sultan

Every half hour this bird whistled.

This man made the falcon beside him release a pellet into the dragon's mouth.

The dragon began to wriggle. The pellet hit a gong inside the elephant before it fell into a bowl.

The elephant driver beats a rhythm every half hour

A new way of measuring time

The first mechanical clock, driven by weights, was made by Gerbert, a French monk who in 999 became Pope Sylvester II. Many further changes were introduced until, in 1300, fairly accurate mechanical clocks were used in Europe. A device called a verge escapement turned the hands.

The verge escapement of a mechanical clock

A balance moved back and forward, controlling the speed of the ticking.

The crown wheel

The verge escapement consisted of a crown wheel and balance, connected by gears to the clock hands. As the weight fell, it set the crown wheel moving around in jerks or ticks. This made the clock hands move around too.

Clock hands

Weight

Pendulums

In 1656, Christian Huygens (1629-95), a Dutch physicist, invented the first accurate pendulum clock. Its design was based on an idea suggested by Galileo Galilei (1564-1642; see page 8). Galileo had observed that pendulums always swing back and forward at regular intervals. Huygens developed a way of keeping a pendulum swinging while linking its movement to the hands of a clock dial through a series of toothed wheels.

A recon-struction of Galileo's pendulum escapement

Pivoted lever

Forked arm

Toothed wheel

Cog wheels

The swing of the pendulum made the pivoted lever and the forked arm turn the toothed wheel.

The movement of the toothed wheel turned the cog wheels.

The pendulum always took an identical period of time to swing backward and forward.

A new kind of map

A map is a two-dimensional representation of the Earth's surface. But the Earth is spherical, which means that the shapes on early maps are distorted. In 1569, Gerardus Mercator (1512-94), a Flemish geographer and mapmaker, introduced a more accurate way of drawing maps than had previously been used. He drew the world as though it was a cylinder divided up by parallel horizontal and vertical lines, called lines of latitude and longitude. In 1585, Mercator published an atlas of maps drawn using his new system. His method is still used in atlases today.

A map of Africa from Mercator's Atlas

Under pressure

Evangelista Torricelli (1608-47), was the son of an Italian textile worker. He experimented with vacuums and pressure. In 1643, he produced a device, now known as a mercury barometer, which is used to measure atmospheric pressure.

How Torricelli's barometer worked

A bowl was half-filled with mercury. The open end of a test tube full of mercury was placed under the surface of the mercury in the bowl.

Some of the mercury in the tube ran out into the bowl. As a result the level of the mercury in the tube fell.

The height of the column of mercury in the tube was directly affected by the magnitude of atmospheric pressure. It could, therefore, be used to measure atmospheric pressure.

Torricelli and his barometer

Measuring temperature

For thousands of years, people measured temperature by noting the expansion of a liquid as it is heated. But by the 17th century there were over 30 scales of measurement, so comparing readings from different thermometers was difficult. In 1742, Anders Celsius (1701-44), a Swedish astronomer devised a standard scale for the measurement of temperature. It is called the Celsius scale and contains a hundred degrees. Each degree is one hundredth of the temperature difference between the boiling and freezing points of water.

One of the first thermometers to use the Celsius scale

Absolute zero

Jacques Charles (1746-1823), a French physicist noticed that when a gas cooled, its volume contracted by 1/273 for every fall of one degree Celsius in its temperature. William Thomson (1824-1907), another physicist, suggested that at −273°C, the energy of motion of gas molecules must have reached zero. Thomson, who was awarded the title Baron Kelvin of Largs for his achievements, devised a new temperature scale in which 0°K (which is called absolute zero) is the equivalent of -273°C. Known today as the Kelvin scale, it helps scientists measure very low temperatures.

Detecting radiation

In 1908, German-born physicist Hans Geiger (1882-1945), invented a hand-held machine used to detect radiation in the air. It is now called the Geiger counter. When radiation is present, the machine makes a clicking noise. The level of radiation is counted and shown on a dial.

An early Geiger counter

Low pressure gas in a copper cylinder

Wire inside the counter

When radioactive particles entered the tube, an electric pulse passed between the wire and the cylinder's walls. The pulses were detected by a counter.

Instruments of observation

eople have always wanted to see things more closely than is possible with the naked eye. The first magnifying lenses were made about 700BC in the Middle East. Since that time, developments have helped people to see the world in greater detail. Today, the electron microscope can even make the invisible visible.

An astronomical lens

One of the first people to make a practical telescope was Hans Lippershey (c.1570-1619), a Dutch optician. It consisted of a long tube with a magnifying lens at each end. The combined effect of two lenses enabled him to see distant objects in greater detail than with the naked eye.

A controversial view

Galileo Galilei (1564-1642), born in Pisa, Italy, studied medicine and became a university lecturer. In 1592, he built a telescope which magnified objects about 30 times. He used it to examine the Moon and the movement of the planets.

Galileo using his telescope

In 1632, Galileo wrote *Dialogue Concerning the Two Chief World Systems*. He supported the views of Copernicus, a Polish monk, who claimed that the Earth revolved around the Sun. This idea clashed with the teachings of the Roman Catholic Church, which said that the planets revolved around the Earth. Galileo was convicted for holding a view contrary to the teachings of the Church.

Eyepiece

Galileo's telescope of c.1609

Reflecting telescopes

In 1668, an English scientist named Isaac Newton (1642-1727) built a new kind of telescope, using mirrors as well as lenses to direct the rays of light from an object onto the observer's eye. This reduced the blurring which had previously been caused by imperfections in the lenses. This is known as a reflecting telescope.

Newton's design was improved by William Herschel (1738-1822), a German astronomer, who studied astronomy in England. He incorporated giant mirrors with diameters of 1.2m (4ft), which collected more light and enabled him to see very distant objects. With this powerful new telescope, Herschel and his sister Caroline (1750-1848) studied the skies. They discovered the planet Uranus and many new stars and comets.

Newton's reflecting telescope (1668)

Light rays from the object were collected by a mirror at the base of the telescope.

Eyepiece

This mirror directed the light to the eyepiece

The telescope was mounted on a wooden ball so that it could be swivelled.

Herschel's giant reflecting telescope

Telescope tube made of iron

The observer stood at the top of the telescope and communicated observations to an assistant in a hut at the base through a speaking tube.

Galileo made sketches of his observations of the Moon. They showed the mountains and "seas" that he had seen.

Examining small objects

The first microscope was probably invented by Hans Janssen, a Dutchman, at the end of the 16th century. It contained one lens that produced a magnified image of an object, and a second lens that enlarged the magnified image.

A prolific inventor of scientific instruments, the Englishman Robert Hooke (1635-1703), built an instrument that produced clearer images than Janssen's device. In 1665, Hooke published a book called the *Micrographia*, which contained beautiful engraved plates of his drawings of objects seen through his microscope.

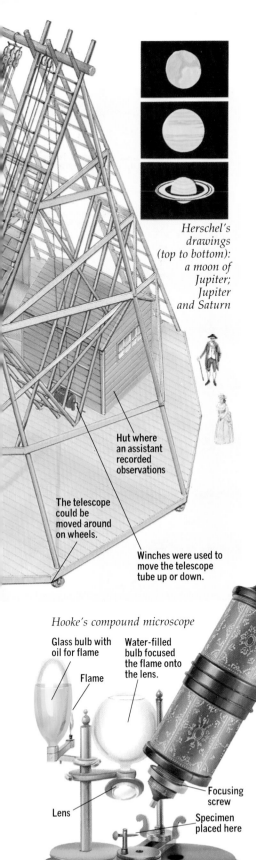

Herschel's
drawings
(top to bottom):
a moon of
Jupiter;
Jupiter
and Saturn

Hut where
an assistant
recorded
observations

The telescope
could be
moved around
on wheels.

Winches were used to
move the telescope
tube up or down.

The electron microscope

All matter is made of atoms which are so tiny that they cannot be seen under ordinary microscopes. In 1933, two German scientists, Max Kroll and Ernst Ruska, developed an electron microscope which could produce an image of an atom. When tiny particles of atoms, called electrons, are fired at a specimen, it too emits electrons. These produce a three-dimensional image of the specimen on a screen.

An electron telescope

Electron emitter

Beam of electrons

Magnets focus the
electrons

*Bacteria cells
magnified 5,000
times*

Electrons emitted by
the specimen produce
a magnified image on
this screen.

Eyepiece

Radar

Robert Watson-Watt (1892-1973), a Scottish physicist, first developed a system called radar (Radio Detecting and Ranging). The system sends out radio waves, and any object they meet reflects them back. The pattern of reflections indicates how far away the object is, its speed and direction.

Watson-Watt first used radio waves to detect storms which were endangering aircraft. In 1935, he built a long-range radar system which could detect aircraft up to 64km (40 miles) away. The system was vital in helping Britain to defend itself from air attack during World War II.

*A radar image
of a hurricane
near Mexico*

*A radar station built on
the British coast
during World
War II*

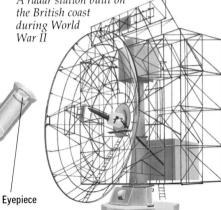

Hooke's compound microscope

Glass bulb with
oil for flame

Water-filled
bulb focused
the flame onto
the lens.

Flame

Lens

Focusing
screw

Specimen
placed here

Spectacles and contact lenses

In 1280, an Italian physicist named Salvino degli Armati (1245-1317) is thought to have made the first pair of glasses. These contained two convex lenses, which magnified objects so that people could see them more easily.

Leonardo da Vinci (see page 45) experimented with the idea of contact lenses. In *Codex on the Eye*, he described a water-filled tube sealed with a lens which could correct eye defects. Da Vinci's idea was tested in the 18th century by Thomas Young and John Herschel (son of William Herschel). A layer of transparent gel was put on Herschel's eye to correct his eye defect.

*Contact lenses made
in about 1930*

*An illustration of hand-
held spectacles (1493)*

Manufacturing and automation

By the end of the 18th century, more people were starting to work in huge factories, manufacturing a variety of goods. The introduction of new inventions led to great increases in the production of cloth, iron, pottery and coal. This period of rapid technological change is called the Industrial Revolution.

Increasing output

Cloth making was the first manufacturing process to be greatly altered by new inventions. In 1733, John Kay (1704-c.1764), an English weaver, mechanized weaving when he invented the "flying shuttle". It doubled the amount of cloth a person could produce in one day.

In 1764, another English weaver named James Hargreaves (c.1722-78) invented the Spinning Jenny.

The Spinning Jenny

Spindles of spun yarn

Wheel turned by hand

Eight spindles could be worked by a hand-turned wheel, so a single operator could spin eight threads. In 1771, Richard Arkwright (1732-92) built a water-powered spinning machine that produced stronger thread than the Spinning Jenny.

Arkwright's spinning machine

Unspun fibre

The spun thread

A bobbin

This wheel operated the machine

A steam-driven toy

The use of steam as a source of power can be traced back as far as the 1st century AD, to a Greek engineer named Hero of Alexandria. He designed a toy consisting of a metal sphere filled with water. The sphere was heated over a fire. When the water inside it boiled, steam began to escape from two holes on opposite sides of the sphere. This produced a force that caused the sphere to rotate.

Hero considered his invention no more than a clever toy.

Steam engines

In the 18th century, giant steam engines were used to power machinery. The first was made in 1698, by Thomas Savery (c.1650-1715), an English engineer. Inside the engine, steam from a boiler passed into the cylinder. A plunger, called a piston, was forced out of the cylinder by the pressure of the steam. Cold water was sprayed onto the cylinder to cool and condense the steam. This produced a much lower pressure inside the cylinder, causing the piston to fall again. His engine was used to pump water out of flooded mines.

Later, Thomas Newcomen (1663-1729), another Englishman, improved Savery's machine, which often broke down. In Newcomen's machine the piston was chained to one end of a wooden crossbeam. The pumping machinery was attached to the other end.

Newcomen's steam engine

Crossbeam

Piston

Cylinder

Boiler

In 1777, an engineer named James Watt (1736-1819) designed an engine with a separate condenser, into which steam from the cylinder was passed and cooled. This allowed the engine to be kept hot, reducing fuel consumption and saving time.

Watt's steam engine became the main source of power in Britain's textile mills.

Coal was burned in a furnace to heat the water in the boiler.

A steam-pipe carried steam from the boiler to the cylinder.

Boiler

The cylinder contained a piston. The piston was driven up and down by changes in pressure inside the cylinder.

Here in the condensing system, exhaust steam from the cylinder was turned back into water. The water was then lifted into a separate tank, and pumped back to the boiler.

Exhaust steam

Water

Tank

Water pumped into the boiler

Sewing machines

The first sewing machine was designed in 1830, by a French tailor named Barthélemy Thimonnier. A wheel, powered by a foot pedal, raised and lowered a needle. It could sew 200 stitches in a minute, compared to the 30 stitches of a tailor. But many tailors feared they would lose their jobs, and an angry mob destroyed 80 of the machines.

Elias Howe (1819-67), an American engineer, also developed a sewing machine. But to support his family he was forced to sell his invention for a small sum of money. Later he found that Isaac Singer (1811-76) was selling sewing machines based on his original design. In 1854, Howe launched a law case against Singer, in which he won the right to receive payment for all sewing machines sold in the USA.

A cutaway picture of a modern sewing machine

Needle thread

Connecting belt

Needle

Presser foot

Bobbin hook

Thimonnier using his sewing machine, patented in 1830

An early sewing machine

Needle

How a sewing machine makes a stitch

The needle pierces the cloth.

A hook on the bobbin catches the needle thread.

The needle thread is looped around the bobbin.

The needle rises and pulls the stitch tight.

Robots

A robot is a machine that can be instructed to perform tasks. One of the first robotic devices was the automatic pilot, invented in 1913, by an American named Elmer Sperry (1860-1930). He developed instruments that were sensitive to a plane's movements. If the plane veered off a certain flight path, the automatic pilot adjusted the controls to correct its direction.

In the 1940s, mechanical arms were used to handle dangerous chemicals behind protective screens. Today increasingly precise robots are being built. Some can be given verbal commands and respond to their surroundings.

A cutaway picture of a robotic arm used for welding

Beam

The up-and-down movement of the piston was converted into rotary (rotating) motion by a beam and a device called a sun and planet gear.

Sun and planet gear

Flywheel

This belt transferred the movement of the fly wheel to power machinery

This pump supplied cold water to the condensing system.

These hoses supply water, air and electricity to the welding gun.

The welding gun is attached to the robotic arm.

This joint allows the arm to move up and down.

This joint called the "elbow" allows the arm to rotate.

These wires supply electricity to the robot.

This is "Wabot", a Japanese-made robot with two legs. It was built to study how robots can walk and balance.

11

Motor cars

Daimler's car

The first horseless road vehicles, built at the end of the 18th century, were huge steam-powered carriages. In 1860, the invention of the internal combustion engine (see below) made smaller, fuel-driven vehicles a possibility. Since then thousands of inventions have contributed to the development of faster, cheaper, readily available motor cars. It is estimated that there are almost 500 million motor cars on the road today.

A steam-driven carriage built in 1770 by French army engineer Nicolas Cugnot

A four-stroke cycle

Air and gas

Piston

Cylinder

Spark

Exhaust valve

1) The "induction" stroke – A piston descends, sucking a mixture of air and gas into the cylinder.

2) The "compression" stroke – The piston is pushed back up, compressing the gas in the top of the cylinder.

3) The "power" stroke – An electric spark ignites the gas at the top of the cylinder. It explodes, pushing the piston down.

4) The "exhaust" stroke – The piston rises again, forcing the burned gases out through an exhaust valve.

Daimler

In 1885, Gottlieb Daimler (1834-1900) and Wilhelm Maybach (1846-1929), two German engineers, developed a lightweight, high speed engine to run on petrol. They attached it to a wooden bicycle, and created the first motorbike. By 1889, they had produced the first four-wheeled motor car. Its wheels were turned by a belt-drive mechanism.

It had a steering column and a four-speed gearbox. Daimler also developed the carburettor, which mixes the air and petrol vapour that ignites in the cylinders and makes an engine run more efficiently. Daimler set up the Daimler Motor Company in 1890, which he then merged with the Benz Company in 1926 to form Mercedes–Benz. (Mercedes was the name of the daughter of one of Daimler's backers.)

Horseless carriages

The first lightweight engine was built in 1860 by Étienne Lenoir (1822-1900), a Belgian engineer. It is called an internal combustion engine because a mixture of air and coal gas was burned in a tube (called a cylinder) inside the engine. The power produced by the burning gases moved a piston which, in turn, rotated the wheels. Lenoir attached his engine to an old cart and drove down a dirt track in a wood.

In 1876, Nikolaus Otto (1832-91), a German engineer, produced a "four-stroke" engine, which takes its name from the four movements made by the piston inside the engine (see panel). Most modern motor car engines are based on Otto's design.

Lenoir's gas engine

Benz

The first motor car ever sold was produced by Karl Benz (1844-1929). He developed an internal combustion engine which ran on petrol. The vehicle he attached it to had three wheels and a horseshoe-shaped steel frame. Benz tested his vehicle in 1885, and it reached a speed of 14.5km / h (9mph).

Benz's petrol-driven car

A steering handle turned the front wheel.

Leather seat for driver and passenger

Seat spring

Hand brake

Fuel tank

Wheels with solid rubber tyres

The engine was fixed behind the seat.

A chain transmitted power from the engine to the back wheels.

Mass production

At the beginning of the 20th century, cars were still extremely expensive because they were built by hand for individual customers. Henry Ford (1863-1947), born into a farming family in Michigan, USA, believed that reducing the price of cars would greatly increase public demand for them. In 1903, he set up his own business called the Ford Motor Company. He standardized the components from which cars were constructed and introduced the idea of a moving assembly-line to build his cars. A car was moved from one worker to the next, each of whom performed a simple task in its construction.

The first mass-produced car, the Ford Model T, rolled off the production line in 1908. By 1913, 1,000 cars were being produced each day.

The Ford Model T

- Roof could be folded back
- Windscreen could be opened
- Steering wheel
- Horn

Petrol tank

Battery

The carburettor mixed petrol and air to create a gas that exploded when compressed in the cylinders.

Wooden spoked wheels with inflatable rubber tyres

Front axle. Behind this was the steering arm which connected with the steering wheel and directed the front wheels.

Fan to keep the engine cool

Starting handle

The assembly line of the Ford Model T

The chassis was a strong steel frame on which the major parts of the car - the wheels, engine and mechanical parts - were attached.

The body unit was assembled separately. Once it was ready it was brought down a chute to a hoist.

The body was picked up by the hoist and lowered onto the chassis with the engine already fitted and bolted into place.

All the accessories were fitted, such as the windscreen, headlights and mudguards.

Once the car was complete it was ready to be driven away. Using mass production methods, a car could be assembled in as little as one hour.

Racing cars

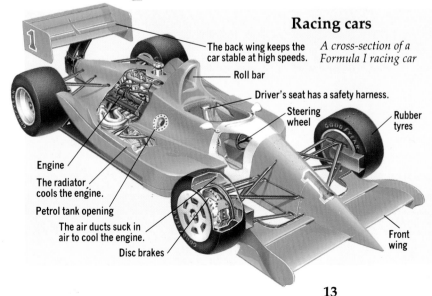

The back wing keeps the car stable at high speeds.

Roll bar

Driver's seat has a safety harness.

A cross-section of a Formula I racing car

Steering wheel

Rubber tyres

Engine

The radiator cools the engine.

Petrol tank opening

The air ducts suck in air to cool the engine.

Disc brakes

Front wing

Racing cars incorporate the latest technology in the motor industry. This technology is often later adapted and used in ordinary cars. For example, disc brakes and turbochargers were first tested on racing cars.

The bodies of racing cars are built of ultra-light materials such as carbon-fibre. A low, streamlined design reduces wind resistance when the car is travelling at high speed. This also means that less power and petrol are needed to drive the car.

Trains and railways

The age of railways began at the end of the 18th century, with the invention of the steam engine and the introduction of cast iron rails. At that time, many people believed that it was dangerous to travel faster than the speed of a galloping horse, and opposed the development of locomotives.

Rail tracks were first used in mines to transport coal.

The first steam locomotive

An English mining engineer named Richard Trevithick (1771-1833) realized that steam engines could be used to propel vehicles along tracks. In 1804, he introduced the *New Castle*, the first steam locomotive ever to run on rails. It pulled wagons containing 70 passengers, and ten freight

The Catch Me Who Can, a locomotive built in 1808 by Trevithick

containers, along a track almost 16km (10 miles) long. It could travel at a top speed of 8km/h (5mph).

A new railway age

One of the most famous early railway engineers was George Stephenson (1781-1848), an Englishman. He was a fireman in a coal mine and a very skilled mechanic. The owner of the mine where he worked asked him to build a locomotive to carry coal.

In 1814, he produced the *Blucher*, a steam engine that could pull a weight of 30.5 tonnes (30 tons) at a speed of 6.5km/h (4mph). But it took a long time for the engine to build up enough power to move.

George Stephenson's Locomotion

Stephenson worked hard on improving both locomotives and the rails they ran on. In 1825, he built the first public railway to carry steam trains. He also designed the *Locomotion*, the steam engine which pulled the world's first public passenger train.

Stephenson's Rocket

Locomotives quickly became an important means of transport. In 1829, the directors of the Liverpool and Manchester Railway offered a prize for the best steam locomotive. Stephenson and his son Robert (1803-59) won the competition with an engine called the *Rocket*, capable of speeds of up to 48km/h (30mph).

Stephenson's Rocket pulling a passenger wagon.

Passenger wagons

The wheels were made of wood with metal rims.

The tender carried coal for the fire and a barrel of water for making the steam.

The advantages of electricity

Some inventors investigated the possibility of building trains powered by electricity. In 1879, Ernst von Siemens (1816-92), a German electrical engineer, exhibited a train that ran on a 274m (300yd) long electrified track. Electric trains are quieter, safer and cause less pollution than steam trains.

Soon Germany and Britain had built tramways. Carriages called trams ran along tracks, powered by electricity. The use of electric railways gradually spread worldwide.

A steam-driven locomotive pulled wagons around wooden tracks.

Passengers paid to travel in the open wagons.

The circular track was built on an area of wasteland in London.

A goods train on the Liverpool and Manchester Railway

The *Rocket* pulled a 14.2 tonne (14 ton) train at nearly twice the speed of rival designs. It proved that steam power was superior to horse power and laid the foundations for the expansion of railways throughout the 19th century. Fast trains went into service on the Liverpool and Manchester Railway in September 1830, transporting passengers and heavy goods.

The boiler had 25 heating tubes leading to it from the fire box. These turned the water in the boiler into steam, which made the train powerful and fast.

Piston driven by steam

Chimney

ROCKET

An iron fire box heated metal tubes running through the water in the boiler.

Driving wheel with a connecting rod.

Underground railways

In 1863, the Metropolitan Railway was opened in London. It was the first underground railway system, using steam locomotives to pull passenger wagons.

The opening of London's Metropolitan Railway in January 1863

An early steam locomotive used on the Metropolitan Railway

The first electric underground railway was opened in London in 1890. The line ran under the River Thames joining the north and south of the city. Today many cities throughout the world have underground railways.

A cutaway picture showing the Train à Grande Vitesse (TGV) which is a high-speed, electrically powered, French passenger train.

Driver's cab

Brake gear

Collision protection

Traction motors

Cooling air vents

This frame connects the train with overhead wires

Baggage compartment

Passenger compartment

Battery compartments

Air conditioning system

Suspension

A bogie is a trolley with four wheels. It swivels to steer the train around bends. These bogies have an elaborate suspension system to provide a very smooth ride.

Sea transport

The first sailors used trees, grass and animal skins to build rafts and canoes. But as sea transport became essential for communication and trade, stronger and faster ships were needed. In time, wooden sailing ships were replaced by vessels made of iron and later of steel. The invention of the steam engine (see page 10) meant that ships no longer had to rely on oars, wind or tides for power.

Steam power

Frenchman Claude Marquis de Jouffroy d'Abbans (1751-1832) built the first steamboat, called the *Pyroscape*, in 1783. The boat had a steam engine which turned its paddle wheels.

In 1836, an English farmer named Francis Pettit Smith (1803-74) designed a screw propeller. It had curved blades which propelled a boat forward by pushing water backward. Unlike a paddle wheel, a propeller stayed under water and was less easily damaged.

The Pyroscape, built in 1783

The Great Eastern was launched in 1858.
Both paddles and engines powered the ship.

Revolutionary ship design

Isambard Kingdom Brunel (1806-59), an English engineer, revolutionized ship design. In 1837, he designed the *Great Western*, the largest wooden ship of its time and the first steamship to sail across the Atlantic regularly.

Brunel's next vessel, the *Great Britain*, was driven by a huge screw propeller and built of iron, making it very strong.

Brunel's largest ship was the *Great Eastern*. It was designed to transport 4,000 passengers in great luxury and carry enough coal to sail from England to Australia and back. It was launched in 1858, but there was an explosion on board, and it proved too expensive to run. Brunel died soon after the launch, overworked and financially ruined. The *Great Eastern* was sold for scrap 30 years later.

Isambard Kingdom Brunel

Submarines

In the 17th century, one of the first boats to travel under water was built for King James I of England by Cornelius Van Drebbel (c.1572-1633), a Dutchman.

The Nautilus was built in 1800. It was driven under water by a hand-cranked propeller and above water by a sail.

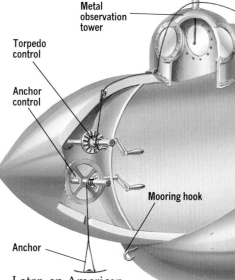

Metal observation tower

Torpedo control

Anchor control

Mooring hook

Anchor

Later, an American engineer and inventor named Robert Fulton (1765-1815) designed the *Nautilus* for Emperor Napoleon I of France. This submarine could carry four passengers and remain submersed for three hours.

The first naval submarine was designed by an Irish engineer named John Holland (1840-1914). In 1900, he made the *Holland VI*, which had an internal combustion engine for travel above water and an electric motor for moving underwater.

A cutaway diagram of the Ben Franklin, a modern research submarine

Surface radio antenna
TV camera
Surface lookout
Hatch
Control panel
Ballast tank
Propulsion motor
Viewing ports

The torpedo could be released under enemy ships.

The sail could be folded when the submarine submerged.

A handle was used to turn the sail when sailing above water.

The pilot turned the propeller using handles and gears.

A propeller drove the submarine underwater.

Rudders directed the submarine up or down when it was in the water.

Pumps to expel water

Deep-sea divers

Deep-sea divers are affected by water pressure. Breathing air that is not at the same pressure as the surrounding water can be extremely dangerous.

In 1819, a German mechanic named Augustus Siebe (d.1872) designed a diving suit that solved this problem. It was made of waterproof canvas and had a screw-on helmet. A pipe supplied air from the surface, and a pressure pump in the pipe kept the air at the same pressure as the water around the diver. The suit enabled people to dive safely to depths of up to 100m (328ft) so that they could build and repair under water structures.

Siebe's diving suit

Hovercraft

The hovercraft was invented in 1959, by a British engineer named Christopher Cockerell (b.1910). He designed a vessel with a long, flexible skirt hanging down beneath it. Large fans on the deck sucked in air. The air was pumped down through the vessel in powerful streams called "peripheral jets". The high-pressure air was captured by the skirt, creating a cushion which lifted up the craft, allowing it to hover above smooth surfaces such as water or ice.

Cockerell carried out an experiment to demonstrate the principle of peripheral jets.

Cockerell testing a model of one of his hovercraft designs

Cockerell's early experiment

Hairdryer

Tin cans

Tin cans

Kitchen scales

A cross-section of a hovercraft

Air blown into cans where it is forced to the edges

Propellers suck in air

Air inflates the flexible skirt, forming an air cushion

He used two tin cans, a hairdryer and kitchen scales. He pumped air into the cans, which lay one inside the other. This created high-pressure air jets which lifted the cans above the kitchen scales.

By 1968, regular hovercraft services were operating between England and France.

Propeller

Fins and rudders

Fan intake

A cutaway diagram of a modern SR-N4 hovercraft

Lift fan

Control cabin

Outer trunk

Engines

Transmission shaft

Buoyancy tanks

Transmission main gearbox

Air transport

The idea of being able to fly has captured people's imagination from the earliest times. In Greek mythology, a man called Icarus tried to fly to the Sun with wings made of feathers and wax. But hot air balloons, the first successful way of flying, were not built until the 18th century. Aircraft were invented in the 20th century and soon revolutionized both transport and warfare.

Balloon flight

Balloons filled with hot air float because hot air is lighter than cold air. The first successful hot air balloon was built in France in 1783 by the Montgolfier brothers, Joseph (1740-1810) and Jacques (1745-99).

The balloon was made from paper pasted onto linen.

A sheep, a duck and a cockerel were among the first passengers. They flew for about eight minutes, covering only a short distance. The first balloon flight with human passengers lasted about 25 minutes and covered a distance of 8km (5 miles).

Later, instead of hot air, balloons were filled with gases that are lighter than air, such as hydrogen. Ballooning became a very popular sport. But when one of the first balloons crash landed, the people who found it thought it was a monster and tried to kill it.

Long-distance balloons

Balloons were very difficult to steer. They often blew a long way off course, or climbed so high above the Earth's surface that pilots had difficulty breathing. In 1852, Frenchman Henri Giffard (1825-82) designed an "airship", a balloon 44m (144ft) in length and pointed at each end. It was steered by a propeller, and driven by a steam engine.

In 1898, Ferdinand von Zeppelin (1838-1917) built an airship with a rigid frame inside made of a lightweight metal. After this, huge airships were built for passenger trips. One, the *Graf Zeppelin*, made 144 transatlantic flights. But in 1937, 35 people were killed when the world's largest balloon, the *Hindenburg*, caught fire. Airships were taken out of service shortly after this.

Wooden struts supported the wings.

Twin rudders at the rear gave directional control.

Gun platform

Observation platform

Winch platform

Bow cabins

Control car

Observation and gun platform

Aircraft compartment

Helium gas cell

Metal frames

An American airship. In Europe, airships were converted into bombers in World War I and carried out air-raids, dropping bombs on London.

A pioneer of flight

A flying machine which successfully imitated a bird's flight was built by a rich English landowner, Sir George Cayley (1771-1857). In 1853 he launched a glider, piloted by his coachman, from a hilltop on his estate in Yorkshire.

Otto Lilienthal (1849-96), a German engineer, made over a thousand flights in monoplane (single-wing) and biplane (double-wing) gliders that he had designed and built. But he was eventually killed when one of his gliders crashed.

The pilot hung below the glider and moved his body and legs to control the direction of flight.

Otto Lilienthal's glider

The Wright brothers' Flyer I was powered by an engine and two propellers.

Wooden propeller

Flexible but strong wooden frame

The pilot had simple handles to control the plane's movement.

The plane was powered by a four-cylinder engine. The power was transmitted from the engine to the propellers by a bicycle chain.

The wings were covered in a cotton fabric.

Thin wires were used to twist the wings to lift one side or the other. This meant that the plane could not only fly level but also bank to either side to make turns.

The first aircraft flights

Orville (1871-1948) and Wilbur (1867-1912) Wright were the sons of an American bishop. They designed an extremely lightweight engine and fitted it to their first aircraft, *Flyer I*.

On December 17, 1903, Orville Wright piloted the first powered and controlled aircraft flight. He made four flights that day. The longest lasted 59 seconds and covered a distance of 260m (852ft). *Flyer III*, built in 1905, was the first efficient plane. It could fly for over half an hour, and was easy to steer and control. In 1909, the American army recognized the importance of the Wright brothers' achievement and ordered a military version of the plane.

Wilbur Wright in Flyer III

From aircraft to helicopters

Igor Sikorsky (1889-1972) was an engineer who emigrated to America from Russia. In 1939, he built the first modern helicopter, *Sikorsky VS-300*. Like helicopters today, it had a single main propeller called a rotor and a small tail propeller. It was able to take off and land vertically, fly backwards and sideways, and hover.

The Sikorsky VS-300

Defying gravity

In the 17th century, the British scientist Isaac Newton (1642-1727) predicted that it would be possible to launch an object into space. Two hundred years later Konstantin Tsiolkovsky (1857-1933), a Russian school teacher, calculated that a

rocket would have to travel at about 40,250km/h (25,000mph) to leave the Earth's atmosphere. He realized that if certain liquid fuels were mixed and ignited, the explosion could propel a rocket into space at such a speed. In 1926, the first liquid fuel rocket was launched by an American named Robert Goddard (1882-1945).

Space travel was made possible by the work of a German engineer, Baron Wernher von Braun (1912-77). During World War II, he designed a number of rockets, including the V-2 missile. It could travel at a speed of 1.6km (1 mile) per second, to a target over 322km (200 miles) away (see page 41).

After the war, von Braun worked on the American space project. In 1958, he built a system called *Jupiter* which launched the USA's first satellite (see page 29).

The Space Shuttle, launched in 1977, was the first reusable spacecraft.

Main launch fuel tank

Launch rockets fall away soon after takeoff.

Parachutes slow the descent of the rockets.

Flight deck

Cargo bay

Cocoon for carrying satellites

Steering engine

Three main engines

Inventions in the home

In the 20th century, many inventions have transformed life in the home. Standards of hygiene have risen with the introduction of new ways of storing and preserving food. Exhausting tasks which had previously been performed by hand are now quickly completed using a variety of electrical devices.

Electric irons

The first irons were metal pans, filled with hot charcoal. They were used in the 8th century by the Chinese to smooth silk. In the 17th century, pieces of cast iron fitted with handles were heated on a fire or stove. In 1882, Henry Seely, an American, made an iron that had an electric element.

An early electric iron

Electric element

High-powered cleaning

Up until the 19th century, people had to clean their carpets by beating or washing them. The first mechanical carpet cleaners were sweepers with rotating brushes, or devices fitted with bellows to suck up dust.

The first successful vacuum cleaner was invented by Hubert Booth (1871-1955), a British engineer, who set up the British Vacuum Company in 1901. His fuel-driven machine, known as the "Puffing Billy", was taken from house to house by a horse-drawn van. Uniformed employees put hoses through windows to clean people's carpets. Booth's machine was such a success that he was asked to clean the ceremonial carpet at Westminster Abbey, London, before the coronation of King Edward VII of England.

In 1908, an American named Murray Spangler patented a new lightweight vacuum cleaner. His design was eventually made and marketed by a firm owned by William Hoover.

An early Hoover "bag and stick" vacuum cleaner

An electric motor turned a large fan, creating a vacuum inside the Hoover. The vacuum sucked in dirt and dust off the carpet, which was collected in a large bag at the back.

A brush at the front picked up and pushed back dirt.

On/off switch

Keeping cool

Food which is kept cool lasts longer than food left at room temperature. People often used ice to preserve things until Karl von Linde (1842-1934), a German inventor, made the first domestic refrigerator. It was powered by a steam motor which pumped a gas called freon into pipes behind a food cabinet. Inside the pipes the gas condensed into a liquid. As this happened, the temperature of the freon dropped, cooling down the food cabinet.

The first electric refrigerator was designed in 1923 by two Swedish inventors, Balzer von Platen and Carl Munters.

A cutaway of a modern refrigerator

Evaporator absorbs heat from the air

Freezer compartment

Cooled air at the top sinks to the bottom; warmer air rises to be cooled.

Compressor

Condenser

A compressor pumps freon gas around the refrigerator inside pipes. When it reaches the condenser it is condensed into a liquid. Its temperature drops, cooling the refrigerator.

A close shave

The first safety razor, in which only the edge of the blade touched the skin, was made in 1771, by Jean-Jacques Perret, a Frenchman. Before this, blades were unshielded, making shaving dangerous. King Camp Gillette (1855-1932), an American salesman, had the idea of a razor blade which was thrown away when blunt. With an inventor, William Nickerson, he patented the disposable safety razor in 1901. In 1908, 300,000 razors and 13 million blades were sold.

An early disposable razor

The head of the razor could be taken apart and a new blade fitted.

Electric toaster

In 1909, the General Electric Company of the USA produced the first electric toaster. A slice of bread was placed on a mesh of wires heated by an electric current. The bread had to be turned over when one side was done, to toast the other side.

An American named Charles Strite designed the first pop-up toaster in 1927. It had heating elements to toast both sides of the bread at once. A clockwork timer turned off the electricity and, at the same time, released a spring which ejected the toast.

An electric toaster, dating from 1938

Coiled wires glowed red hot when the electricity was switched on.

The bread was placed here and pushed into the toaster.

Washing machines

The world's first electric washing machine was built in 1906 by an American, named Alva Fisher. Dirty clothes were placed in a horizontally-mounted metal drum, which was rotated by an electric motor. As the clothes tumbled they gradually became clean. The first combined electric washer and tumble dryer was introduced in 1924 by the Savage Arms Co. of the USA.

A modern tumble dryer

Heating element

Drum

Hot air is pumped into the rotating drum. This heats the water held in the clothes causing it to evaporate.

An electric motor turns the drum

A condenser unit dries the moisture in the air inside the drum.

Pump

Electric kettles

The first electric kettles contained wires in separate compartments beneath their bases. The water did not come into contact with the wire and therefore took a long time to heat up. In 1923, Arthur Large made a breakthrough. He developed a copper tube containing a wire that could safely be covered by water in a kettle. It heated water quickly.

An electric kettle made in about 1920

Electric element

Canned food

Food preserved in tin canisters was introduced by an Englishman named Peter Durand. His idea was bought by a company called Donkin, Hall and Gamble. They set up a canning factory in 1811 and canned foods were sold in London shops by 1830.

This can of roast veal was taken on an expedition to the Arctic in 1824. When scientists opened it 114 years later, the meat was in perfect condition.

Microwave ovens

In 1945, the idea of making an oven which used radio waves to heat up food was patented by an American inventor named Percy Spencer. In a microwave oven, food is bombarded with radio waves, called microwaves. These make the molecules inside the food vibrate, producing heat which cooks the food quickly.

A modern microwave oven

The microwaves are directed onto a fan. This spins around and spreads the waves throughout the oven.

A special metal mesh across the oven door prevents the microwaves from escaping, but allows the food to be viewed safely.

A turntable rotates so that the food will be cooked evenly.

The microwaves are generated in a vacuum tube called a magnetron.

Control panel

A revolution in the office

With the mass-production of a selection of tiny electronic components, many sophisticated devices have become commonplace in offices. Word processors, photocopiers and facsimile machines have simplified business transactions all over the world. This new equipment also enables more and more people to work from home.

Mechanical writing

The first practical typewriter was designed in 1867, by Christopher Sholes (1819-90 an American newspaper editor and politician. He spent much of his spare time inventing. With his friend Carlos Glidden, he invented a numbering machine, which they later decided to convert into a lettering machine.

Sholes built about 30 different machines and designed a keyboard layout similar to that used today. But he did not make money out of his invention. He sold it to a company named Remington and Sons, who sold their first typewriter in 1874. Typewriters soon became very popular. The author Mark Twain, an early enthusiast, typed his own manuscripts.

An early Sholes typewriter

Drum carrying paper

Small hammers with inked letters strike the paper.

Cutaway showing rods connecting the keys with the letters.

Christopher Sholes with one of his typewriters

Keyboard

Personal computers

In 1964, a US company called IBM produced the first word processor. It was a typewriter with a computer memory that could store text on magnetic tapes. When a tape was played back, the typewriter printed out the text. In 1978, another US company, called Qyx, introduced a machine which used magnetic disks to store text. These disks could store more information than the tapes, and allowed the user to retrieve stored information quickly.

In the 1980s, personal computers running special word processing programs began to replace typewriters. Today computers can be used to produce many types of publications, such as this book, to keep accounts and to store and organize huge amounts of office information of all kinds.

A modern personal computer

Monitor

System unit, inside which are the workings of the computer

Floppy disk drive into which floppy disks can be inserted.

Hard disk drive

Graphics card

Keyboard

Mouse

Paper clips

The paper clip was invented in 1900 by Johann Vaaler of Norway. The design, which has remained almost the same ever since, consisted of a simple double loop of wire which could hold sheets of paper tightly together. Before, loose pieces of paper had to be pinned together.

Sticky tape

In 1928, Richard Drew an American, produced a general-purpose sticky tape. It was known as "Scotch tape", but in Europe it was sold under the name "Sellotape". It consisted of a strip of clear plastic called cellulose, with glue on one side.

Photocopying

In 1938, an American inventor named Chester Carlson (1906-68) invented the xerographic copier, now known as the photocopier. Modern photocopiers work in the following way:

1. An image of the page to be copied is projected onto a metal plate using a light source and lenses. The plate is electrically charged, creating positive and negative charges on its surface.

2. Light areas of the image destroy the positive charges on the plate. Where the image is dark, the positive charges remain. The plate is then coated with toner powder.

3. The toner powder sticks to the positively charged areas of the metal plate. It is then transferred onto a sheet of paper which comes from the feed tray.

4. The toner powder is then sealed onto the sheet of paper as it passes between two heated fusing rollers.

Mirrors

Fusing rollers seal the toner powder onto the paper.

Photo-receptor drum

Toner powder

Paper feed tray

Photographic exposure lamp

Photographic lens

Chester Carlson with his invention

The picture above shows a cutaway of a modern photocopier

Facsimile transmission

A facsimile (fax) machine can transmit text and photographs by telephone to a receiving machine a few seconds later. The first fax machine appeared in 1843. It consisted of a pendulum which scanned raised lettering and sent out electrical pulses. Modern machines use diodes (see page 32) which detect light reflected from the document being sent.

In 1922, Arthur Korn, a German physicist, sent photographs by radio transmission across the Atlantic. The first fax service was set up in 1926.

How a modern fax machine works

1. The document to be faxed is fed in here.

2. A fluorescent tube bounces light off the document, reflecting its image onto a lens.

3. The lens passes the light to a microprocessor. This breaks the image down into a series of lines.

4. The lines are then changed by another microprocessor into white and black dots. These are converted into a number code - "1" for white and "0" for black.

5. Another microprocessor converts this information into signals which are sent down a telephone line.

6. At the receiving fax machine, the telephone message is converted back to a number code.

7. The code is sent to a printer, which contains a line of dots which heat up or cool down according to the electrical current supplied by the number code.

8. An image of black dots is formed on a piece of paper, matching the information given by the code.

The ballpoint pen

In 1938, a design for the first ballpoint pen was patented by Lazlo Biro (1900-85) a Hungarian artist and journalist, and his brother Georg, a chemist. They called their pen the biro. Ink from a reservoir inside the pen flowed onto a free-moving steel ball.

A special ink was invented for use in ballpoint pens. It dried instantly when it was exposed to air. The pen was first used by the British Royal Air Force, because it did not leak at high altitudes.

A ballpoint pen, 1940s

Ink in a plastic tube

Ink flows onto a small metal ball.

Construction and buildings

In the 18th and 19th centuries, millions of people left rural areas to work in the world's growing industrial cities. Many traditional building methods had to change in order to provide accommodation for the new urban population. The work of many inventors enabled architects to design and construct much bigger, brighter and safer buildings.

Cranes

The earliest description of a crane appears in a handbook written in about 10BC by the Roman architect Vitruvius. It consisted of a pole held in position by ropes, with a pulley at the top. A rope running through the pulley was attached to heavy loads such as building materials or ships' cargoes. The loads were then lifted by slaves in a treadmill.

The crane described by Vitruvius

- Pulleys
- Ropes held the crane steady.
- Load
- A treadmill was turned to raise the load.

A more efficient crane, known as the derrick crane, was designed in Italy during the 15th century. Steam-powered cranes were built in the 19th century by a Scots engineer named John Rennie (1761-1821).

Building the Tower of Babel – an illustration of the mythical tower, from an English book published in 1425

A bucket being raised with ropes and pulleys

Elevators for high-rise buildings

During the 19th century, architects designed such tall buildings that machinery was needed to transport people and goods up and down them. Elisha Otis (1811-61) was an engineer from Vermont, USA. In 1852 he took a job in a factory in New York, where he designed a steam-powered safety elevator. It included a spring operated safety mechanism to hold the passenger platform securely if the elevator cables broke. Otis demonstrated his new invention to the public. He was lifted high up in the air in an elevator and then its cables were cut. In 1857, the first safety elevator was installed in a New York department store.

Elevators were installed at the Eiffel Tower in Paris in 1889.

- Ticket collector
- Passengers going up a leg of the Eiffel Tower.
- A driver controlled the speed.
- Elevator controls
- One of the elevators carried sightseers up 160m (146ft) to a viewing platform.
- The elevator was hydraulically powered, which means the car was pushed up rails using a liquid under pressure.

Moving staircases

In 1894, the world's first escalator was installed as a tourist attraction on a pier at Coney Island, New York. It was named the "inclined elevator" and was designed by Jesse Reno, a businessman from New York. A conveyor belt pulled around a sloping ramp. But the ramp sloped at an angle of about 30 degrees to the ground, which made it dangerous for passengers. So Reno replaced the ramp with a set of rotating steps.

In the early 1980s, a Japanese company named Mitsubishi built the first spiral escalator. It was installed in a department store.

Toilets

As the population in cities increased, a hygienic way of disposing of sewage was urgently needed. In 1778, Joseph Bramah (1748-1814), an English cabinet maker whose job was fitting water closets (an early kind of toilet), designed and patented a new toilet. A valve shut the toilet off from the main sewer pipes when it was not in use. This stopped poisonous gases from seeping into houses.

Lifting this handle opened two flaps. One flushed water into the bowl, and the other let it drain away.

Bramah's toilet

Locks

Bramah also invented a complex lock. He offered a reward to anyone who could open it. 75 years later, at London's Great Exhibition of 1851 (a fair at which the world's newest technology was shown), a visitor finally picked it open; even then it took 51 hours.

Locks were first used in Ancient Egypt. They were made of wood and were opened using a key. The key had cylindrical pins of different lengths which fitted into grooves in the lock. Inspired by the Egyptian ideas, Linus Yale (1821-68) produced a modern pin lock, known as a Yale lock.

Bramah's original lock of 1787

How a Yale lock works

Springs
Plug
Tumblers
Key
Cylinder

The lock consists of a brass cylinder with a central plug, both with a row of holes. In each hole is a moveable pin made in two pieces called a tumbler. Springs hold down the tumblers.

The key has a serrated top edge. When it is inserted, it pushes up each tumbler against its spring so the holes in the tumbler align with the edge of the central plug.

When the key is turned, the central plug also turns. A lever attached to the central plug draws in a bolt and the lock opens.

Gas lamps

Mantle

Most early gas lamps were simply holes in gas pipes. When lit, the escaping gas gave off a very weak light. In 1885, an Austrian chemist, Carl Auer (1858-1929), designed a new kind of gas lamp. It contained a device known as a mantle, which consisted of a mesh of carbonized cotton that glowed brightly when heated in a gas flame.

Auer's gas mantle of 1885

Electric lighting

In 1878, an English scientist named Joseph Swan (1828-1914) invented an electric light bulb. It consisted of a glass bulb containing a filament made of carbonized cotton. He removed air from the bulb, because without air the filament would never burn away.

The following year, Thomas Edison (1847-1931), a prolific inventor from the USA, also produced a light bulb. After experimenting with filaments of carbonized thread, he used carbonized paper filaments. In 1880, he began manufacturing light bulbs that were safe to use in houses, and sold them for $2.50 each. Eventually Thomas Edison combined forces with Swan to form the Edison and Swan United Electric Light Company.

Edison's light bulb of 1879

Glass bulb with partial vacuum

Carbon filament glowed when heated by electric current

Swan's light bulb of 1878

Filament of carbonized cotton thread.

Edison with his light bulb

Printing

Before printing was invented, texts had to be copied out by people called scribes. Only a small number of books could be produced, which made them very expensive. In one day, a printer could produce the amount of material that a scribe took a whole year to complete. Books and pamphlets became widely available, and knowledge and new ideas spread more quickly.

Blocks and types

The first printed pages were prayer sheets, produced in Japan in the 8th century. They were made from blocks of wood, carved with raised characters or pictures. But each block took a long time to make, and could only be used for one page.

The Diamond Sutra, the oldest known printed book, AD868

In about 1045, Pi Cheng, a member of the royal court of China, invented movable type. He used baked clay to make single Chinese characters, which were then fitted into an iron frame ready for printing. The characters could be used again to make up new pages.

Early blocks of reusable Turkish type

Printing in Europe

In the 15th century, Johannes Gutenberg (c.1400-68), a German printer, who was unaware of the techniques used in China, developed his own version of movable type. He made individual letter blocks from metal. The letters required for each page of text were arranged in a wooden frame and fitted into a press. They were then inked and paper was pressed onto them. Thousands of copies could be printed and the type could then be rearranged for a new page.

A reconstruction of Gutenberg's press

An engraving of Johannes Gutenberg, and a page from his Bible

Conflict and loss

Gutenberg's work won him the support of Johannes Fust, a businessman. Fust was impatient for financial success. In 1455, he successfully sued Gutenberg and seized all the printing equipment. He set up a printing business with his son-in-law, who had trained as one of Gutenberg's apprentices.

Before his death in 1468, Gutenberg saw his invention used throughout Europe and watched other people making rich profits. By 1500 there were 100 German presses in Italy, and 30 in Spain.

A wooden screw enabled the press to be raised and lowered.

Metal letters were arranged into pages in a metal frame called a forme. They were then covered in ink by a hand roller.

Padded wooden hammers were used to make all the letters level.

Paper was placed in a frame called a tympan.

The tympan hinged over the forme and both were slid under the press.

The press was screwed down so that the inked letters printed clearly onto the paper.

The steam press

By the end of the 18th century, newspapers and books had become so popular that hand-worked presses could not keep up with demand. Friedrich König (1774-1833), a printer and engineer from Saxony (now part of Germany), and his partner Andreas Bauer designed a steam-driven press. It printed 1,000 sheets an hour, four times the speed of a hand-worked press.

König's machine, produced in 1814, contained two large cylinders on which paper was placed. After one sheet had been printed on each, the cylinders rotated, bringing new blank sheets into position. The plate holding the type was automatically re-inked when necessary.

König's printing press of 1814

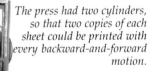

The press had two cylinders, so that two copies of each sheet could be printed with every backward-and-forward motion.

Feeding board

Feeding board

Sheet of paper placed here

Paper carried around printing cylinders

Inking rollers

Delivery table receives printed sheets

The invention of Linotype

In 1886, Ottmar Mergenthaler (1854-99), a German watchmaker, invented a way of setting type mechanically, called the Linotype system. Text was typed on a keyboard like a typewriter. The machine produced complete lines of type, with each letter and word correctly spaced, at four times the speed that was previously possible.

Mergenthaler using a Linotype machine

Computer typesetting

In 1965, a computer-controlled method of setting type, called Digiset, was developed in Germany. Text was typed on a keyboard and stored in a computer's memory. The text was then scanned by a laser and an image of the letters projected onto photographic paper, which was developed. The Digitek system of computer typesetting shown below was developed in the 1980s. Text stored in a computer's memory is scanned and converted into a code of pulses of light. An image of the text is projected onto photographic paper by the exposure head.

Photographic paper

Image projected onto paper

Exposure head

The Digitek system of typesetting

Communication machines

Before message-sending machines were invented in the 19th century, communication was a very slow and difficult process. People could only send letters by messengers, or signals using drums, smoke, fires, church bells and flashing mirrors. Most of these methods were only effective over a short distance, and correspondence over long distances was a very time-consuming operation. Even with the invention of steamships, it took months for a letter sent from Europe to arrive in Australia.

Communication towers

Claude Chappe (1763-1805), a Frenchman, introduced a system called the telegraph, which means "writing at a distance". A network of towers was built on hilltops. Each tower housed a machine with two long pointers that could be set in 49 different positions. Each of the positions corresponded to a letter or number. Operators could send messages from one tower to the next. The system was very successful. By the mid-19th century, the network of towers stretched at least 4,828km (3,000 miles) throughout France.

One of Chappe's towers

Messages along wires

The first electric telegraph machine was produced in 1837 by the British inventors William Cooke (1806-79) and Charles Wheatstone (1802-75). Electrical currents were sent along a wire to a receiving device. The currents then moved several needles that were mounted on a dial on the receiver. The needles pointed to letters, spelling out the message.

A later version of Cooke and Wheatstone's telegraph machine

Morse code

In 1843, an American artist by the name of Samuel Morse (1791-1872) designed a new telegraph code which replaced the one used by Cooke and Wheatstone. He gave every letter of the alphabet a coded equivalent of dots and dashes. When messages were transmitted, long electrical pulses stood for dashes and short pulses for dots. Morse code, as it is known, is still used today.

Morse publicized his code by erecting a telegraph wire 6km (37 miles) long, which stretched from Baltimore to Washington. He used this to transmit news of the presidential election.

In 1858, Charles Wheatstone devised a system in which an operator punched messages in Morse code onto long paper tapes which were fed through a telegraph transmitter. At the other end of the wire, a pen drew the code on to another tape, which was read and translated.

Eventually, the pen was replaced with a "sounder", which converted the dots and dashes into long and short sounds. Operators could listen to the coded message and write down the translation.

A	·—
B	—···
C	—·—·
D	—··
E	·
F	··—·
G	——·
H	····
I	··
J	·———
K	—·—
L	·—··
M	——
N	—·
O	———
P	·——·
Q	——·—
R	·—·
S	···
T	—
U	··—
V	···—
W	·——
X	—··—
Y	—·——
Z	——··

The alphabet and its equivalent in Morse code

Roller pulled tape along

Clockwork motor

Clockwork key to wind up receiver

Paper tape fed out from a reel in the drawer

Electromagnet

A message was tapped out with this key.

Morse's telegraph machine printed the dots and dashes of Morse code.

An alphabet called semaphore, invented in 1812

A B C D E F G H I J K L M N O P Q R S T U V W X Y Z

Spoken messages

Some inventors concentrated on producing a device that would enable people to talk over very long distances. A breakthrough was made by Alexander Graham Bell (1847-1922), a Scotsman who lived in Boston, Massachusetts in the USA. He ran a school for the deaf, and later went on to work at the city's university.

He and Thomas Watson (1854-1934), an electrical engineer, made an instrument consisting of a transmitter (or mouthpiece) and a receiver (or earpiece). The transmitter turned voice sounds into a varying electric current. This was sent along a wire to the earpiece, where it was changed back into voice sounds.

Bell's telephone - the mouthpiece and earpiece were identical devices.

Used as a mouthpiece – the speaker's voice vibrated a diaphragm, causing an electric current passing through it to vary in strength.

Diaphragm

Used as an earpiece – the varying current passed along the wire to the earpiece, which also contained a diaphragm. The electric current made the diaphragm vibrate, reproducing the voice sounds.

Bell made the first telephone call ever on March 10, 1876. He had spilled acid on his trousers and spoke to his colleague, "Mr Watson, can you come at once, I want you." The world's first telephone exchange opened in Connecticut in 1877. Operators had to connect the lines between one caller and another by hand. New York and Boston were linked by telephone in 1883.

The mouthpiece and earpiece of a Bell telephone in use

Telephones through the ages

Over the last century, the design of the telephone has undergone many changes.

A selection of different styles of telephones

An Edison receiver, 1879 – the user turned the handle while listening.

A Crossley telephone, 1880 – the user spoke into the top of the box and listened through the receiver.

A Gower-Bell telephone, 1880s

A design introduced in the 1890s – the speaker turned the handle to call the operator.

A 'Candlestick' telephone, 1905 – the operator was called by lifting the receiver.

A 'cradle' telephone, 1930

A portable phone – these can be used without a cable.

Satellite communications

Satellites are unmanned spacecraft that orbit the Earth. They can transmit telephone calls and television pictures across the world. They can also send information about weather and navigation conditions. In 1957, the USSR launched *Sputnik I*, the first man-made object to orbit the Earth.

Sputnik I

In 1960, the USA launched the *Courier* and *Echo* satellites. They relayed the first satellite telephone calls between the USA and Europe. In 1962, the USA launched *Telstar*, the first satellite to relay live television shows as well as telephone calls. It could transmit 60 calls or a single television channel at any one time.

The Telstar satellite

Today, an elaborate network of satellites links areas all over the globe. Companies can now buy private satellites for their own communication needs.

A modern communications satellite

Solar panels power the communications system.

Communications antennae send out and receive messages.

Units for telephone and television transmissions

Photography and film

People have been drawing and painting the world around them since the first cave paintings. During the 10th century, Arab astronomers used an early camera obscura (see box below) to look at images of the Sun without damaging their eyes. From the 15th century, this idea was used by artists to project images onto canvases to help them draw accurately. But only the invention of the camera in the 19th century has enabled people to produce exact replicas of the things we see.

The camera obscura

The camera obscura is a box or darkened room into which light passes through a tiny pin-hole, forming an image on the opposite inside wall. You can make your own camera obscura.

How to make a camera obscura

Make a box out of black cardboard which does not let in any light. Cut a square window into one side.

Cover the window with paper to make a screen. Make a tiny hole in the side of the box opposite the screen.

Light rays from a bright object will pass through the pinhole and form an image on the paper screen.

The first photographs

By the 18th century, people began to realize that certain chemicals are affected and changed by light. They discovered that materials coated with these substances would record patterns of light which fell across them. The world's first photograph was taken in 1826, by a French physicist named Joseph Niepce (1765-1833). He used a camera obscura to project an image onto special sheets of pewter, called plates. These had been coated with a light-sensitive substance called bitumen. It took eight hours for a blurred image to form. The length of time that light is allowed to fall on photographic plates or film is called the exposure time.

A conical camera of 1841

Focusing dial

Two lenses to focus the image

The image is focused onto a screen. The camera is then dismantled and the screen replaced with a light-sensitive plate.

A magnifying lens to help focus the image.

An early camera c.1850

Lens

Light-sensitive copper plate

Niepce's photographic techniques were improved by his partner Louis Daguerre (1789-1851). By 1839, Daguerre was obtaining clear photographs after an exposure time of only 20 minutes. His pictures were known as daguerreotypes and were very popular, particularly for portraits. But people sitting for a portrait had to have clamps around their heads to stop them from moving. The metal plates were very expensive and the pictures could not be copied.

Photography comes of age

William Fox Talbot (1800-77), an English scientist, invented a new method of developing pictures. He soaked paper in light-sensitive chemicals. When an image was projected onto the paper, the brightest areas turned it black, and the darkest parts left it white. This version of the image is called a negative. Fox Talbot then shone light through the negative onto another sheet of light-sensitive paper. This produced positive prints which he called calotypes, from the Ancient Greek words meaning "beautiful pictures".

William Fox Talbot

Photography for all

George Eastman (1854-1932), an American inventor, realized the commercial potential of making photography available to ordinary people. He produced a simple, hand-held camera called the Kodak no. 1, which was sold already fitted with a roll of film.

George Eastman's Kodak camera of 1888

Lens

The cylindrical shutter was operated by pulling a string.

After taking one picture, the user wound the film on, ready for the next shot. When the film was finished, the camera was returned to the Eastman factory where the pictures were developed. Eastman's company motto was "You press the button, we do the rest".

Arrangement of film roll holders seen from above

Key operated take-up roller

Main roll of film

The film passed the exposing aperture.

Metering roller

The take-up roller was turned by a key.

The main roller carried the film.

The film was fed past a circular exposing aperture.

A metering roller controlled the amount of film being wound on.

The Polaroid camera

The Polaroid camera was invented in 1947, by an American, Edwin Land (1909-91). It contained a tiny processing laboratory which produced positive black and white prints in less than one minute. The first Polaroid cameras that could take colour photographs became available in 1963. Today, Polaroid cameras can develop prints in a few seconds.

Edwin Land's Polaroid camera of 1948

Print paper

Rollers broke open a pod of processing chemicals.

Negative paper

Sequential photographs

In 1872, Eadweard Muybridge (1830-1904), a British photographer, was hired by a Californian horse owner. To settle a bet, Muybridge was asked to discover whether a trotting horse lifts all its hooves off the ground at once. He set up 48 cameras on a racing track and rigged them to be triggered by clockwork or by threads which were broken as the horse passed. He produced the sequence of photographs shown here, which settled the bet.

Photographs from Muybridge's famous experiment

The birth of moving pictures

Any image produced in our eyes takes a moment to fade. So if many pictures of an object which is changing position are viewed in rapid succession, the brain perceives the object to be in motion. This phenomenon is called "persistent vision". It is the principle on which motion pictures work.

In 1894, two French brothers, Auguste (1862-1954) and Louis (1864-1948) Lumière, heard about the Kinetoscope, a machine invented by Thomas Edison (see page 34). It was a box containing a strip of moving photographs. When the viewer looked into the box, the objects in the pictures appeared to be moving. The brothers built a similar machine called a *Cinématographe* which projected images onto a screen. In 1895, they showed 10 films.

The first Cinématographe used in Britain

Far right: Stills from an early film of a man sneezing

31

Radio and television

Unlike the telephone or telegraph, radio and television do not need cables or wires for signals to be transmitted. Today sounds and images can be sent rapidly via satellites from one side of the world to the other. This has dramatically affected communications as events can be reported around the world as soon as they happen.

Making waves

In the 19th century, scientists began to suspect that electrical and magnetic effects were transmitted in waves, like light. Heinrich Hertz (1857-94) a German scientist, proved this in 1885. He showed that the waves emitted by an electric spark on one side of his laboratory could be detected by a loop of wire on the other.

Messages without wires

Guglielmo Marconi (1874-1937), an Italian inventor, discovered a way in which waves could be used to send messages from one place to another without wires or cables. At the age of 20, having read about Hertz's work with electromagnetic waves, he began to carry out his own experiments. In 1894, he successfully sounded a buzzer 9m (30ft) away from where he stood.

Guglielmo Marconi with his wireless telegraph.

He pressed a key which was not connected by wire to the bell. The electromagnetic waves that made this happen are called radio waves.

Marconi moved to London, where he patented his ideas and demonstrated his equipment to the British Post Office, who decided to

A "Marconiphone" patented in 1896

finance his work. After improving his equipment, Marconi was able to send a message in Morse code (see page 28) from England to a radio receiver 50km (31 miles) away in France.

In 1902, Marconi sent a radio signal across the Atlantic – the letter 's' in Morse code. Five years later, a Canadian scientist, Reginald Fessenden, transmitted a human voice by radio for the first time.

The Marconiphone broadcaster-receiver wireless sets (1922)

Spinning discs

In 1884, Paul Nipkow (1860-1940), a German engineer, developed a disc with a spiral pattern of square holes. When the disc was rotated in front of an object, each hole captured the light from a small area of the object. These fragments could be transmitted through another disc which reformed them as a whole image on a screen. The Nipkow disc was an important step in the invention of television.

A diagram demonstrating the principle of the Nipkow disc

Light from the object passes through a spinning Nipkow disc to a photoelectric cell.

Object

Diodes

An important contribution to the development of radio and television was made in 1904 by a British engineer named John Fleming (1849-1945), who designed the diode. Diodes are used to convert radio waves into electrical signals which can be transmitted over long distances.

Fleming's diode of 1904

Glass bulb containing a vacuum

Negative electrode

Positive electrode

The photoelectric cell turns the energy in the light into electrical signals. These signals vary according to the amount of light falling on the cell - strong light produces a strong electrical signal and weak light produces a weak one.

The cell is linked to a lamp, which varies in brightness according to the strength of the electrical signal. This information about the light and dark areas of the object is then flashed to a second Nipkow disc.

Photoelectric cell

Lamp

Screen   Image

A second Nipkow disc spins at exactly the same speed as the first. Light from the lamp is projected through holes in the disc onto a screen behind. The viewer's brain blurs all the fragments of light together and sees a complete image of the object.

Hi-tech television

High definition television (HDTV) was first broadcast on June 25, 1990. It was a transmission of the football match between Italy and Uruquay in the 1990 World Cup. HDTV was developed by a group of companies called Eureka 95. Television pictures are made up of lines and tiny dots called pixels. On an ordinary television set there are 625 lines and 120,000 pixels. On a HDTV there are 1,250 lines and 480,000 pixels giving the picture greater detail and clarity.

HDTV produces very realistic images.

The large number of pixels makes the image on an HDTV clear and detailed

HDTV screens can be much larger than normal TV screens.

The height/width ratio of a normal TV screen is 3:4, while that of an HDTV screen is 9:16.

HDTV viewing conditions

Range of vision

The best viewing distance for HDTV is three times the height of the screen, compared with seven times for normal televisions.

Live television

In 1926, John Logie Baird (1888-1946), a Scottish inventor, made the first television transmission of a human face. His apparatus included an old box, a cake tin, knitting needles, a bicycle lamp and a cardboard Nipkow disc. In his laboratory, he transmitted a blurred image of the face of a boy named William Taynton. As Baird improved his equipment, the pictures he produced became less distorted. Later that year he gave the first public demonstration of television.

After this breakthrough, many television systems were developed. The British Broadcasting Corporation (BBC) began operating a black and white television service from London in 1936, and by 1939 there were television receivers in 20,000 homes. In the USA in 1953, the first successful transmission of colour television was made.

A television picture of a face was achieved in 1926

Baird's transmitting equipment of 1926

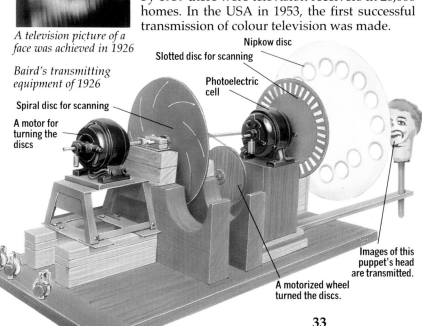

Spiral disc for scanning

A motor for turning the discs

Slotted disc for scanning

Photoelectric cell

Nipkow disc

Images of this puppet's head are transmitted.

A motorized wheel turned the discs.

Recording sound

After the invention of the telephone in 1876, many scientists began to research the possibilities of saving or storing sound. Once this had been achieved, inventors continually tried to improve methods of recording sound and playing it back. The machinery has become more and more sophisticated and the sound quality better and better.

A prolific inventor

During his lifetime an American-born inventor named Thomas Edison (1847-1931) registered 1,093 patents. In 1876, he set up the world's first industrial research laboratory, which he called his "invention factory". However, some inventors accused Edison of stealing their ideas.

In 1877, he produced the phonograph, one of his most famous inventions. This machine could record sounds and play them back. At first it was sold as a toy, but before long Edison and other inventors had improved its design so that it could be used to record music.

Edison's phonograph of 1877

A horn focused sound onto a metal diaphragm which touched a steel needle, called a stylus.

Sound made the diaphragm vibrate, causing the stylus to make indentations of different depths in tin foil wrapped around a wax cylinder.

The gramophone

Émile Berliner (1851-1929) was a German scientist who emigrated to the USA to seek his fortune. He set up a laboratory where he researched into acoustics (the science of sound) and electricity.

In 1887, he patented a new device which he called the gramophone, after the Greek for "recorded voice". Instead of the cylinders used by Edison, Berliner stored sound in grooves on flat discs made of a substance called shellac (a resin produced by insects). The discs were played back using a needle which vibrated between the walls of the groove on the disc. The recording was played back through a loudspeaker. Berliner's discs produced a much clearer sound than Edison's cylinders.

Berliner's gramophone of 1895

Recording an early Berliner disc

This man is speaking into a mouthpiece and his voice is recorded on a disc.

Horn

Needle

Disc

Tin foil

Stylus

Diaphragm

Cylinder

Mastering

In 1891, Berliner introduced "mastering", a system used to produce many copies of a disc. A glass disc coated with shellac (called a negative) was used to engrave a recording pattern onto flat metal discs (positives). Later, he developed a system in which shellac positives were pressed from a nickel-plated negative. By 1908, Berliner's German factory was producing over six million discs a year. For the first time, people were able to listen at home to music recorded in concert halls.

Mastering a modern vinyl disc

1. Grooves are cut into a master disc made of a very hard plastic called lacquer.

2. The master disc is coated with nickel which is peeled off to be used as a negative.

3. Hot plastic is pressed between two negatives, to produce a positive.

Horn

Cylinder wrapped in tin foil

When the cylinder was played back, the indentations in the foil made the stylus vibrate. The vibrations were changed into sound by the diaphragm.

Handle

Tape recording

The forerunner of modern tape recorders was designed in 1898, by Valdemar Poulsen (1869-1942), a Dane. He developed a machine called the telegraphone, which converted sound waves into magnetic patterns stored on a wire. To play back the sound, the wire was wound past a magnet. It generated tiny electric pulses which corresponded to the sound originally recorded. These pulses were converted back into sound waves, heard through headphones.

This 1903 Poulsen telegraphone recorded sounds on wire.

The invention of plastic tape turned the tape recorder into a commercial success. It was introduced in 1935 by AEG, a German company. The tape was coated with magnetic particles. It was light and compact, and enabled people to make longer recordings than on discs.

Today, recordings can be made on small audio cassette tapes.

Protective case made of hard plastic

Reel of plastic tape coated with magnetic particles.

The replay head of a tape recorder touches the tape at this point. It reads the magnetic patterns on the magnetic tape.

Compact discs

In 1982, a Dutch company called Philips, and the Japanese firm Sony, introduced the first compact discs. On a compact disc, sound is stored as digital information in tiny pits on the surface. A laser beam scans the pits, and the information is converted into electrical signals and then into vibrations. There is no contact between the laser scanner and the disc, so compact discs do not wear out. They are also unaffected by scratches and dust. A compact disc can store about an hour of music.

A compact disc scanned by a laser

Microscopic pits

Laser beam

Instead of a stylus there is a laser beam. It scans the disc and "reads" the pattern of pits.

Digital audio tapes

Digital audio tapes (DAT) were introduced in 1987. They are half the size of previous audio cassette tapes, yet they can record two hours of music on each side. Sound is recorded onto these tapes as a numbered code.

Recording sound on to digital audio tapes

A digital audio cassette

Number code

To record music onto DAT, sound is converted into a code of numbers. Inside a DAT recorder this code is converted into a magnetic pattern.

The magnetic pattern is recorded onto the DAT.

To play back the music on a DAT, this process happens in reverse. The magnetic patterns on the tape are converted into sound signals reproducing the original music.

Movie soundtracks

In 1889, Thomas Edison's assistant Charles Batchelor experimented with combining moving pictures and sound. Over the next 40 years other inventors, many of them associated with the new motion picture industry, developed methods for synchronizing film and speech.

Diagram showing how a film's soundtrack works

1. A stripe along the edge of a movie film carries the soundtrack. The width of this sound stripe varies according to the sound signals produced during the recording.

2. A light is shone through the sound stripe toward a photoelectric cell. The varying width of the stripe varies the amounts of light reaching the photoelectric cell.

3. The photoelectric cell converts the light into sound signals, which are the same as those of the original.

4. The sound signals travel down a cable to the cinema loudspeakers, where they are converted into sound waves.

Lifesavers

Life in the home and at work has always been fraught with dangers. Inventions and technological advances, such as motor cars or aircraft, create new dangers for the people using them. Inventors have had to develop safety devices to compensate for these hazards.

A miner's lamp

Working in mines has always been dangerous. Before the beginning of the 19th century, many miners were killed or injured by explosions when the candles they carried underground ignited pockets of gas. In 1815, an Englishman named Humphry Davy (1778-1829), produced a lamp in which the flame was enclosed by fine wire mesh. This stopped the lamp's flame from igniting gas in the air. The number of gas explosions in mines fell dramatically soon after the lamp was introduced.

A cutaway of Davy's safety lamp

The wire mesh absorbed the heat of the flame before it could come into contact with the gas in the air.

Wick in oil

Extinguishing fires

In 1816, an English inventor named George Manby, designed a fire extinguisher. It consisted of a metal cylinder containing water. The water was forced out of the cylinder by compressed air.

Alexander Laurent, a Russian inventor, designed the first chemical fire extinguisher in 1905. Foam which smothered flames was pumped by hand out of a metal container.

A modern fire extinguisher uses carbon dioxide gas. When the handle is pressed, a valve opens. This releases the pressure inside, and allows the carbon dioxide to turn into a gas which shoots out of the nozzle.

Handle

Valve

Carbon dioxide gas

Carbon dioxide liquid

Nozzle

Carbon dioxide gas can be directed at the flames with the nozzle.

Hidden points

Brooches made of bronze and of a similar design to modern safety pins were used to fasten cloaks in western Europe in the 12th century BC. The modern safety pin itself was designed in 1849, by Walter Hunt of New York.

Hunt's 1849 patent for the safety pin

Today's safety pins look very similar to Hunt's originals.

Jumping safely

There is a design for a parachute among the drawings of Leonardo da Vinci (see page 45). However, it was not until 1783 that a parachute was used. A Frenchman named Louis Lenorand used one to jump from a high tower. Many early parachutes looked like umbrellas.

Silk parachutes which fold away were introduced in the USA in about 1880. The first parachute with a ripcord was used in the USA in 1908.

Leonardo da Vinci's design for a parachute

In 1797, a Frenchman named André-Jaques Garnerin used a parachute to jump from a hydrogen balloon.

Green for go

In 1868, a traffic signal arm used to indicate stop and go was first used in London. It had red and green gas lamps for use at night. But the signal was abandoned after an incident in which a gas lamp exploded, killing a policeman.

In 1914, the first electrical traffic light, hand-operated and using red and green lights only, was installed in Cleveland, Ohio, in the USA. The first automatic traffic lights with red, green and amber lights were installed in London in 1925.

The first traffic signal, installed in London in 1868

Arms lowered meant "go"

Arms extended meant "stop"

Martin-Baker Mk16
ejection seat

Parachute
container

Ejection guns
unit

Auxiliary
oxygen handle

A pilot ejector seat

In 1921, James Martin (1893-1981), an Irish engineer, set up a company to build lightweight monoplanes. During World War II, he designed a fighter aircraft. It included a device that ejected the canopy of the cockpit, allowing the pilot to escape quickly if the plane caught fire.

After the war, Martin tackled the problem of getting pilots out of fast-moving aircraft, and he produced the ejection seat. The pilot pulled a handle above his head, and a seat powered by a compressed spring shot him out of the cockpit. Once the seat was clear of the aircraft, a mini parachute reduced its speed and a large chute allowed the pilot to descend safely. Ejection seats became standard in jet fighters from the 1950s.

The ejection sequence of a Mk16 ejection seat

1. The pilot pulls a handle which triggers the ejection seat.

2. Guns attached to the ejection seat fire, and all locks and connections to the chair are automatically released.

3. A mini parachute, called a drogue, opens to slow the seat down.

4. The seat descends with the pilot still in a sitting position.

5. The drogue is released and the lines connecting it to the seat are cut.

6. A large parachute inflates. The pilot is pulled out of the ejection seat, which is then abandoned.

7. The pilot descends on the parachute. A life-raft is automatically inflated, in case of a landing in water.

Saved by a cat

An Englishman named Percy Shaw (1890-1976) made a fortune from one simple invention. One foggy night in 1933, he almost drove his car off the edge of a cliff. He was only saved by seeing his headlights reflected in the eyes of a cat sitting at the side of the road. Inspired by this incident, Shaw invented reflecting devices that he called "cat's eyes". They were soon fitted on roads in many countries.

How a cat's eye works

A glass stud is mounted in a rubber case with a metal surround. The mounting is raised above the level of the road.

When a car passes over it, the stud descends into its rubber casing. This reduces obstruction to the car's wheel.

Once the car has passed, the stud rises again and the glass is wiped clean by a rubber pad.

Strapped down for safety

Many inventions have attempted to make people's chances of surviving a car collision greater. In 1903, Gustave Liebau, a Frenchman, patented a design for protective braces, used in cars and aircraft. This formed the basis of the modern seat belt. The Swedish car manufacturer Volvo first fitted seat belts to their cars in 1963.

In 1988, the Japanese car manufacturer Toyota fitted an electrical system in some of its cars that automatically fastens the belt. The following year, Kim Nag-Hyun of South Korea developed a system that, in the event of a collision, automatically releases the belt 30 seconds after impact.

Piston

Explosive charge

Seat belt

Stages in a head-on collision of a car and a wall

Head-on collisions cause deceleration from running speed to zero in an instant.

As the front of the car crumples it absorbs some of the impact of the collision.

But passengers not wearing seat belts will be thrown forward at high speed.

Stages in the activation of an airbag safety system.

Automatic belt tensioners – On impact, the piston is pushed up by an explosive charge, tightening the belt.

An airbag system contained in the driver's steering wheel is activated on impact.

The airbag inflates to further absorb the energy of sudden deceleration.

When the driver is thrown forward the airbag protects him or her from serious injury.

Medical inventions

Many important inventions have helped doctors to diagnose and treat diseases. Some devices have been developed by doctors themselves, others have been produced as a result of technological advances in other fields which have then been applied to medicine.

Helping nature

Forceps are a surgical instrument used to help in the delivery of babies. They were invented by an English doctor named Peter Chamberlen (d.1631). For many years they remained a well-kept family secret, until Chamberlen's nephew, also named Peter Chamberlen (1601-83), inherited them. His use of forceps made him internationally famous in the field of childbirth.

Chamberlen's original forceps. They were like large pincers, operated by hand.

Ambulances

Dominique Larrey (1766-1842) was a French surgeon who received a gold medal for inventing a curved surgical needle. He is also famous for the invention of the ambulance. In 1792, France was at war with Prussia and Austria. Larrey saw that heavy wagons could not get to the battle front to collect wounded soldiers. He designed a light-weight carriage to transport people to hospitals quickly.

Larrey's ambulance carriage of the 1790s

Patients were placed on a thin mattress

Listening to the body

While out walking in Paris in 1816, a French doctor named René Laënnec (1781-1826) saw two children playing. One child held a stick to his ear, while the other child tapped the opposite end with a pin. The sound of the blows was transmitted along the wood. Later, Laënnec rolled up a sheet of paper and tied it with string. When he placed the tube on a patient's chest he could hear a heartbeat. He called his instrument a stethoscope, after the Greek word *stethos* meaning chest.

Try making a stethoscope of your own.

Laënnec's wooden stethoscope

Take a large, rectangular piece of stiff paper or cardboard and roll it into a long tube.

Tie the tube securely with pieces of string or rubber bands to keep it in shape.

Hold one end of the tube to your ear and place the other end against a friend's chest.

Painless operations

An anaesthetic is a drug that causes a temporary loss of feeling in a part of the body. Before anaesthetics were invented, patients had to be held down by force during painful operations.

The pain-numbing effects of nitrous oxide were first noticed in 1799 by Humphry Davy (1778-1829), an English scientist. In 1846, an American dentist, William Orton, used a powerful anaesthetic called ether to perform an operation on a patient's jaw. The following year, a Scottish doctor used a liquid called chloroform to reduce the pain of childbirth. In 1853, chloroform was given to Queen Victoria of England during the birth of one of her children.

A patient inhaling nitrous oxide through a mask.

The "Letheon" ether inhaler was produced in 1847.

Pieces of sponge were soaked in ether.

A mouthpiece was placed over the patient's mouth.

A flexible rubber tube

Ether fumes

Valves in the mouthpiece enabled the patient to breathe in and out.

Injecting beneath the skin

The hypodermic syringe, used to inject drugs into blood vessels or muscles, was invented in 1853 by Frenchman Charles Pravaz.

In 1987, another French doctor, Jean-Louis Brunet, patented a device which is attached to syringes when taking blood samples. The device automatically seals the needle as soon as it is withdrawn from the patient. This reduces the risk of doctors and nurses becoming contaminated by blood infected with dangerous viruses such as AIDS or hepatitis.

A selection of syringes

19th-century syringes

Needle

In this modern syringe fluid is forced out through the needle by a plunger.

Scale

Monitoring the heart

In 1903, Willem Einthoven (1860-1927) a Dutch doctor, invented the electrocardiograph (ECG) machine. It measures and records the electrical impulses produced by the heart's activity and is used to detect irregularities which can indicate heart disease. In 1924, Einthoven was awarded a Nobel Prize for his invention. An electrocardiograph machine produces a photographic chart of the heart's pulses, which is known as an electrocardiogram.

Einthoven demonstrating equipment which monitored the heartbeat of a dog.

From submarines to babies

By 1918, French scientists led by Pierre Langevin (1872-1946) had developed the sonar (sound navigation and ranging) system. The system sends out beams of sound waves and any object they meet reflects them back. The pattern of reflections forms a picture of the object. Sonar was installed in submarines and ships to detect other vessels. The principle was used in medicine in the 1950s by Ian Donald, a Scottish doctor. He discovered he was able to study the shape of an unborn baby's body and internal organs by passing pulses of sound through its mother's abdomen. This process, called ultrasound scanning, is used to check the health of unborn children.

Ultrasound image of a human fetus in the womb

Assisted breathing

In 1929, Philip Drinker, an American engineer, designed a device called a respirator, or iron lung, which helps people with breathing difficulties. It consists of an airtight box enclosing the patient's body from the neck down. Changes of pressure inside the box force air in and out of the lungs.

Early respirator of the 1930s

A 1950s respirator

The patient lies with his or her head outside the airtight box.

Tube to the air pump

A pump created a vacuum inside the airtight box.

Each time a vacuum is created inside the box, the pressure of the atmosphere outside forces air into the patient's lungs. The air is forced out of the lungs when there is no vacuum.

Surgery using lasers

Doctors often use technology developed for non-medical purposes. Lasers, for example, were first used in industry for drilling, welding and engraving. They are now used in surgical operations to cut through flesh and seal off tiny blood vessels to reduce bleeding. The theory of laser light was suggested in 1958 by Charles Townes (b.1915) and Arthur Schawlow (b.1921), American physicists. The first laser was built in 1960 by Theodore Maiman (b.1927).

How a ruby laser works

A rod of ruby inside a spiral shaped flash lamp.

Mirror

The ruby crystal absorbs white light from the flash lamp.

It re-emits the energy as a strong red beam which can travel great distances without becoming spread out or weak.

The laser beam increases in strength as it bounces between the mirrors.

Flash lamp

Weapons and warfare

Weapons are among man's earliest inventions. The first warriors made spears and axes by tying bones and flints to sticks. The Romans used sophisticated mechanical weapons, and by AD1000 the Chinese were making gunpowder for fireworks and sending signals. In the 13th century, Europeans began using gunpowder to fire cannons and hand-held guns.

A Colt revolver

The hammer was cocked (pulled back) by hand.

Cartridge containing a bullet

When the gun was fired, the hammer struck a firing pin on the cartridge. This detonated an explosive charge and shot the bullet out of the gun barrel.

Barrel

Trigger

Cartridges were placed in the cylinder. After each shot the cylinder rotated, bringing a new cartridge in front of the hammer ready for firing.

A patent for one of Colt's rifles

A 16th-century machine gun. Each barrel had a bullet and was fired by hand.

Today, science and warfare are very closely linked. New and increasingly deadly weapons have been invented by both chemists and physicists.

A fast-firing revolver

Early handguns were very difficult to fire. Before each shot, a gun had to be loaded with gunpowder and pellets, and a fuse lit to ignite it. A more efficient gun was patented in 1836, by Samuel Colt (1814-62) who was born in Connecticut, USA. His gun designs included one called a revolver which could fire six shots before it needed to be reloaded. At first, revolvers were considered very complicated, but later they were extensively used in the American Civil War (1861-65) and by settlers making their way westward across the USA.

This man with two fast-firing revolvers is thought to be Black Jack Ketcham, an outlaw.

A quick killing

Richard Gatling (1818-1903) was an inventor from North Carolina, USA. After the outbreak of the American Civil War in 1861, he designed a gun, called a machine gun, which could be fired rapidly. It had ten barrels arranged as a cylinder around the central shaft. The cylinder was rotated using a hand crank. A cartridge on top of the gun dropped bullets into position for firing. The multiple barrels enabled the gun to be fired many times without overheating. It could fire 350 bullets in a minute.

Gatling's design was improved by Hiram Maxim (1840-1916) who introduced the first fully automatic machine gun in 1884.

A cutaway of a Maxim machine gun

Dynamite and peace prizes

Alfred Nobel (1833-96), a Swedish chemist, owned a factory that made an explosive called nitroglycerin. When the factory blew up in 1865, killing several people, Nobel began to look for a way to make explosives safer to handle

By mixing nitroglycerin with a chemical called *kieselguhr*, he produced a more stable substance. He sold the mixture in tubes of waxed cardboard and called it "dynamite", after the Greek word *dynamis* meaning power.

Though Nobel made his fortune manufacturing explosives, he was a dedicated pacifist. He left the bulk of his large fortune to fund the Nobel Prizes, awarded annually to people who make major contributions in the fields of literature, chemistry, physics, medicine and world peace.

A water-filled jacket kept the gun-barrel cool.

Muzzle

Water emptying plug

Used cartridges were ejected from the gun by a spring.

Cartridge belt

Rear sight

Crank

Safety catch

Trigger mechanism

Handle grip

War rockets

In 1942, a long-range rocket called the V-2 was launched (see page 19). Designed by Wernher von Braun (1912-77), it flew at several times the speed of sound, giving no warning of its approach. It had a range of 320km (200 miles). It had a warhead that weighed about 1.02 tonnes (1 ton) and was packed with explosives.

Today, many missiles are guided to their targets by electronic devices. Some have a range of 9,600km (6,000 miles), and can strike within 30.5m (100ft) of their target.

Nose fuse
Warhead
Fuse conduit
Guidance chamber
Radio control
Nitrogen bottles

A V-2 rocket

This fuel tank contains a mixture of ethyl alcohol and water.

This fuel tank contains liquid oxygen to speed up burning of fuel.

The two fuels are forced by pumps into the combustion chamber. The mixture is then ignited by gunpowder.

The exhaust fumes escape at supersonic speed.

Steerable rudder

Chemical warfare

Fritz Haber (1868-1934) was a German chemist. His early studies involved converting nitrogen (a gas found in air) into ammonia, a substance used in crop fertilizers. He won the Nobel Prize for chemistry in 1918 for this work. But many people objected to the award because Haber had been involved in developing poisonous gases for use in warfare. He produced chlorine gas, which attacks the lining of the nose, throat and lungs. During World War I, both sides used poisonous gases.

Haber also devised a gas mask to protect both civilians and soldiers from harmful gases.

Gas masks were introduced in 1915.

Tight-fitting mask made of cotton pads soaked in chemicals

Connecting pipe

A box containing charcoal and lime-permanganate granules filtered the poisoned air.

Nuclear warfare

By the outbreak of World War II, scientists realized that if the nucleus of an atom was split in two, a huge amount of energy would be released. If this energy was uncontrolled there would be a massive explosion. A bomb based on this principle is called an "atomic bomb".

In 1942, Enrico Fermi (1901-54), an Italian scientist, built a nuclear reactor, in which he produced controlled nuclear energy. The first atomic bomb was developed under the supervision of American physicist Robert Oppenheimer (1904-67). He was in charge of the Los Alamos Science Laboratory, in New Mexico, USA, when the

atomic bomb was tested in 1945. The USA was at war with Japan and later that year they dropped two atomic bombs on the Japanese cities of Hiroshima and Nagasaki, killing many thousands of civilians. When they saw the huge destruction the bomb caused, many scientists spoke out against American plans to build another more powerful bomb, known as the hydrogen bomb or "H" bomb.

Oppenheimer (left) at a bomb testing site

This atomic bomb, called "Fat Boy", was dropped on Nagasaki, Japan.

Inside the bomb was a substance called plutonium. All the atoms in the plutonium split, releasing huge amounts of uncontrolled energy.

Stabilizing fin

Nose fuse

The nuclear explosion was detonated by charges inside the bomb.

Calculators and computers

Counting and calculating systems have been needed for as long as people have bought and sold goods. One of the earliest adding machines, the abacus, was invented about 5,000 years ago, in Babylonia (now the area occupied by Iran and Iraq).

A 19th-century engraving of an abacus being used in China

Special numbers

In 1614, John Napier (1550-1617), a Scottish mathematician, invented logarithm tables. The principle of the tables was that every number had an equivalent special number called a logarithm. Logarithms made mathematical division and multiplication quick and easy. For example, to multiply two numbers their logarithms were simply added together. The resulting logarithm was looked up in the tables to find its corresponding number.

An early calculator

Blaise Pascal (1623-62) was a French mathematician. In 1642, he designed an adding machine to help his father, a tax inspector, whose job involved carrying out many complicated calculations.

Convinced that the machine would make their fortunes, father and son invested a lot of money in it. But their work was opposed both by clerks who feared they would lose their jobs, and by employers who preferred to pay low wages rather than buy Pascal's expensive machine.

Cogs for calculating

Charles Babbage (1792-1871), the son of a rich banker from Devon, England, was a very talented mathematician. He was concerned about errors in Napier's logarithm tables. In 1821, he began to design a "difference engine", a very large and complicated machine, designed to calculate logarithms automatically. But it was difficult to make the machine's parts accurate enough to prevent errors in its calculations.

For about ten years the British government poured money into Charles Babbage's project. But, finally, they lost patience and stopped.

Next, Babbage began to design an "analytical engine", which could carry out many different types of calculation. Working with him was mathematician Ada Lovelace (1815-52). She devised several computer programs for the engine, which were coded on cards with holes punched in them.

A modern reconstruction of Babbage's analytical engine. It was designed to be driven by steam.

Numbers were stored in columns by wheels which could be put in any of ten positions corresponding to the digits 0 to 9.

Punched program cards

Babbage devoted the last 37 years of his life to building the analytical engine. He refined his design again and again, and applied for extra funds to pay for the work. He became increasingly frustrated by what he considered a lack of public recognition and support for his work. In 1871, he died before he had completed the machine. In fact, his engine was well beyond the technology of the time and it is unlikely that it would ever have been finished.

Lady Ada Lovelace became the first computer programmer.

Pascal's mechanical adding machine

Cogwheels turned dials next to each other in a mechanical gear system

Numbers appeared in these windows.

Dials representing units

Census collection

In the USA during the 19th century, a census of the population was taken every ten years. This became increasingly complicated as the population grew. In 1887, officials were still struggling to compile the results of the 1880 census. A competition was held to find a quicker method of analysing the figures. It was won by Herman Hollerith (1860-1929), an engineer who designed an electric counting machine. Information about each citizen was stored on a card as a series of punched holes. The position of the holes corresponded to particular characteristics, such as age or marital status. The cards were inserted into the machine. Inside, a set of wires was pushed up against them. When a wire passed through a hole, an electric circuit was completed, making a counter advance by one unit. Hollerith's invention sped up methods of processing data so much that the results of the 1890 census were compiled in only six weeks.

The Hollerith tabulator used to compute the results of the 1890 census.

A card used in the 1900 USA census

Electronic computers

An early electronic computer was ENIAC (Electronic Numerical Integrator and Calculator). It was developed by John Mauchly (1907-80) and John Eckert (b.1919) for the American army. Compared with modern computers it was huge, filling an entire large room. Yet it could perform fewer tasks than a modern desk-top computer.

As technology has advanced, computers have become smaller and smaller,

Eckert (right) holding one of ENIAC's components

yet they are capable of performing an increasing number of tasks.

In 1948, the glass valves, called diodes, used in the first computers (see page 32), were replaced by minute electronic devices called transistors. They were invented by three scientists: John Bardeen (b.1908), Walter Brattain (1902-87) and William Shockley (1910-89), who were jointly awarded the Nobel Prize for physics in 1956. Today, pocket calculators and computers contain tiny electrical circuit boards (called silicon chips) which include thousands of transistors.

Today, computers are used for many tasks, from composing music and creating graphics, to guiding aircraft and milking cows. You can find out more about computers and the tasks they perform on page 22.

Handles and cogwheels set the position of the numbers

The engine was programmed by a sequence of punched cards carrying data and instructions. The cards were placed here.

A cutaway picture of a pocket calculator

Liquid crystal display (LCD)

Solar cells convert light energy into electricity to power the calculator.

Button

Switch   Contact pad

When a button is pressed, a switch touches a metal contact pad. This completes the electronic circuit and relays the message to the silicon chip.

0.258

MR   M

7

√   4

C   1

AC   0

The power of the imagination

Throughout the centuries, inventors have imagined machines that were beyond the technological capabilities of their time. Other inventors imagined machines which we now know are beyond the realms of possibility. Some of these inventions never went further than the drawing board; others were built, tested and rapidly forgotten.

Wishful thinking

Some of the machines that inventors have believed possible in the past may seem ridiculous to us today. For example, some people believed that it was possible to build a machine which would go on working forever, without an outside power source. This was known as a perpetual motion machine. In 1618, an English doctor named Robert Fludd (1574-1637) designed a perpetual motion watermill. He believed that once the machine was moving it would continue forever. We now know that it is impossible to achieve perpetual motion. The moving parts of a machine rub together and produce friction. This wastes energy and slows the machine down.

Science fiction

Science fiction writers create imaginary worlds, filled with weird inventions. Sometimes the creators believe that in the future, with new materials and greater scientific knowledge, their vision may become reality.

A century before men walked on the Moon, the French author Jules Verne (1828-1905) wrote about space travel. Perhaps writers today, when they describe imaginary worlds are predicting how we will live in the future.

A propeller-driven skating outfit designed by William Heath Robinson

Some writers have made fun of science and invention, by dreaming up machines which could not possibly be built. The writer Jonathan Swift's book *Gulliver's Travels* is full of mock inventions, including a magnetic flying island.

Flights of fancy

In 1867, two English inventors, Edmund Edwards and James Butler, designed an aircraft based on the shape of a paper dart. It was fitted with a rudder for side-to-side control and flaps for up-and-down control. But it was powered by a steam engine and needed a furnace and boiler that would have been so heavy that the machine could never have flown.

A steam-powered aircraft designed by Edwards and Butler

Landing springs

Star wars

Archimedes (287-212 BC) was a mathematician born in Sicily. He invented many very efficient devices. He also tried to design a weapon which used giant mirrors to capture and focus the Sun's rays to destroy enemy ships. We now know that Archimedes' idea would not have worked; but even today scientists sometimes attempt projects which are beyond the capabilities of modern technology. In the 1980s the USA announced plans to build the Strategic Defense Initiative (SDI), known as "Star Wars", which involved a system of satellites used to shoot down enemy missiles with lasers. Some scientists believe the system will never work successfully.

A design for Dr. Fludd's perpetual motion watermill

A channel carried the water back to the water-wheel

The water-wheel was perpetually driven around by the circulating water.

A rotating screw inside a hollow tube raised water from a tank to the channel.

Millstones for grinding corn were turned by an axle connected to the water-wheel.

The propeller was turned by steam jets on the end of each blade.

Rudders were used to move the aircraft from side to side.

A water tank was heated by a furnace to produce the steam needed for power.

The pilot's compartment contained a furnace and boiler. It would also take one passenger.

Wires provided support

Wooden frame

Anchor for docking

Pratt's helmet-gun

Gun barrel

An air tube led to the gun's trigger.

Sights helped the wearer aim the gun for firing.

A helmet gum

In 1917, Albert Pratt, an American inventor, patented a helmet fitted with a gun. To fire it, the wearer blew through a tube leading to a bulb beside the trigger. The bulb expanded, squeezing the trigger. It could also be turned upside-down and used as a cooking pot. In reality, the recoil of the gun when it was fired would have broken the wearer's neck.

The Renaissance man

Leonardo da Vinci (1452-1519), born near Florence in Italy, was one of the world's greatest artists, as well as being a talented musician and sculptor. He was also a prolific inventor. Throughout his life, he filled notebooks with drawings of many things: the human body, birds in flight and the strange machines he had invented.

Da Vinci's inventions included a flying machine with wings like a bird, vessels to travel under water, a giant crossbow, a spinning wheel, a helicopter and powerful guns. Some of these were built; but many others could not have worked and remained hidden away in his sketch books for centuries.

Leonardo's design for a tank. He was also a military engineer, designing war machines and fortifications.

A portrait of Leonardo da Vinci shortly before his death

Viewing turret

Wheel driven by hand cranks

Gun barrels

A design for a missile-detecting satellite system

Solar panels provide power

Infrared telescope

This shield protects the telescope from radiated heat.

Infrared grid locates and monitors aircraft and missiles.

Superfluid helium cooling system

A reconstruction of a giant crossbow sketched in Leonardo da Vinci's notebook

A lever was pulled and a rope holding the arrow was released. The arrow flew off.

A soldier operated a gear mechanism which pulled back the arrow.

The crossbow could be moved into position on three pairs of wheels.

Key dates in the history of invention

Dates BC

4241BC The first year in which events can be precisely dated. This is made possible by the introduction of the Egyptian calendar.

c3200BC The Sumerians in Mesopotamia are the first people to use writing and to draw a picture showing a wheel.

c3000BC The Babylonians invent the abacus, the first adding machine.

c1300BC The Syrians develop their own alphabet.

700BC Coins are used in Lydia (Turkey) for buying and selling goods.

287BC The birth of Archimedes, who invents many valuable mechanical devices using screws and levers.

c10BC The Roman architect Vitruvius describes a crane.

Dates AD

999 The first mechanical clock is invented by a monk.

c1000 The Chinese use gunpowder for fireworks and sending signals.

c1045 In China, Pi Cheng invents movable type.

1280 The first pair of glasses is made in Italy.

1450s Johannes Gutenberg's printing presses revolutionize the production of books. This, in turn, speeds up the spread of information about new inventions.

1452 The birth of Leonardo da Vinci, an artist who invents numerous machines.

1569 Mercator a Flemish mapmaker, introduces a new method of drawing maps.

1592 Galileo builds a telescope which magnifies things 30 times.

1614 John Napier, a Scottish mathematician, invents his logarithm tables.

1642 Blaise Pascal designs an adding machine to speed up his father's tax calculations.

1643 Evangelista Torricelli makes a device now known as the mercury barometer for measuring air pressure.

1656 Christian Huygens designs an accurate pendulum clock, based on Galileo's ideas.

1665 The illustrations in Robert Hooke's *Micrographia* reveal the power of new microscopes.

1668 Isaac Newton builds a reflecting telescope.

1698 The first steam engine, built by Thomas Savery, is used for pumping water out of flooded mines.

1733 The flying shuttle, invented by an English weaver, doubles the amount of cloth a person can produce in one day.

1771 Richard Arkwright's water-powered spinning machine produces much stronger cotton thread than was previously possible.

1778 Household sanitation is greatly improved by the introduction of Joseph Bramah's new toilets.

1783 The Marquis de Jouffroy d'Abbans launches the first steamboat.

1783 The Montgolfier brothers successfully fly a hot air balloon.

1797 The value of parachutes is demonstrated by a Frenchman jumping from a hot air balloon.

1801 The *Nautilus*, an early submarine, completes its maiden voyage.

1804 Richard Trevithick builds the first steam locomotive to run on rails.

1814 Friedrich König develops the steam-driven press, which works far more quickly than hand-operated printing machinery.

1815 Humphry Davy invents a miner's lamp, which makes it far safer to work in mines.

1819 Augustus Siebe designs a pressurized diving suit enabling people to dive to greater depths.

1821 Charles Babbage starts work on his difference engine, designed to draw up complicated mathematical tables automatically.

1826 Joseph Niepce, a French physicist, takes the world's first photograph.

1829 George Stephenson wins a competition to design and build the best steam locomotive. He produces a locomotive called the *Rocket*.

1830 The first sewing machine is designed by Thimonnier, a French tailor.

1836 Samuel Colt patents his fast-firing revolver.

1837 Isambard Kingdom Brunel launches the first transatlantic steamship.

1837 Two British inventors named William Cooke and Charles Wheatstone make the first electric telegraph machine.

1839 Louis Daguerre invents daguerreotype photographs, which become very fashionable for portraits.

1843 Samuel Morse designs his famous dot-dash code for use when sending telegraphic messages.

1846 An American dentist uses ether to numb pain during a jaw operation.

1848 The first escalator is opened in New York as a tourist attraction.

1849 The safety pin is invented.

1857 A New York store becomes the first shop to have a safety elevator.

1860 The Belgian Étienne Lenoir builds the first internal combustion engine.

1863 The first underground railway line opens in London.

1868 A newspaper editor, Christopher Sholes, builds the first practical typewriter.

1872 Photograprapher Eadweard Muybridge takes the first set of sequential photographs.

1876 Alexander Bell sends the first telephone message.

1876 America's most prolific inventor, Thomas Edison, sets up his invention factory.

1877 Edison produces the musical phonograph.

1878 Joseph Swan invents the electric light bulb.

1879 Ernst von Siemens demonstrates the first train to run on electrified tracks.

1881 Émile Berliner patents a gramophone using flat discs.

1884 Hiram Maxim introduces an automatic machine gun.

1885 Physicist Heinrich Hertz demonstrates the existence of electromagnetic waves.

1885 An Austrian chemist named Carl Auer invents a gas mantle, which is easier and safer to use than candles.

1886 Linotype machines enable the text for printed books and newspapers to be produced far more quickly.

1888 George Eastman produces the Kodak no.1 camera and develops customers' films.

1889 Edison's assistant Charles Batchelor experiments with the idea of movie soundtracks.

1890 The Daimler Motor Company starts to manufacture four-wheel, fuel-driven cars.

1890 The American census is rapidly completed with Herman Hollerith's electric counting machine.

1895 In Paris, the Lumière brothers put on a show with ten moving films.

1898 Valdemar Poulson designs the forerunner of the modern tape recorder.

1901 King Camp Gillette patents the disposable safety razor blade.

1902 Italian Guglielmo Marconi transmits a radio message across the English Channel.

1903 The American Wright brothers make the first powered aircraft flight.

1903 Henry Ford introduces mass-production techniques with his new car factory.

1903 Willem Einthoven invents the electrocardiograph machine to record the heart's activity.

1904 John Fleming's glass diodes become an essential part of radio equipment.

1908 Named after its inventor, the Geiger counter is used for detecting and measuring radiation.

1909 The General Electric Company introduces the electric toaster.

1923 Two Swedish engineers design the first refrigerator.

1925 Traffic lights are installed in London.

1926 John Logie Baird successfully transmits the first television image of a human face.

1926 Robert Goddard launches the first liquid fuel rocket.

1928 The American invention "Sellotape" becomes an everyday item.

1929 Philip Drinker invents the iron lung to help sick people breathe.

1933 Two German scientists named Max Kroll and Ernst Ruska introduce the electron microscope.

1933 Inspired by seeing his headlights reflected in an animal's eyes, Percy Shaw invents "cat's eyes" for marking roads.

1935 The German company AEG introduces magnetic plastic tape for recording sound.

1937 People begin to stop using airships after the *Hindenburg* catches fire and passengers are killed.

1938 A Hungarian inventor Lazlo Biro introduces the first ballpoint pen is called a biro.

1938 An American, Chester Carlson, invents the first photocopying machine.

1839 The first helicopter is built by a Russian engineer named Igor Sikorsky.

1942 Wernher von Braun launches the first long-range V-2 rocket.

1942 In Chicago, USA, controlled nuclear energy is successfully produced.

1945 An American inventor named Percy Spencer patents his design for the first microwave oven.

1945 The USA drops two atomic bombs on Japanese cities.

1946 ENIAC, America's first electronic computer, is publicly demonstrated.

1947 Edwin Land's Polaroid camera produces black and white photographs in under one minute.

1948 Three American scientists named John Bardeen, Walter Brattain and William Shockley miniaturize electronic circuitry by inventing a device called the transistor and win a Nobel Prize for their work.

1957 The Russian *Sputnik I* is the first artificial object to orbit the Earth.

1959 The hovercraft, designed by Christopher Cockerell, is publicly demonstrated.

1960 Theodore Maiman builds the world's first laser.

1962 *Telstar* is launched, the first satellite to relay live TV as well as telephone calls.

1977 America launches the Space Shuttle, the world's first reusable spacecraft.

1982 Philips and Sony introduce compact discs.

1987 Digital audio cassettes are introduced.

1990 The first transmission of high definition television.

The *Inventors* quiz

The answers to all the following questions can be found between pages 3 and 45 of this book. You will also find the answers upside down at the bottom of this page.

1. What is the name of the central heating system invented by the Romans?

2. Name of the 16th century map maker whose methods are still used in atlases today.

3. Name one of the universally accepted scales of temperature measurement.

4. Which planet did William and Caroline Herschel discover?

5. Who first experimented with the idea of contact lenses?

6. Why did an angry mob destroy 80 sewing machines designed by Barthelmey Thimonnier?

7. Who produced the first motor car to be sold?

8. In what city was the first underground railway opened?

9. Can you identify the following inventors?

a)   b)   c)

10. Which ship, designed by Isambard Kingdom Brunel, carried enough coal to sail from England to Australia and back?

11. What equipment did Christopher Cockerell first use to demonstrate the principle of peripheral jets?

12. Which of the two Wright brothers piloted the first powered and controlled aircraft flight?

13. What was the name given to Hubert Booth's first fuel-driven vacuum cleaner?

14. Why did Christopher Sholes, the inventor of the typewriter, not make any money out of his invention?

15. Identify these inventions and name their creators.

a)   b)

c)

16. Why was the first ballpoint pen so useful to the British Air Force?

17. How did Elisha Otis demonstrate the spring-operated safety mechanism in his elevator?

18. What happened to Johannes Gutenberg's printing equipment in 1455?

19. How many sheets of paper could Friedrich König's machine print in an hour?

20. What does the word "telegraph" mean?

21. Who took the world's first photograph?

22. What bet did photographer Eadweard Muybridge settle?

23. What was the first radio signal sent across the Atlantic Ocean?

24. Who made the first television transmission of a human face?

25. Which important invention designed by Thomas Edison in 1877 was first sold as a toy?

26. Émile Berliner's discs were made of shellac. What is shellac?

27. Why were the first gas-powered traffic signals abandoned?

28. What animal saved Percy Shaw's life in 1933?

29. Name the process used to check the health of unborn babies which has its origins in a device used by submarines and ships.

30. How many bullets could the Maxim machine gun fire in a minute?

31. Who invented the explosive called dynamite, yet left much of his fortune to fund a series of prizes including one for world peace?

32. In 1642 Blaise Pascal invented an adding machine. Why was it particularly useful for his father?

33. An early electronic computer was called ENIAC. What does ENIAC stand for?

34. Can you recognize the inventions from these close-ups?

a)   b)   c)

35. Name one of the reasons why the aircraft designed by Edwards' and Butler would not have been able to fly.

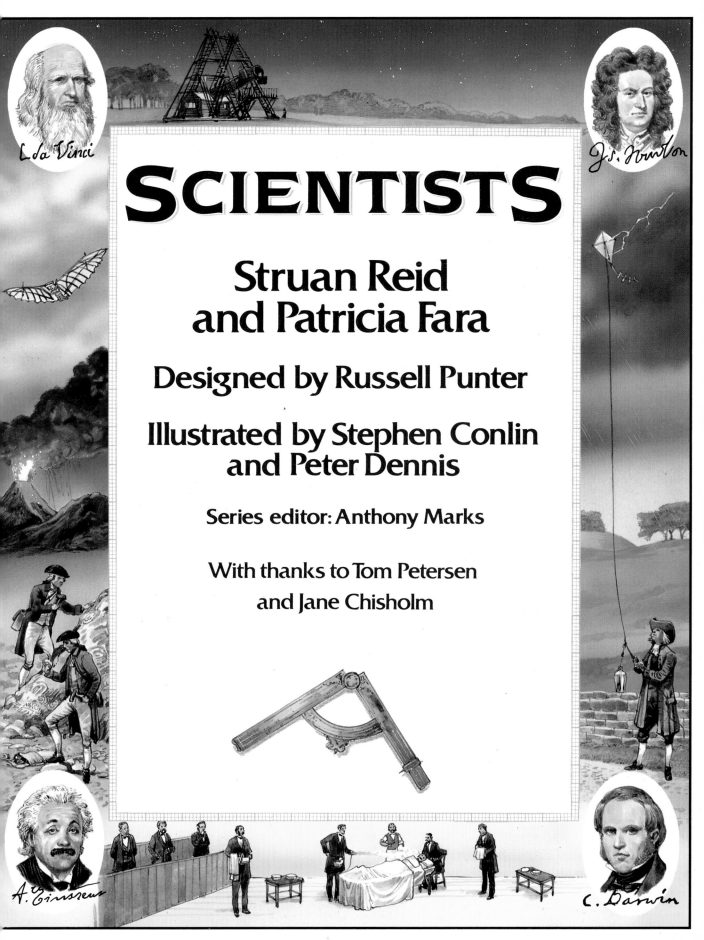

SCIENTISTS

Struan Reid
and Patricia Fara

Designed by Russell Punter

Illustrated by Stephen Conlin
and Peter Dennis

Series editor: Anthony Marks

With thanks to Tom Petersen
and Jane Chisholm

Contents

Introduction

This section of the book is about the lives and work of some of the world's greatest scientists, from the earliest observations of the skies to modern theories of the universe. It is not a comprehensive history of science, but it describes in detail the breakthroughs and discoveries that have had the greatest impact on the lives of people through the ages.

What is a scientist?

Scientists are people who gather knowledge about the world and how it works. To do this they ask questions, then try to answer them by using observation and experiment. Today there are many different types of scientist, but until about 200 years ago people did not distinguish between the scientific disciplines. In fact, the word "scientist" was not invented before 1830.

For thousands of years most people believed that the earth lay at the middle of the universe, as this 16th-century engraving shows.

How science began

Science began as a search for knowledge that arose out of a need for survival. For example, early hunters studied the habits and variety of animals they hunted. They discovered the uses of plants and herbs as food and medicine, and worked out how to make use of natural substances such as metals and minerals. By experimenting with these materials, people developed ways to improve the quality of their lives.

16th-century illustration showing liquids being heated and collected in bottles

Today we depend upon science for many of the things we take for granted, for comfort, health and entertainment. This section of the book is about the people who made these scientific developments possible.

Expanding frontiers

Scientific knowledge is always expanding, and the scientific truths of one age are often questioned by people of the next. Scientists today generally accept that their theories will be revised in the future. New inventions and discoveries also change the way we look at the world. For example, many 15th-century Europeans believed that the sky was made up of crystal spheres which carried the stars and planets around the earth. But discoveries such as those made possible by the invention of the telescope forced people to reject that idea. They began to regard the universe as larger than had previously been thought. This in turn altered people's ideas of their own position in the universe.

A map of our galaxy formed from radio waves

Historical arrangement

This section of the book is arranged historically, beginning with the earliest scientific ideas and medical skills used in the ancient world. It then considers medieval Arab thinkers and the vital role they played in preserving and developing classical learning and passing it on to Renaissance Europe. From this point on, the development of science into the individual disciplines familiar to us today is revealed. It discusses the changing relationship between science and religion, and the difficulties that many earlier scientists faced. There are also pages on scientific societies and the very important but underrated role of women scientists. A chart on pages 94-95 outlines the main events described in this section of the book.

Dates

Some of the dates are from the period before the birth of Christ. They are indicated by the letters B.C. Early dates in the period after Christ's birth are indicated by the letters A.D. Some of the dates begin with the abbreviation "c". This stands for *circa*, the Latin for "about". It is used when historians are unsure exactly when an event took place.

Early scientific ideas

Science is the process of gathering knowledge and answering questions about the world and how it works. Today, science is divided into different branches, such as chemistry and biology. But in ancient times people did not make the distinction between science and other forms of investigation. Many questions that we would now regard as scientific were then given religious or philosophical explanations. Very few early "scientists" are known by name, but we do have evidence of their ideas.

This Egyptian painting depicts the constellations (groups of stars) as gods.

The Ancient Egyptians

One of the first civilizations in the history of the world was that of Ancient Egypt. It began over 5000 years ago and lasted for more than 3000 years. The Egyptians were very practical, and were especially skilled as builders and craftspeople. But they were also great thinkers, with theories and ideas about the world around them.

This wall painting shows an Egyptian surveyor taking measurements.

Egyptian priest-astronomers used the position of the Moon and stars like a giant clock, to work out the timing of their religious festivals. This enabled them to calculate when the River Nile would flood each year. This was the most important event in the agricultural year. They also used their knowledge of the stars to work out several calendars. The first calendar to divide the year into 365 days may have been introduced by an Egyptian man called Imhotep (see page 56).

The Mesopotamians

The region of Mesopotamia (now in modern Iraq) was the site of several ancient civilizations, including those of Sumer and Babylon. The Sumerians flourished from about 4000B.C. They were skilled astronomers and mathematicians, and built huge temples called ziggurats.

The Sumerians also devised a system of writing known as cuneiform ("wedge-shaped"). This was the first form of writing in which abstract signs, rather than pictures of objects, were used to represent sounds. The Sumerians also used two counting systems. One was a decimal system based on units of ten. The other was based on units of sixty.

The Babylonian civilization flourished in Mesopotamia for over 1300 years from 1900B.C. Babylonian astronomers made many observations of eclipses, the Moon and the planets Venus and Mercury. They named the constellations after their gods and divided the skies into areas. This later formed the basis for Greek astrology.

The Babylonians were able to predict future movements of the planets by consulting detailed lists

of planetary motions which they had compiled over many years. The purpose of this work was not to explain the motions, but rather to put together calendars and to make predictions about the future. The Babylonians saw the world as a flat disc floating on the seas. Babylon was ringed by mountains.

A Babylonian stone map of the world, c.600B.C.

Central America

From about 2000B.C., several civilizations grew up in Meso-America (Mexico and parts of Central America). One of the greatest was that of the Mayans (300B.C. to A.D.900). Later civilizations included the Toltecs and Aztecs.

Mayan observatory at Chichen Itza, Mexico

This is part of a Mayan calendar. The Mayans used dots, dashes and curved lines to indicate dates.

This Aztec stone depicts the stars and planets. The Aztecs (c.1300-1521) adopted the Mayan calendar.

The Mayans divided the world into four "directions", or sections, each associated with a tree and a bird. They believed the world was made up from the back of a giant crocodile lying in a pond.

The earliest Greek science

Scholars in Ancient Greece were known as philosophers, which means "lovers of knowledge". Apart from the subject we now know as philosophy (the study of ideas), they also studied scientific subjects such as mathematics, biology, astronomy and geography. They carefully collected as much information as possible to help their studies.

Thales of Miletus

The first important place of Greek learning was based in the eastern Mediterranean. One of the most influential philosophers there was Thales, who came from the port of Miletus, which is now in Turkey.

Thales of Miletus (c.624-546B.C.)

A mathematician and astronomer, he taught that water was the main ingredient of all things and that the earth was a disc floating on water. The work of Thales is very significant because he tried to give natural explanations to puzzling phenomena. For example, he said that earthquakes were not caused by the anger of the gods, but by eruptions of hot water in the oceans.

Pythagoras

Pythagoras was born on the island of Samos and became one of the most highly respected of the early Greek philosophers. As a young man he visited Egypt and Babylon, and was greatly influenced by many of the ideas he found there. He became an important religious leader whose followers were known as the Pythagorean Order.

Pythagoras' ideas about the universe were based on his emphasis on the importance of particular numbers and symmetry in everything. Because of their love of beauty and order, he and his followers believed that the planets moved in circles, and that the heavens and earth were spherical. These ideas were still extremely influential 2000 years later.

An Athenian coin depicting Pythagoras (c.560-480B.C.)

Pythagoras worked out how the size of bells relates to the sounds they make.

Science in Ancient Greece

The people of Ancient Greece used stories about their gods to explain things they found puzzling. For example, the god of the sea, called Poseidon, was also known as "the earth-shaker" because he was thought to cause earthquakes when he was angry. But from the 6th century B.C. some people started to look for more practical explanations of how and why things look and behave as they do. In order to obtain this knowledge, they asked lots of questions and made many observations and calculations about all sorts of things in the world around them.

Greek coin showing Poseidon

The Academy at Athens

Plato is regarded as the founder of western philosophy. He was born in Athens and later studied under another famous philosopher called Socrates. When he was in his thirties, Plato decided to travel abroad. He visited many of the lands bordering the Mediterranean Sea and met other philosophers.

By the time he returned to Athens in 388B.C., Plato had decided to become a teacher. The following year he founded a school called the Academy which became famous throughout the Greek world. It lasted for over 900 years until it was closed by the Roman emperor Justinian in A.D.529.

Mosaic showing philosophers at the Academy

Plato's work and influence

Plato developed a set of teachings known as the Doctrine of Ideas, which were handed down to us via the Arabs. They were very important for later thinkers because they linked scientific thought with religion and philosophy. Plato argued that everything we detect with our five senses (sight, hearing, taste, smell and touch) is only an outward appearance. He believed that reality is something that we can never observe but only contemplate with our minds. This became one of the foundations of later western thought.

Although Plato had a great influence on later philosophers and scientists, today his views are often regarded as a hindrance to modern experimental science. This is because Plato did not encourage experiment, thinking that observation only confused the search for pure theoretical knowledge. For

Plato (427-347B.C.)

example, he believed that the movements of the planets are best understood by the mind, not by accurate observations. He emphasized mathematics as the key to all knowledge but, unlike Archimedes (see below), was not interested in its practical use.

Tutor to Alexander

Aristotle (384-322B.C.) was born in Macedonia in northeastern Greece. His parents died when he was a boy and he was sent by his guardian to study at Plato's Academy. On Plato's death, he left Athens and journeyed for twelve years in Greece and Asia Minor. He returned to Macedonia in 343B.C., and for three years he served as tutor to the young Prince Alexander of Macedonia (later Alexander the Great). After Alexander succeeded his father as king,

This fragment of a mosaic shows Alexander in battle.

Aristotle moved back to Athens and set up his own school, the Lyceum.

Illustration from a Greek cup showing students at work

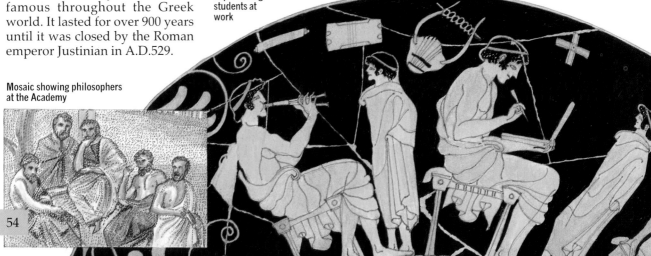

After Alexander's death in 323B.C., Aristotle left Athens for the last time and retired to his estate at Chalcis on the island of Euboea where he died.

Teaching at the Lyceum

Aristotle's beliefs were very different from Plato's. Unlike Plato, he thought it was necessary to gather as much information as possible. His writings, passed down to us through the ages via the Arabs, laid many of the foundations of modern scientific study.

According to Aristotle, the gods had given a fixed position to every object in the sky above and the earth below. He believed that nothing could change by itself without displacing everything else in the system. Aristotle devised a "Ladder of Nature", with living things placed above inanimate matter such as stones. Human beings were placed above the animals and the gods ruled over them all.

A medieval illustration showing Aristotle's Ladder of Nature

Aristotle believed that the universe consisted of a series of spheres fitting one inside the other, arranged around a spherical earth. Immediately around the earth was the sphere of the atmosphere, followed by spheres containing earth, water, air and fire. Beyond the fire sphere lay a region containing a substance he called the *aether* (from the Greek for "shining"). Farther out

Medieval version of Aristotle's view of the universe

still were spheres carrying planets and stars, and finally, around them all, lay a sphere which controlled the movement of the whole system.

Aristotle's influence

Aristotle's main contribution to science was his emphasis on careful observation and very detailed classification. His ideas were highly influential in Europe for about 1500 years. It was not until the Renaissance that they were questioned, most notably by Galileo (see page 66).

Aristotle's system was not in itself rigid. But it was used by many people in the Middle Ages to justify and maintain the feudal system, a strict social order by which kings ruled over lords, who in turn ruled over peasants.

This illustration shows the three main occupations in the Middle Ages: priests, warriors and peasants.

Mathematician and inventor

Archimedes was born in the Greek colony of Syracuse in Sicily. He was a brilliant mathematician and studied at a famous school of learning in Alexandria in Egypt called the Museum. He was killed in 212B.C. when the Romans captured Syracuse.

Archimedes
(287-212B.C.)

He is best known for a law called Archimedes' Principle. This states that when an object is immersed in a fluid it is subject to an upward force equal to the weight of the fluid displaced. It is said that Archimedes shouted *Eureka* ("I have found it") when he saw that his body displaced the water as he climbed into his bath.

Medieval picture of Archimedes in his bath

Practical mathematics

Archimedes used geometry to measure curves and the areas and volumes of solids. He designed leverage systems such as the Archimedean screw for removing water from flooded ships. This principle is still used to raise water from one level to another.

Mosaic showing the murder of Archimedes by a Roman soldier.

Medicine in the ancient world

People have always had to deal with illness, disease and death, but explanations and treatments have varied from area to area throughout history. In many places, illness was seen either as the invasion of the body by some poison or spell, or it was attributed to angry gods who had stolen the person's soul. Early physicians were part doctors and part priests. They believed that medical treatment could relieve the illness, but that the main cause could only be removed by praying to the gods and offering them sacrifices.

Egyptian medicine

The Ancient Egyptians were extremely good surgeons and used a variety of drugs and surgical techniques. Their knowledge of human anatomy was excellent because of their practice of embalming (the preservation of the dead). They believed that the dead person's spirit, or *Ka*, would die if the body rotted away. In order to provide a home for the spirit, the body was preserved as carefully as possible.

This Egyptian wall painting shows part of the embalming process.

First the corpse was cleaned, then the brain and internal organs (such as heart, liver, lungs) were removed and washed in wine. They were then stored in special jars, called canopic jars, with preserving herbs. The body was next

A brightly painted Egyptian canopic jar

stuffed with perfumes and sweet-smelling resins and sewn up. It was covered with natron (a mixture of sodium salts that absorbed moisture) and dried for about 35 days. Finally it was coated with resin, wrapped in linen and placed in an airtight coffin. The most famous Egyptian doctor was called Imhotep (lived c. 2650B.C). He was also an architect and high priest.

Imhotep

Indian medicine

The best-known ancient Indian medical text is the *Ayurveda*, originally compiled in India around 700B.C. In it, disease is seen as an imbalance of substances in the body. Doctors used medicines to drive out harmful substances, and replace them with ones that were more in tune with the body. The *Ayurveda* also shows that Hindu doctors had a good understanding of diet and the digestive system.

The Ancient Indians excelled in surgical treatment, and the *Ayurveda* describes many different types of surgical instrument. Their doctors knew how to perform many operations, especially on the stomach and bladder. They could also remove cataracts (clouded lenses) from eyes, and were famous for their plastic surgery (rebuilding wounded parts of the body). They used hairs to stitch up torn lips.

An Indian illustration showing a type of plastic surgery of the nose.

Chinese medicine

In the 6th century B.C., a Chinese philosopher called Confucius (551-479B.C.) taught that people are closely linked to a universe dominated by two opposing types of force known as *yin* and *yang*. *Yin* was regarded as a negative force, while *yang* was positive. He claimed that the harmony of the universe and the health of people depended on keeping a balance between the two forces. Today, many Chinese believe that these two forces circulate around the body in the form of spirits or fluids.

Chinese illustration showing how to take a patient's pulse

By inserting needles at specified points on the body, the correct flow of the two spirits can be maintained. This technique, known as acupuncture, is used to ease the pain of surgical operations instead of drugs. Today in China, and increasingly in the West, acupuncture and other alternative medicines are used with drugs and surgery.

A 17th-century Chinese wooden acupuncture figure

Greek medicine

In the 5th century B.C. a medical school on the small Greek island of Cos became very influential. The physicians at Cos were good at treating bone injuries but knew little about internal organs. They believed that disease was caused by a lack of balance in the body between four fluids - which consisted of blood, black bile, yellow bile and phlegm - and four related qualities - heat, cold, dryness and dampness.

A 14th-century portrait of Hippocrates (c.450-370B.C.)

The island was the home of Hippocrates, a doctor who is often known as "the father of medicine". Like modern doctors, he insisted on keeping medical records, noting when treatments failed, as well as when they were successful.

Hippocrates emphasized the importance of letting the body heal naturally, so he used few drugs, instead recommending treatments such as warm relaxing baths and a simple diet. At that time many people thought that an illness such as epilepsy was a punishment from the gods. But Hippocrates rejected

This medieval illustration shows a Greek patient being treated for a dislocated arm.

A selection of 2nd-century B.C. Greek surgical instruments

this, and suggested instead that it had natural causes.

Greek medicine was very influential in medieval and Renaissance Europe. Hippocrates' teachings were gathered by Greek scholars to form a massive medical work called the Hippocratic Collection. Parts of it were still being used as textbooks in European medical schools as late as the 19th century. Today, doctors make a promise to work for the benefit of the patient at all times. It is known as the Hippocratic Oath, after Hippocrates.

Roman medicine

The most famous of all doctors in Roman times was Galen. He was born at Pergamum in Asia Minor (now in Turkey) the son of a Greek architect. In A.D.161 he moved to Rome, where he spent nearly all his active life. He set up a medical practice and became so successful that he was eventually appointed physician to the emperor's family.

Galen's work dominated medieval medical thought in the Arabic world and Europe. He did important research into the physical structure and functions of the body. He could not learn anatomy by cutting up dead humans, as this was illegal, and had to use carcasses of apes and pigs. But because animals are different from humans, his anatomical theories contained many errors which were accepted until the work of Vesalius in the 16th century (see page 64).

Bust of Galen (c.A.D.129-200)

Galen's system was wrong in several ways. He put veins (carrying blood to the heart) on the right side of the body and arteries (carrying blood from the heart to various parts of the body) on the left. He believed that blood seeped through pores in the septum (internal wall) of the heart.

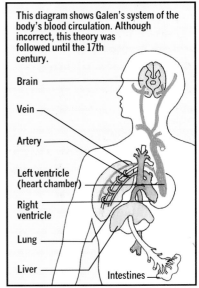

This diagram shows Galen's system of the body's blood circulation. Although incorrect, this theory was followed until the 17th century.

- Brain
- Vein
- Artery
- Left ventricle (heart chamber)
- Right ventricle
- Lung
- Liver
- Intestines

Galen taught that the heart pumped blood through the arteries mixed with something he called "pneuma" (a sort of spirit which the lungs obtain when air is breathed in). He proposed that the blood was sent to the organs that needed it, but not in a circulatory motion. This theory is incorrect, but it was not until the 17th century that an English doctor called William Harvey (see page 65) correctly worked out how the blood circulates continuously all the way around the body.

Islamic science

In Arabia in the 7th century A.D., the Prophet Mohammed founded a new religion called Islam. Within a century of his death in 632, his followers (known as Muslims) had conquered a huge empire that stretched from Spain to the borders of China. The arts and sciences flourished in the Arab world, particularly between 900 and 1200. As well as making their own contributions to science, the Arabs absorbed scientific ideas from many different parts of their great empire, particularly from the Greeks and Persians. In this way Islamic thinkers helped to transmit the ideas of the ancient world to medieval Europeans. Without them, much of this information would have been lost.

An Islamic manuscript showing a dentist extracting a tooth

This Islamic illustration shows the Greek philosopher Aristotle (see page 54) with a student.

A great thinker

Ibn Sina, known in Europe as Avicenna, was an extremely learned and versatile man who wrote about 270 books on a huge range of subjects. He was born at Bokhara in Iran. At the age of only 16 he was working in medicine. At various times during his life he was a lawyer and teacher of science. He was also involved in politics and acted as adviser to the Iranian ruler. He died of colic

Ibn Sina (980-1037) teaching a class of students

(inflammation of the abdomen), but there were suspicions that he may have been poisoned.

Ibn Sina wrote the *Canon*, a huge book about medicine. This work influenced medical teaching in Europe until the 17th century. Islamic law forbade the dissection of the human body, so the book was mainly about how to recognize and treat diseases, and how to prepare drugs. Another of ibn Sina's major works was a large encyclopedia entitled *The Cure*, which covered a wide range of subjects from philosophy to mathematics and physics.

The master of alchemy

Alchemy was a very important part of Arabic thinking. Alchemists mainly looked for a way of changing non precious metals such as iron into gold. Alchemical studies were important because although they used magic and spells, they also involved the use of experiment. This laid the foundations for several modern sciences, including chemistry and mineralogy (the study of minerals).

An alembic, a vessel used in distillation

Al-Razi (c.854-935), known in medieval Europe as Rhazes, was born at Rayy in Iran. He was the greatest Muslim alchemist and one of the most famous figures in medicine of the 9th and 10th

centuries. But al-Razi also questioned religious teachings, and so made himself unpopular with the powerful clergy.

Al-Razi devoted the first part of his life to alchemy. He rejected much of the magic and spells performed by alchemists and concentrated more on their experimental ideas. He was very interested in the use of chemical substances and clearly described some of the techniques used in alchemy, such as distillation (boiling a liquid until it becomes gaseous, then cooling it back into a liquid again).

These brass instruments were used in geomancy, a method of prophesying the future.

He also made some of the earliest suggestions for equipping a laboratory, listing some of the instruments.

Al-Razi was appointed director of the hospital in Rayy and then moved to become director of the hospital in Baghdad. He was one of the first of the Muslim writers on medicine, producing over a hundred works on the subject. His most famous publication was the huge *Comprehensive Book* which covered the whole of medical practice known at that time, including Greek, Indian and Chinese medical knowledge.

Islamic surgical instruments

Islamic astrological signs. From left to right: Aries, Taurus, Gemini, Cancer, Leo, Virgo.

Astronomer and courtier

Abu Rayhan al-Biruni (973-c.1050) was born in Khwarazm, Armenia. He began his scientific studies while still very young and by the age of 17 had designed and made an instrument for observing the sun. But in 995 a civil war forced him to flee abroad.

The observatory at Samarkand, c.1420

Al-Biruni returned home two years later and held a number of official positions at royal courts. He continued his scientific studies and astronomical observations, and designed and built many instruments for observing the sun, the moon and the stars.

This Turkish astronomer is observing a meteor with an instrument called a quadrant.

But al-Biruni's interests and studies were not limited to astronomy. In all, he wrote about 13,000 pages of highly technical material about geography, mathematics, optics (the study of light and the eye), medicines and drugs, precious stones and astrology. His interest in alchemy also led him to study the composition of minerals and metals, and his writings in this field later proved very influential as the science of chemistry developed. He also wrote a huge work on mineralogy called *The Book of the Multitude of Knowledge of Precious Stones*. Although he was ill for many years, by the time of his death at the age of 80 he had written over 140 books on many different subjects.

A page from an Islamic book about mineralogy

Lenses and light

Ibn al-Haytham (965-c.1040) was the greatest of all the Islamic physicists. He was born at Basra in Iraq and became known in Europe as Alhazen. He moved to Cairo where he worked at a school called the Academy during the reign of the Caliph al-Hakim (996-1020).

Al-Haytham wrote on a range of subjects, including optics, astronomy and mathematics. His work on optics was so extensive and detailed that it formed the basis of many later European studies of the subject. In his book called *The Treasury of Optics* he rejected an earlier Greek idea that the eye sends out rays of light to the object it is looking at. Instead he suggested that rays of light come from the object to the eye.

A 16th-century illustration of al-Haytham's study of the structure of the eye

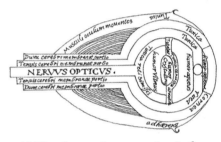

Al-Haytham also examined the effect of light through lenses. He concluded that the refraction (bending) of light is caused by light rays moving at different speeds through different materials, such as air, glass and water. This idea was used in the 17th century by Kepler (see page 63) and Descartes (page 67). Al-Haytham was also the first person to develop the *camera obscura*, a box in which images from outside are projected onto a wall. He used a hole in a wall to reproduce the image of the sun during an eclipse.

A 19th-century English camera obscura, based on al-Haytham's principles.

Islamic astrological signs. From left to right: Libra, Scorpio, Sagittarius, Capricorn, Aquarius, Pisces.

Science in medieval Europe

The period from about A.D.400 to 1400 in Europe is often known as the medieval age. For much of this time the Christian Church was very powerful and ruled all aspects of life. As most scholars were Christian monks, they had to follow the teachings of the Church. People who contradicted the Church's views were often persecuted.

From the end of the 11th century, many ancient Greek, Roman and Arab books reached northern Europe through Muslim Spain (see page 58). Bishops feared that the new knowledge

Pope Innocent III (1198-1216), a very powerful Church leader

contained in these books would make people question the Bible's account of the creation of the world. Over the years, however, much science and philosophy from the classical and Arab worlds was slowly reconciled with Christian teachings.

Religion and philosophy

Thomas Aquinas was an Italian monk. In 1264 he wrote a book, *Summa contra gentiles*, in which he stated that while everything was created by God, knowledge and truth could also come from other sources. He said that on religious questions the Church and the Bible were the only authorities, but that in scientific matters the work of the Greeks and Arabs could also help to explain the world that God had created. These ideas enabled the Church to come to terms with the teachings of the ancient world.

Thomas Aquinas (1225-74)

The rise of new learning

From the late 12th century, places of learning called universities were founded all over Europe. The most important were those at Bologna, Oxford, Cambridge and Paris. Many of the people who taught and studied there were associated with the Church, so the universities became important in developing ideas about religious matters.

Illustration showing man at the middle of the universe which is embraced by God

Robert Grosseteste (c.1168-1253) was born in Sussex, England. He became a leading figure in scientific studies in the first half of the 13th century. He studied at Oxford University and then, from 1209, taught at the University of Paris. In 1214 he returned to Oxford, where he acted as tutor to some of the students, including a community of monks.

A class in progress at the new university at Bologna in Italy.

A supporter of Aristotle

Grosseteste always stressed the great importance of testing all scientific propositions. In this he was a supporter of Aristotle who recommended the use of careful observation and analysis. He wrote on a wide range of subjects, including astronomy and music. His most famous work was on optics and how light behaves, and in this he was influenced by the work of the Arabic scientist ibn al-Haytham (see page 59).

Grosseteste's drawing of light passing through a lens

Grosseteste's pupil

Roger Bacon (c.1214-c.1294) was born in Somerset, England. He studied at Oxford University and in 1241 moved to Paris. In 1247 he returned to Oxford where he was one of Grosseteste's pupils. He taught for the rest of his life in England and France.

Bacon did not experiment himself, but he did carry out some research into optics and the eye. He described ibn al-Haytham's account of the eye as a device for forming images. He also understood the causes of the refraction (bending) of light and was one of the first people to suggest that lenses could be used as spectacles for magnification.

This illustration of 1352 is the earliest known picture of lenses being used as spectacles.

Conflict with the Church

When he was almost 40, Bacon became a Franciscan monk. He had an argumentative nature and had many disputes over astronomy and astrology with John of Fidanza (later Saint Bonaventure), the head of the Franciscans.

In 1267, at the invitation of his friend Pope Clement IV, Bacon wrote a work called *Opus majus*, an important volume of papers covering all areas of knowledge. In addition, it condemned the teaching methods of both the Franciscans and the Dominicans, claiming that they were out of date and narrow-minded. This made him still more unpopular with the authorities and even the Pope was outraged. In 1277 Bacon was put on trial and sent to prison in Paris for several years. The charge was that he regarded reason and philosophy as more important than the established teachings of the Christian Church.

Science supporting religion

Bacon is a major figure in the history of science, not because he challenged the authority of the Church, but because of his scientific approach. He believed that the study and advancement of science could complement and support religion. He thought that scientific study would enable people to understand all aspects of the world. In this way, he argued, they would gain a better knowledge of God and his works.

This medieval illustration shows the Church (at the top) controlling the different areas of knowledge (below).

The signs of the Zodiac. During the middle ages Astrology played an important part in people's lives.

Aristotle's work is questioned

By the 14th century scholars had adopted many ancient ideas, especially Aristotle's. But they interpreted these rigidly, taking them to mean that the universe was unchanging and perfect, with the earth fixed at the middle.

Jean Buridan (c.1300-85), a teacher at Paris University, adopted a Greek idea called the "impetus theory". His version stated that God had set the planets and stars moving around the earth at a speed that would continue forever. This was an important step toward a physical explanation of planetary motion, because it rejected supernatural causes. Buridan was afraid to publish his work because it contradicted Aristotle's teaching that divine beings pushed the planets along.

The friend of princes

Nicolas Oresme (c.1320-82) was born in Normandy in France and became Bishop of Lisieux. From about 1340 he studied in Paris under Buridan. Oresme went much further than Buridan in questioning Aristotle's work. He suggested that the earth might not be fixed but might actually rotate daily on its own axis. He also used mathematics to work out planetary movements. Oresme's ideas helped later scientists to formulate new ideas about the structure of the universe. This eventually led to the overthrow of the Aristotelian system by Galileo and others in the 17th century (see page 66).

This medieval engraving depicts a mathematics class.

The earth and the sun

From the earliest times, people have wanted to understand the mystery of the stars and planets. Early civilizations charted the movements of the sun and the moon to construct calendars.

This picture shows Nut, Egyptian goddess of the sky, bending over gods of the earth and air.

The Ancient Egyptians arranged the stars into groups called constellations, which they often gave religious significance. The science of astronomy developed as people gradually learned more about the world beyond them. Astronomers examine the skies in order to answer questions about space and the movements of the planets and stars.

The Ptolemaic system

In about A.D.150 Ptolemy, a Greek astronomer living in Alexandria in Egypt, wrote an important textbook now known as the *Almagest* (Arabic for "the greatest work"). In this, he described a system of the universe in which the earth lay stationary and the moon, the sun, and the planets all moved around it in circular paths called orbits. All the stars were fixed to the surface of a rotating sphere. This idea, which was based on the work of Aristotle (see page 54), is known as the geocentric (from the Greek for earth) theory. It

This brass sphere, based on Ptolemy's ideas, was used to work out the positions of the stars.

became the accepted view of the universe for nearly 1400 years. But as new and more efficient instruments were invented to examine the skies, the findings of astronomers became more and more accurate. The new evidence began to contradict Ptolemy's geocentric theory.

Ptolemy (c.A.D.90-170) as shown in this medieval engraving

Doubts are raised

Niklas Kopernik was a Polish monk more commonly known by his latinized name of Copernicus. He studied mathematics, medicine and law in Poland and Italy and became a canon at Frauenburg Cathedral in Poland. There he became interested in astronomy, and he began to doubt that the earth lay at the middle of the universe. Instead, he suggested a system with the sun lying at the middle and the planets, including the earth, orbiting around it in circles. This is known as the heliocentric (from the Greek for sun) theory.

Copernicus (1473-1543)

Copernicus recorded this theory in a book called *De revolutionibus orbium caelestium* ("Concerning the revolutions of the heavenly spheres"). The Church, however, taught that the earth was the heart of the universe, which was the view that had been presented in the Bible. Because

he was a clergyman, Copernicus decided not to publish his book for fear of being criticized and punished by the Church.

In 1543, shortly before he died, Copernicus was finally persuaded to publish his book. But without his knowledge, the publishers added a preface in order to protect themselves from criticism by the Church. It stated that Copernicus' scheme was not a real picture of the universe, but only a theory. This reduced the impact of the book when it came out. But while his book contained many ideas we now know to be incorrect, it provided a structure for the work of such later astronomers as Kepler (see opposite) and Galileo.

Engraving of the Copernican, heliocentric system of the universe

A new star appears

Tycho Brahe was born in Skåne, then in Denmark but now Sweden. He was a very quarrelsome man and had most of his nose cut off in a duel. While studying at Copenhagen University, he became very interested in astronomy.

In 1572 astronomers noticed that a new star had appeared in the sky. (It was probably an exploding object now known as a supernova.) Brahe calculated that the new star lay beyond the moon. This conflicted with the Aristotelian theory that only the skies between the earth and the moon could change.

Brahe's observatory on Hven

A contemporary drawing of the 1572 supernova

An island observatory

In 1574 Brahe set up an observatory on Hven, an island in the Baltic Sea given to him by King Frederick II of Denmark. His observations of a comet (see page 71) in 1577 showed that it moved among the planets lying beyond the moon. This again proved that changes did occur in the skies. Although his findings contradicted Aristotle's view of the universe on several fundamental points, Brahe would not accept Copernicus' view because it opposed the teachings of the Church. Instead he proposed a compromise, a system in which the planets orbited the sun, and the sun orbited the earth, which lay still at the heart of the universe.

When Frederick died in 1588, the Danish royal family withdrew the money used for the upkeep of the Hven observatory. The following year Brahe moved to Prague. He remained there for the rest of his life, continuing his work as an astronomer.

Tycho Brahe
(1546-1601)

Medallion commemorating the great comet of 1577

New theories

Johannes Kepler was born in Germany. He taught mathematics at Graz in Austria, then moved to Prague to become Brahe's assistant. When Brahe died he left his astronomical findings to Kepler, instructing him to use them to disprove Copernicus' theories.

Kepler worked for years on the orbits of the planets, but the information he had collected did not fit with the theories of either Brahe or Copernicus. He worked out that although the planets did indeed move around the sun, they moved not in perfect circles but in extended circular paths called ellipses. He also realized that the speed of the planets varies as they travel, according to their distance from the sun. These ideas are the basis of Kepler's three laws of planetary movement. He also understood that the sun has a very strong influence on the movement of the planets.

Johannes Kepler
(1571-1630)

Kepler published many of his theories in his books *The New Astronomy* (1609) and *Epitome of Copernican Astronomy* (1621). At the time most people did not realize the significance of his ideas, but his writings influenced many later scientists. Newton used Kepler's laws when he formulated his theories of gravity (see page 70).

Understanding the human body

During the Middle Ages medical knowledge in Europe remained based on the work of Galen and other early doctors (see pages 56-57). In the 12th century, however, new ideas began reaching western Europe, as Greek and Arab medical texts were translated into Latin. Doctors and medical scientists began to question ancient theories and later to replace them with new ones of their own.

A flamboyant personality

Aureolus Philippus Theophrastus Bombastus von Hohenheim, otherwise known as Paracelsus, was born near Zürich in Switzerland. He studied at the University of Ferrara in Italy, then worked as a surgeon in the army. Paracelsus was a violent man who angered even his closest friends. He charged rich people huge fees, but treated the poor for free. He took the name Paracelsus because he disagreed so much with the Roman physician Celsus and other traditional doctors. (*Para* is the Greek word for "beyond" or "against".)

Paracelsus
(1493-1541)

A restless doctor

In 1527 Paracelsus became professor of medicine at Basle University, where he also had a successful doctor's practice. But he had many arguments with the medical authorities and, after publicly burning books by Galen and Avicenna, he had to leave Basle. For the rest of his life he journeyed around Europe, never staying more than two years in one place, and died in Austria.

This picture shows Paracelsus performing a surgical operation.

Paracelsus did not believe in the old Greek idea that disease was caused by an imbalance of the four fluids (see page 57). Instead he thought it was caused by a poison entering the body. He sometimes treated people with drugs that produced symptoms similar to those of the disease they had. This was an early form of homeopathy, a method that claims to heal the body by reinforcing its natural defences.

The great anatomist

Andreas Vesalius was born in Brussels, the son of an apothecary (pharmacist) to the Holy Roman Emperor, Charles V. He first studied at Louvain (now in Belgium), then at the University of Paris, but war forced him back to Louvain. By this time Vesalius was very interested in human anatomy, the science of the structure of the body. In order to study this thoroughly, he needed to dissect (cut up) dead bodies. As this was forbidden by law, he sometimes had to rob graves to get the corpses he required, or take the bodies down from gallows. In 1537 he attended the medical school at Padua in Italy,

16th-century illustration showing Paracelsus lecturing

one of the most famous in Europe. His knowledge was already so extensive that he was awarded his doctorate after only two days of exams, then appointed lecturer of anatomy. He later became physician to Charles V, but in 1564 he drowned in a shipwreck on his way back to Madrid from a pilgrimage to Jerusalem.

Galen's work is questioned

While he was at Padua, Vesalius carried out as many dissections as possible, using animals as well as human bodies. He did all the dissections himself and used large anatomical diagrams as guides for his students. But these drawings were still based on Galen's theories.

Andreas Vesalius
(1514-64)

Vesalius gradually discovered many differences between Galen's ideas and the results of his own dissections. By 1539 he was able to prove that Galen's descriptions fitted an ape's body rather than a human being's. In 1543 he published *The Fabric of the Human Body*, one of the greatest scientific books ever written. It gave anatomy the status of an academic pursuit, and by the 17th century Vesalius' theories were accepted almost everywhere in Europe.

A drawing from *The Fabric of the Human Body*

This illustration from *The Fabric of the Human Body* shows the body's muscles.

A royal physician

William Harvey was born in Folkestone, England. After studying arts and medicine at Cambridge University, he went to Padua to continue his medical training with a famous professor of anatomy called Fabricius. In 1602 he returned to London and set up a medical practice. He was appointed physician at St Bartholomew's Hospital, London in 1609. In 1618, he was made physician to James I in 1618, and later to Charles I, and was a staunch royalist during the English Civil War.

William Harvey (1578-1657)

A new theory of circulation

In 1628 Harvey published a book, *De motu cordis* ("On the movement of the heart and blood"). It was the product of many observations and set out his theories about how blood travels around the body.

Harvey's diagram showing valves in the veins

At that time, most doctors believed Galen's idea that blood was passed from one side of the heart to the other through small holes. From his own experiments, Harvey introduced the concept of circulation, showing that blood flows away from the heart through the arteries, and back to the heart through veins. Fabricius had found valves in the veins, but had not understood their function. Harvey realized that the valves in large veins direct the blood back toward the heart, and that the valves of the heart keep the blood flowing around the body in one direction only - to the lungs from the right side, and to the rest of the body from the left. He also realized that the heart acts as a pump to circulate the blood.

This diagram shows blood circulation according to Harvey.

Lung

Vein from upper parts

Artery to upper parts

Liver

Artery to lower parts

Vein from lower parts

One more puzzle

Harvey's discovery was a brilliant piece of reasoning based on observation. But there was still a final question: how did blood that left the heart through the arteries enter the veins? Harvey guessed that tiny blood vessels must connect the veins and arteries, but he was unable to prove it. In 1661, while examining a frog's lungs under a microscope, an Italian called Marcello Malpighi (1628-94) found the tiny linking vessels (called capillaries) and the puzzle was finally solved.

Science during the Renaissance

I n Europe in the 14th century there began a period of about 200 years that became known as the Renaissance (meaning "rebirth"). During this time people began to rediscover the arts and learning of Ancient Greece and Rome, and to develop new ideas about the world around them. They began to look at things more critically and observation and experiment in all areas became more important. They also challenged the established Aristotelian teachings, which combined Greek and Christian philosophy (see page 60).

The universal man

Many thinkers during the Renaissance believed in the ideal of the "universal man", someone who combined a wide range of talents and interests. Leonardo da Vinci was a painter, sculptor, musician, architect, scientist and an ingenious inventor who typified this ideal.

Leonardo was born near Florence, the son of a legal clerk called Pietro da Vinci. His father noticed Leonardo's artistic talents and sent him to work in the studio of a painter called Andrea del Verrochio. Although he only completed a relatively small number of paintings, Leonardo is now recognized as one of the world's greatest artists. One of his most famous pictures is the *Mona Lisa*, which he painted in 1503.

Leonardo da Vinci (1452-1519)

Leonardo's sketchbooks

Leonardo dissected about 30 human bodies (a practice that was illegal at the time), and produced anatomical drawings that were much more accurate than anything that had been done before. He studied the properties of light and the movement of water, and his sketchbooks are filled with his designs for mechanical devices, including flying machines. We now know that many of these would not have worked, but they demonstrate Leonardo's ability to combine detailed observation with powerful imagination.

Sketches by Leonardo showing various anatomical features

This is a reconstruction of a design by Leonardo for a flying machine. Below are his sketches of a mechanical wing and birds in flight.

Leonardo's later years

From 1483 Leonardo worked in Milan as an inspector of fortifications, and then in Florence as a military engineer. In 1507 he moved to Amboise in France, where he spent the rest of his life.

Despite his enormous range and creativity, Leonardo's work had little influence on the progress of science. His studies were made for his own satisfaction; most of his contemporaries knew nothing of them. His many sketches and notebooks were dispersed after his death and remained largely unknown for centuries.

Copernicus' champion

Galileo Galilei (1564-1642) was born in Pisa in Italy, the son of a composer. He played a vital part in establishing Copernicus' view (see page 62) that the earth rotates around a stationary sun. A pioneer of the experimental approach to science which was developing at this time, he was also a gifted teacher.

At the age of 17, Galileo enrolled as a medical student at the University of Pisa.

While he was attending a service at the cathedral, he noticed that the chandeliers were swinging in a wind, and used his pulse to time their movements. He found that though the swings slowly got smaller they always took the same amount of time. This led him to suggest that pendulums could be used to measure time. This idea was the basis of the first mechanical clocks.

Galileo left Pisa to continue his work in mechanics and mathematics, but he later returned there as professor of mathematics. The results of his experiments at this time provided increasing evidence to contradict many of Aristotle's theories about the organization of the universe (see page 54).

"And yet it moves!"

After hearing about the invention of the telescope in Holland, Galileo designed and built some more powerful models himself. In 1610 he published his observations of the stars and planets in *The Starry Messenger*, a book which became both popular and influential. In it he described mountains on the moon, and dark spots which occasionally move across the face of the sun. He also showed that some planets, like Jupiter, have their own small orbiting planets. Galileo's work demonstrated the uses of the telescope. But more importantly, all his findings supported the view of Copernicus that the earth rotates around the sun.

Two of Galileo's telescopes

In 1632 Galileo published his *Dialogue Concerning the Two Chief World Systems*, which summed up his observations. The work was seen as a masterpiece all over Europe. But in Italy it clashed with the teachings of the Church, which upheld the traditional view of the earth lying in the middle of the solar system.

Paintings by Galileo of the surface of the Moon

In 1633 Galileo was charged with heresy (holding a view contrary to the established teaching of the Church). He was brought before a Church court in Rome known as the Inquisition. Having been found guilty, he was threatened with torture unless he publicly denied his claim that the earth moved round the sun. Appearing old and frail, Galileo did as the Inquisition demanded. He was ordered to retire to the countryside for the rest of his life. But it is said that as he was leaving the court he murmured "And yet it moves!" because he still believed in his theory.

Galileo's sketch of the method of measuring the height of mountains on the Moon

The mathematical philosopher

The ideas of René Descartes were very influential in both mathematics and philosophy. He was born in Brittany in France, the son of a lawyer. In 1628 he moved to the Netherlands, where the Protestant Church took a more relaxed view of new ideas. He worked there for the next 20 years.

René Descartes (1596-1650)

One of the most important contributions Descartes made to philosophy was his concept of doubt. He did not accept an unquestioning belief in biblical and classical sources of knowledge. He declared that his own existence was the only thing he could be certain about: *Cogito ergo sum* ("I think, therefore I am"). In his major scientific work, *Principles of Philosophy*, he suggested that the movement of the universe could be described in terms of moving particles of various sizes.

Drawing by Descartes which shows the universe as whirlpools of matter

Descartes laid the basis for co-ordinate mathematics, a system that enables different quantities, such as age and height, to be related to each other in graphs or charts. His ideas on the structure of the universe were very influential, though they were later challenged by Newton (see page 70).

Scientific societies

In Europe from the middle of the 17th century, groups of men began to meet regularly in such cities as London, Florence, Oxford and Paris to discuss their scientific experiments and ideas. They were mostly wealthy people who experimented at home and who wanted to share their discoveries. These very informal meetings developed into the first scientific societies. During the following centuries, these societies grew stronger and more influential, often helped by an increasing government interest in science. Partly as a result of their influence, science gradually divided into specialized subjects such as geology and astronomy, and many people began to take up the activity of scientific research as a paid career.

The coat of arms of the Royal Society, the earliest scientific society

A belief in experiment

Francis Bacon was the son of a courtier to King Henry VIII of England. He trained as a lawyer, eventually becoming a politician under Queen Elizabeth I. In 1617 King James I appointed him Lord Chancellor of England, but in 1621 he was convicted of taking bribes, dismissed from office and banished from the royal court.

Bacon wrote about his views on scientific methods in a series of books and essays. He felt that it was important to find the answers to scientific problems by means of experiment. In his book *Novum organum* he argued that careful experiment and observation

Francis Bacon (1561-1626)

would lead to new scientific discoveries and enable people to develop new theories. He suggested that scientists should collect facts and figures on each subject and from as many sources as possible. In 1627 he published *The New Atlantis*, his last book. This described his vision of a world in which scientists were dedicated to improving the lives of everyone in the community.

Although Bacon did not carry out any scientific experiments himself, his ideas remained very influential for many years. During the 17th century, his writings and his philosophy of experiment stimulated people all over Europe to establish new scientific organizations.

The Royal Society

The establishment of the Royal Society in London was extremely important because for the first time it offered a permanent meeting place for the scientific community. Members were no longer isolated individuals but now felt that they belonged together in a social group where they could discuss their latest experiments.

The Society was founded in 1662, at the beginning of the reign of Charles II. It received the personal backing of the king, who granted it a Royal Charter that outlined its purposes and gave it certain rights. The founding members were

This engraving shows Gresham College, a scientific college founded in 1596 which was a forerunner of the Royal Society.

Part of the Charter of the Royal Society, granted by Charles II

mainly doctors, philosophers, and important officials. They included the architect Christopher Wren and the writer Samuel Pepys. The Royal Society is still in existence today and is an important forum for ideas.

This illustration of Louis XIV visiting the Académie Royale des Sciences was issued by the French government in the 17th century.

Académie Royale des Sciences

The Académie Royale des Sciences was founded in Paris in 1666. Although it was based on the Royal Society, it was very different from its counterpart in England. The French king, Louis XIV, was keen to use science to increase his own power and influence, and he took a close interest in the running of the Académie.

Membership was strictly limited to those people who had proved themselves to be academically excellent and who also had the king's approval. However, unlike the members of the English Royal Society, who never received a salary, the French academicians were paid by the government. This marked the beginning of the age of the salaried scientist.

The Académie produced a lot of excellent scientific work, especially in the second half of the 18th century. But because of its strong links with the monarchy it was abolished during the French Revolution. It was replaced by the Institut de France, which was founded by Napoleon.

A giant burning lens made and used by Lavoisier (see page 78) in experiments at the Académie Royale des Sciences.

Specialist societies in Britain

Until scientific study became common in universities in the second half of the 19th century, scientists tended to discuss their ideas in learned societies. The members included people from a range of backgrounds, including industry, chemistry and medicine. This interaction of people and skills contributed to the Industrial Revolution, which happened earlier in Britain than in the rest of Europe. From the end of the 18th century, many countries in Europe were transformed into industrial nations.

Specialist societies grew up in London, such as the Linnean Society (biology and natural history) in 1788, the Geology Society in 1807, and the Astronomical Society in 1831. They quickly became professional organizations with their own journals and limited membership.

Germany in the 19th century

Justus von Liebig was one of the greatest chemists of the 19th century. He was born in Germany, the son of a chemist. In 1822 he moved to Paris to study chemistry. He visited laboratories in France and was very impressed by the standards of chemistry he found there. On his return to Germany he set up his own research laboratory in 1824 at the University of Giessen. Here teamwork rather than individual research was encouraged.

Justus von Liebig (1803-73)

Liebig's laboratory was one of the best equipped in Europe. (He invented the Liebig condenser, a cooling device that turns gases into liquids.) His work influenced the development of Germany's industries, particularly those that produced of dyes and drugs. In the 19th century German universities became centres of scientific research that acted as the models for new universities all over the world.

Bottles of artificial dye, produced in Germany in the 19th century

The rise of experiment

Today experimentation is regarded as one of the main activities of scientists, but for many centuries this was not the case. Scientific ideas were often based on religion and philosophy rather than experiment. But at the end of the 17th century scientists began to stress the importance of experiment as a valid way of gaining knowledge. They examined the natural world in a new light, trying out new ideas and instruments. Their methods and achievements were to shape western scientific thinking.

Physicist and mathematician

Isaac Newton, one of the most famous scientists in the world, was born into a farming family in Lincolnshire, England. He went to Cambridge University in 1661 to study mathematics and graduated in 1665, the year of the Great Plague. When the plague spread to Cambridge, the university was closed down and Newton returned to Lincolnshire.

Newton's house in Lincolnshire

Newton went back to Cambridge in 1667 and two years later became professor of mathematics there. He later moved to London, where from 1703 until his death he was President of the Royal Society (see page 68).

Isaac Newton
(1642-1727)

Motion and gravity

Newton's stay in Lincolnshire was very productive, but it was not until 1687 that the material he worked on while he was there was published as a book. The full title, translated from the original Latin, was *The Mathematical Principles of Natural Philosophy*, but it is usually known as the *Principia*.

Pages from Newton's book the *Principia*

The first volume included Newton's three Laws of Motion and his theory of gravitation. He is said to have begun wondering about this when he saw an apple fall. He noted that there is a force between the earth and all objects which pulls them together. The earth pulls things like the apple toward it by force of gravity.

A device designed by Newton to illustrate his Third Law of Motion

With the use of mathematical calculations, Newton was able to solve the age-old problem of how planets move in space. He demonstrated that, in the same way as the apple was pulled to earth, the planets were pulled around the sun by gravitation. This proved Kepler's laws of planetary motion (see page 63), which had been based on observation. Newton brought the whole of the universe - the earth as well as the stars and planets - under one set of mathematical laws, organized under the principle of universal gravitation. This has had a major influence on scientific thinking up to the present day.

Experiments with light

In 1704 Newton published another famous work, entitled *Opticks*. This described his experiments with light. In one, he directed a beam of sunlight through a glass prism in a dark room. He noticed that the light was split into the different shades of the spectrum, ranging from violet to red.

Newton's sketch of his light experiments

Newton's experiment showed that sunlight is not white, but a mixture of violet, indigo, blue, green, yellow, orange and red.

An 18th-century cartoon mocking Newton's Laws of Gravity

Pumps and pressure

Robert Boyle, the fourteenth child of the Earl of Cork, was born at the family's castle in Lismore, Ireland. He went to school in England and then journeyed throughout Europe, accompanied by tutors. There he first read the works of Galileo (see page 66) which had a great influence on him.

The vacuum pump designed by Boyle and Hooke, with other scientific equipment

An illustration of a louse from Hooke's *Micrographia*

In 1654, while at Oxford University, Boyle became interested in investigations being carried out in Europe on the nature of the vacuum. (A vacuum is a closed space from which everything, including air, has been removed.) By 1658, with the help of Robert Hooke (see below), he had designed and built a new kind of air pump. The two scientists used it to create a vacuum by pumping air out of a glass globe. It was used mainly for research into air and air pressure, and to study how animals and plants breathe.

Robert Boyle
(1627-91)

An atomic theory of matter

Boyle's work with air and gases enabled him to formulate a law that describes the relationship between the volume of a gas and its pressure. He showed that if an amount of gas is stored at a constant temperature, and the pressure on it is doubled, its volume reduces by half.

This illustration shows one of Boyle's experiments on the pressure of liquids.

In 1661 Boyle published a book called *The Sceptical Chymist*. One of his conclusions was that if air could be compressed it must be made up of tiny particles. He suggested that everything was made up of "primary particles" that could collect together to form larger "corpuscles". He was in fact describing what scientists now call atoms and molecules, though these terms were not introduced until later by Dalton and others (see page 79).

A mechanical genius

Robert Hooke (1635-1703) was an outstanding experimenter and inventor of new instruments. He was born on the Isle of Wight, off the south coast of England. While at Oxford University he met Robert Boyle, who employed him as an assistant.

Hooke moved to London in 1660, and two years later became the curator of

Hooke's compound microscope

experiments at the Royal Society. In 1665 he published *Micrographia*, a book containing illustrations of some of the specimens he had viewed under microscopes (instruments which magnify small objects). It also showed several instruments that he had designed. These included the compound microscope which was much more accurate than early microscopes.

The return of a comet

Edmond Halley (1656-1742) was the son of a London businessman. His experimental work in astronomy and magnetism was of great importance. He first became interested in comets (giant balls of ice and dust that move around the solar system) with the appearance of the Great Comet in 1682.

Halley's comet also appeared before the Battle of Hastings in 1066, as shown here (top) in the Bayeux Tapestry.

Applying Newton's theory of gravitation, Halley noted that the orbits of the comets seen in 1531, 1607 and 1682 were very similar and that the comets appeared at regular intervals. He believed that they must all be the same comet and correctly predicted its return in 1758. It is now named after him and its reappearance helped support Newton's picture of the universe.

Classifying the natural world

Ever since people first hunted animals and gathered plants, they have been aware of the great variety of living things. From the earliest times people tried to arrange the different types into groups according to their characteristics, in order to understand them better. This is known as classification. Over the years, however, so many new varieties were discovered and identified that new classification systems were needed to accommodate them.

This is a page from an Arabic version of a classification of animals by Aristotle.

Pages from Gesner's *Historiae animalium*, written between 1551 and 1558

Edward Topsell's *The Historie of Foure-footed Beastes* (above) was the English translation of Gesner's work.

An early naturalist

Konrad Gesner (1516-65) was born in Switzerland. In 1537, at the age of only 21, he was appointed professor of Greek at the newly-founded Lausanne Academy. He eventually worked as a physician in Zürich, and died there in a plague epidemic.

Gesner is famous for the huge five-volume work he compiled entitled *Historiae animalium* (History of animals). In it, he listed alphabetically every creature he could find from his own observations and from books.

Although this work included such mythical creatures as the bishop-fish, it was an important step toward a new understanding of animals. It gave many details of the appearance of the animals, what they ate and where they lived.

Classification takes shape

One of the most outstanding developments in classification was made by John Ray in the 17th century. He was born in Essex, England. His mother was a well-known medical herbalist who encouraged her son's interest in botany. Ray lectured on botany at Cambridge University for more than ten years, but had to leave for religious reasons. He then toured Europe with a biologist called Francis Willughby. After returning to England in 1660, Ray produced a botanical catalogue entitled *Plants Growing in the Neighbourhood of Cambridge*.

John Ray (1627-1705)

Between 1686 and 1704 Ray wrote an enormous book called *A General Account of Plants* which contained descriptions of 17,000 different types. His system of classification of the plants in this work was organized according to their fruits, flowers and leaves. This was an important advance on Gesner's method of classifying animals, which merely listed particular features. Ray's system, however, detailed different features of the plants and then grouped them according to the characteristics they shared. This gave a clearer idea of how they were related to each other.

An illustration from Ray's *Flora of Britain*

Modern classification

The Swedish botanist Carl von Linné is often known by his latinized name of Linnaeus. He studied medicine at the University of Uppsala in Sweden, but spent much of his time there studying plants in the university gardens.

Linnaeus then settled at Leiden in the Netherlands for three years. While he was there he published a vast number of works, including *Systema naturae* (System of nature).

Linnaeus
(1707-78)

Two years later he wrote *Genera plantarum* (The Genera of plants).

Linnaeus worked at Uppsala from 1741 until his death in 1778. He was first appointed professor of medicine, but became professor of botany the following year.

A page from *Systema naturae* by Linnaeus

In 1753 Linnaeus published his *Species plantarum*, which is now regarded as the starting point for the modern system of classification of plants. In it he developed a method of classification called "binomial nomenclature" (two-part naming system), a method which is still used in a modified form today.

Linnaeus' house at Uppsala

The binomial system gives each plant two names. The first indicates the genus, or large family group to which it belongs, and the second gives the species, or smaller specific type within the genus. In this way a lemon tree is named *Citrus limon*, while an orange tree is a *Citrus aurantium*.

The publication of *Species plantarum* made Linnaeus famous throughout Europe and greatly influenced the study of natural history. When Linnaeus died, an English admirer shipped his collection and papers to London.

Although Linnaeus was aware of the differences between wild and domesticated plants, he still claimed that the universe had remained the same since God's creation. He regarded each species of plant and animal as fixed and unchanging. This view was challenged by Buffon.

Evidence of change

Georges-Louis Leclerc, Comte de Buffon, was born into a wealthy family living near Dijon, France. He became very active in scientific circles and studied mathematics and botany. In 1739 he was appointed superintendent of the royal botanical garden in Paris, the Jardin du Roi.

Georges de Buffon
(1707-88)

Buffon wrote two major works: the *Mémoires* (1737-52), scientific treatises on a range of topics in mathematics, astronomy and physics; and the 36-volume *Natural History* (1749-88). The second book was a survey of the natural world and a history of the Earth. In it, Buffon suggested that fossils provided evidence of extinct species of animal life.

Researchers at the Jardin du Roi

Contradicting Linnaeus, Buffon claimed that fossils showed that the natural world had not remained unaltered, but had changed over the years. The *Natural History* was very important because it was the first book to propose that species had developed over long periods of time. But much more work was needed before the theory of evolution could be devised (see page 76).

Buffon claimed that fossils showed evidence of change.

The age of the earth

This 16th-century illustration shows God creating the world in six days.

Before the 19th century, most theories about the earth and its history were based on biblical accounts. But people gradually began to find evidence that the earth was much older than the Bible suggested. It was discovered that some strata (layers) of rock were older than others, and evidence from fossils indicated many extinct species of plants and animals. Volcanoes and earthquakes showed that the surface of the earth did in fact change. A new science, called geology, developed as people tried to answer questions about how old the earth really is. Geology is the study of the earth's origins, structure and history.

The Neptunist theory

Abraham Werner was born into a wealthy German family with connections in the iron and mining industries. He entered university to study law, but gave this up to study geology. In 1775 at Freiberg in Saxony, Werner founded an institute for studying mining and mineralogy. He worked out the first widely accepted system for classifying types of rock and landscape.

Toward the end of the 18th century many people thought the earth had been shaped by the action of volcanoes and earthquakes. But Werner proposed instead that the earth had once been covered by a huge ocean, created by the flood described in the Bible. This water slowly receded, leaving behind layers of rocks which were formed from minerals in the water. This is known as the "Neptunist" theory, after Neptune, the Roman god of the sea. One of Werner's most important conclusions was that this process must have taken a very long time, as much as one million years. This had a great influence on the work of later geologists.

Abraham Werner (1749-1817)

The Plutonist theory

Although he trained first as a lawyer in Scotland and then qualified as a medical doctor, James Hutton became a famous geologist. In 1795 he published a book called *The Theory of the Earth*. In this he did not include the biblical idea of a flood. Instead he suggested that the earth had changed very slowly over millions of years, and was continuing to do so. According to his theory, the earth's crust was first eroded by natural forces like wind, water, earthquakes and volcanoes. Then the material from this erosion formed a layer and hardened into the earth's surface. Lastly, heat from the middle of the earth caused the movement of rocks, which in turn formed new continents. He suggested that this cycle goes on all the time so that the earth is constantly renewing itself. Hutton's idea is known as the "Plutonist" theory, after Pluto, the Greek god of the underworld. It encouraged a new way of thinking. While Werner's theory had also suggested that the creation of the world took an extremely long time, it could still be related to the flood of the Bible. Hutton's theory, on the other hand, questioned the literal interpretation of the biblical account of the creation.

James Hutton (1726-96) collecting rock samples

This is an early illustration of an eruption of Mt Vesuvius, a volcano in southern Italy.

Fossils

Fossils are the remains of plants and animals preserved in rocks. They are as old as the rocks in which they are found and some were formed more than 600 million years ago. By studying fossils closely, it is possible to build up a picture of life as it was on earth many millions of years ago.

Promicroceras Lower Jurassic

Ornia Ordovician

Uniform change

Charles Lyell was born in Scotland. He studied law at Oxford University, but became interested in geology at the age of 21. In 1831 he was appointed professor of geology at King's College, London. He helped turn the subject from a hobby for rich amateurs into a science in its own right.

Lyell thought that geological features were caused by natural processes acting over very long periods of time. Winds wore away mountains, glaciers moved huge rocks, volcanoes erupted, valleys were eroded by rivers and cliffs by the sea. This theory is known as "uniformitarianism" because it claims that nature acts uniformly in a set pattern. The theory had first been proposed in a general way by Hutton. But it was much more convincingly argued and illustrated by Lyell who used new information gathered after Hutton's day to support his ideas. In time it became the view of most geologists and remains so today.

Charles Lyell
(1797-1875)

Supercontinents

Alfred Wegener was a German meteorologist (someone who examines weather conditions). He studied at the universities of Berlin, Heidelberg and Innsbruck. In 1910, looking at a map of the world, Wegener noticed that part of the west coast of Africa appeared to fit the shape of the east coast of South America. From this and fossil evidence he suggested that the two continents had once been joined together in one "supercontinent", which he called Pangaea. He then suggested that Pangaea had broken up and that the present continents were formed from the drifting pieces. This is known as the "continental drift" theory.

From 1960 Wegener's ideas were extended to make up the new theory of "plate tectonics". This claims that the earth's crust is not one solid mass, but is cracked into giant pieces (known as "plates") carrying the continents. The theory describes a never-ending process, in which molten rock is forced up between the plates to the earth's surface, where it solidifies. Similarly, the edges of the plates slide down beneath the adjacent ones and become molten again. If this does not happen and two plates collide, earthquakes occur along the point of impact.

Continental drift

These illustrations show the gradual break-up of Pangaea into the continents we see today.

200 million years ago — Africa, America

65 million years ago — Africa, America

2 million years ago — Africa, America

According to the continental drift theory, the continents of the southern hemisphere once fitted together as one giant continent, as did those of the northern hemisphere. Because the earth's crust has drifted, the continents have not always been in the same place, and are still moving. For example, according to the theory, North Africa was once covered in a sheet of ice and was situated where the South Pole is today. The South Pole was once covered with tropical forests.

Lyell's drawings of fossil shells

Alfred Wegener (1880-1930)

Fig. 1.

Fossil Chara from the Rock-marl.

Isastrea
Middle Jurassic

Evolution

U ntil the end of the 17th century, most Europeans believed that everything in nature was exactly the same as it always had been; they thought that plant and animal species were fixed, remaining in the state in which they had originally been created by God. In the 18th century, however, an increasing amount of evidence built up which contradicted this. People started to suggest that the characteristics of plants and animals could have changed over very long periods of time. This is now known as evolution.

Early evolutionary ideas

Jean-Baptiste de Monet, Chevalier de Lamarck, was born in France, the eleventh and youngest child of aristocratic but poor parents. He had a difficult life and died poor and blind, his work forgotten. At the age of 16 he joined the army but he had to leave because of ill health. Lack of money forced him to work in a bank rather than taking up his preferred career in medicine.

Chevalier de Lamarck (1744-1829)

Botanist to the king

In his spare time, Lamarck took up the study of plants and became so good at the subject that eventually, in 1781, he was appointed botanist to the French king. Ten years later, after the French Revolution, he was elected professor of zoology at the new Museum of Natural History in Paris. There he gave lectures, arranged the displays and organized exhibitions.

Noticing the differences between fossils and modern forms of animals, Lamarck became convinced that plant

Fossil fish

Living fish

and animal species were not fixed forever, but could change from one generation to the next. His ideas were influenced not only by fossils but also by other geological evidence that suggested that the earth's surface had changed over many years (see page 74).

The Jardin du Roi in Paris where Lamarck studied

Lamarck concluded that within their own lifetimes, animals' characteristics could alter in order to cope with their surroundings. He suggested that these changes were then passed on to their offspring. For instance, he argued that the neck of the giraffe would become longer during its lifetime as a result of stretching for leaves in trees, and that this change would then be passed on to the next generation.

This theory is now thought to be incorrect, though aspects of it were used in the theory of evolution presented 50 years later by Darwin and Wallace.

A South American expedition

Charles Darwin was born in Shrewsbury in England, the son of a successful doctor. He attended school in Shrewsbury and went on to study medicine at the University of Edinburgh. But he did not enjoy the subject and, at his father's insistence, moved to Cambridge University to study for the priesthood. But although he managed to gain a degree, again he was unhappy with the

Charles Darwin (1809-82)

subject. However he showed a great interest in botany and entomology (the study of insects). In 1831 a professor of botany called John Henslow noticed his abilities and found him a place as the naturalist on an expedition to South America. Before leaving, Darwin read works by the geologist Charles Lyell (see page 75). These books made a great impression on him and later influenced his own work.

A page from one of Darwin's notebooks

One of the two types of iguana from the Galapagos Islands

Darwin's discoveries

The expedition left in a ship called HMS *Beagle* and was away for five years. During that time it visited Brazil, Argentina, Chile, Peru and the Galapagos Islands, ten rocky islands lying off the coast of Ecuador in the Pacific Ocean, each with different wildlife.

Darwin's drawing of types of finch from the Galapagos Islands

Along the way Darwin built up a huge collection of rocks and fossils as well as samples of plants, birds and animals. He also made very detailed notes of everything he saw on the journey. He later used much of this material, particularly the observations he made on the Galapagos Islands, in the formulation of his theory of evolution.

Beetles collected by Darwin on the expedition

The *Beagle* returned to England in October 1836. Darwin spent the next 20 years writing up his findings. In 1858 he received a manuscript written by Alfred Wallace (1823-1913), a scientist with very similar ideas to his own. Although they presented their ideas together, Darwin's role was seen as more important than Wallace's.

In 1859 Darwin published *On the Origin of the Species by Means of Natural Selection*, which set out his theories on evolution. The book was an immediate success. But it also led to an uproar because it challenged traditional beliefs on the beginning of life on earth. One of the most revolutionary ideas was that all living things had evolved over many millions of years. This rejected the biblical teaching that the world was created in six days and had remained unchanged ever since. Today, most scientists accept a form of the Darwinian theory to explain biological change, although the theory is still being modified. Some people, however, still object to Darwin's ideas on religious grounds.

Cartoon mocking Darwin's idea that humans are descended from apes

Natural selection

Darwin realized that organisms have to compete with each other for food and shelter. He noticed that within each species, some individuals are born with features that by chance make them more able to survive than others. Their offspring inherit these features, which gradually become more common. If other individuals do not have the helpful features, they are more likely to die out. So over many generations the entire species adapts to its environment. This process, called natural selection, can be seen in the way the peppered moth adapted to environmental changes in the 19th century.

At first, the moths were silver and blended with light tree-trunks. But as trees became blackened with pollution, the moths were more visible, and so more likely to be eaten by birds. Some individuals, born slightly darker than the others, were less visible and so survived better. They passed on their darker shading to their offspring, and so the entire species became darker.

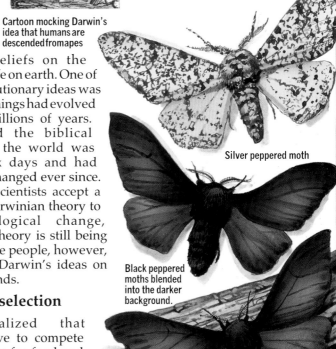

Silver peppered moth

Black peppered moths blended into the darker background.

Chemistry (the study of the substances that make up the world around us) has its origins in the ancient practice of alchemy (see page 58). But alchemy was closely connected to magic and superstition, and is not currently regarded as a true science. Chemistry also has its roots in industrial processes such as iron-working and the making of drugs for medicine. With the growth of experiment and research, the practice of chemistry devloped into a modern science.

An experiment in a 16th-century laboratory

Studying chemical reactions

In 1756 a Scottish experimenter called Joseph Black (1728-99) made an important study of a chemical reaction (the change that takes place when a new substance is formed). Black discovered that when he heated a substance called magnesium carbonate it lost weight. He then suggested that this was because the substance gave off a gas during the heating process. He named the gas "fixed air"; today we know it as carbon dioxide.

A newly discovered gas

Joseph Priestley was born in Yorkshire, England. He trained as a Church minister but soon became interested in scientific research. His work made him famous, but political pressures forced him to leave England for the USA in 1791. In 1774 Priestley made his most important discovery. He noticed that when he heated a chemical called mercuric oxide, a gas was given off. When he placed a lighted candle in the gas, he saw that the flame burned very brightly. At this time, many scientists believed that when something burned it lost a substance they called phlogiston (from *phlox*, the Greek for "flame"). Priestley called his gas "dephlogisticated air" because it seemed to have lost phlogiston. But in fact he had identified the gas we now know as oxygen.

Joseph Priestley (1733-1804)

A late 18th-century cartoon of "Doctor Phlogiston"

The founder of modern chemistry

Antoine Lavoisier (1743-94) was born in Paris. He trained as a lawyer but became interested in science and worked as a tax collector in order to support his scientific research. Tax collectors were very unpopular with the leaders of the French Revolution and Lavoisier was one of many people to be executed at the end of the revolution.

Arrest of Lavoisier by French revolutionaries

Priestley's microscope

The naming of oxygen

Lavoisier performed a series of experiments designed to examine the process of combustion (burning). He heated a number of different substances in air, carefully weighing them before and after heating. His results showed that, rather than losing weight, the substances often became heavier. He reasoned that they must therefore have absorbed something from the air. He showed that this unknown substance was the same gas as the one that Priestley had identified, and renamed it oxygen.

Apparatus used by Lavoisier to investigate combustion.

By successfully explaining some of the phenomena scientists had observed, Lavoisier's results helped to disprove the phlogiston theory, which had been held for nearly a hundred years. His definition of burning - as the uniting of a substance with oxygen - is still used today. He was the first person to demonstrate that all kinds of burning (including the breathing of animals and plants) involve the addition of oxygen. His work helped to overthrow many of the incorrect ideas inherited from alchemy.

Chemical building blocks

In 1789 Lavoisier published *Methods of Chemical Nomenclature*, which built on the work of Robert Boyle (see page 71). In it he developed the idea of elements (substances that cannot be split into simpler substances) as chemical building blocks. Lavoisier listed 33 elements, arranged to show how they combine to form compounds (substances made of more than one element). The book also introduced a new system of naming substances based on their chemical content. Before, they had often had confusing names, some derived from alchemy.

A modern atomic theory

John Dalton was born in a small village in the north of England and taught himself science. His ideas led to a greater understanding of the most fundamental chemical process: the way elements combine to form compounds. In 1808 he published a book called *A New System of Chemical Philosophy*. It had two main points.

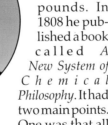

John Dalton (1766-1844)

One was that all chemical elements are composed of very small particles called atoms, which do not break up during chemical reactions. The other was that all chemical reactions are the result of atoms joining together or separating. Another important feature of the book was its proposal that different atoms weigh different amounts.

The relationship between elements

Dmitri Mendeleev was born and brought up in Siberia in Russia, the last in a family of 14 children. He was a brilliant student of science at the University of St Petersburg and later became professor of chemistry there. He studied the relationship between different chemical elements. At this time, a few scientists had noticed that some elements had similarities that related to their atomic weights. The atomic weight of an element is the weight of one of its atoms compared with the weight of a hydrogen atom.

Dmitri Mendeleev (1834-1907) and part of his *Periodic Table*

In 1869 Mendeleev published his Periodic Table of Elements. This grouped the elements into "families" according to their atomic weights, the smallest (hydrogen) on the left, and the largest (lead) on the right. It showed how the elements are related to each other. Mendeleev identified gaps in the periodic table which he claimed represented elements still to be discovered. He was right. Four years later, the first of these, gallium, was discovered. Over a hundred elements have so far been listed.

Some of the equipment used by Dalton

Studying electricity

Electricity plays a very important part in our lives. There are two types: static (not moving) and current (moving). People have known about the effects of electricity since ancient times. But until the end of the 18th century, the only kind they knew how to make was static electricity. The study of electricity became very popular, and during the 19th century people gradually learned more about it and its uses.

Early experiments

In 1705 an English scientist called Francis Hauksbee (c.1666-1713) discovered that if he rubbed a glass globe containing a vacuum (an airless space), it flashed with light. The light was caused by electricity and the globe was acting as an electrical generator.

Hauksbee's static electricity generator

Another man, Stephen Gray (1666-1736), devised experiments which showed that electricity could be conducted (transmitted) through a number of different materials. These included the human body.

An early demonstration of static electricity.

He made electricity travel along a string suspended from cords hung on poles in his orchard.

This French playing card of c.1750 shows a demonstration of static electricity.

Storing static electricity

In 1745 a German priest called Ewald von Kleist (c.1700-48) designed an instrument that could collect and store static electricity. It became known as the Leiden jar, after being used and perfected at the University of Leiden. This was a major development in people's knowledge about electricity. The Leiden jar consisted of a glass jar held in one hand. The inside glass surface was charged (electrified) with static electricity by dipping a brass wire connected to a generator, very similar to Hauksbee's, into the water inside the jar. Once charged, the jar could store the electricity and could also transmit a shock if the wire was touched.

This illustration shows a Leiden jar being charged with static electricity from a generator.

Making electricity useful

One of the first people to study electricity in detail was Benjamin Franklin. He was born in the USA, one of 17 children of a Boston candlemaker. During his long life he had several successful careers: as printer, publisher and politician. At the age of 40 he became interested in electricity, which at that time was mainly used as a form of entertainment in displays. In

Benjamin Franklin (1706-90)

1752 Franklin showed that lightning was a form of electricity. He flew a kite fitted with a metal key into a storm cloud. When lightning hit the key, sparks flew off it.

This experiment was very dangerous and another scientist was later killed doing the same thing. But with it Franklin was able to prove that storm clouds are charged with static electricity. It also showed that lightning is caused by the discharge of that electricity in the form of a very powerful spark. In the same year he fitted the first lightning conductor to the outside wall of a house. This attracted lightning and carried it safely to the ground, preventing damage to the building.

18th-century lady wearing a lightning conductor hat

Animal electricity

Luigi Galvani (1737-98) was professor of anatomy at Bologna University. He realized that an electric ray fish gave a shock similar to that from a Leiden jar. He then wanted to find out whether electricity existed in all forms of life. In 1780, while he was dissecting a dead frog, he noticed that its legs twitched when his scalpel blade touched a nerve. He also noticed that the leg muscles twitched when

Galvani's experiment with frogs' legs

they were in contact with two different metals, in this case brass and iron. Galvani concluded, mistakenly, that the frog's legs produced electricity and that animals must contain electricity in their muscles and nerves.

Electricity from metals

Alessandro Volta (1745-1827) showed that the frog's legs did not contain their own form of electricity and that Galvani's results were in fact due to the contact of the two different metals in a damp atmosphere. Using this information, in 1799 Volta succeeded in building the first electric battery. This became known as a "voltaic pile" and was made up of discs of silver and zinc with damp card between them. It generated a steady current of electricity. The volt, a measurement of electricity, is named after him.

The first battery, known as a voltaic pile

Popular science

Michael Faraday was born near London, the son of a blacksmith. His first job was in a bookshop, but in 1813 he started work as a laboratory assistant at the Royal Institution in London. In 1833 he was made professor of chemistry there. Many people now regard Faraday as the greatest of all experimental physicists. He was one of the first people to try to make science popular with the general public. In 1826 he gave the first lectures about science for children, at the Royal Institution. These are still held every year.

Michael Faraday (1791-1867)

Electricity and magnetism

Faraday became very interested in the relationship between electricity and magnetism. People had known about magnetism for thousands of years, and many believed that electricity and magnetism were related in some way. Then, in 1820, a Danish scientist called Hans Oersted (1777-1851) noticed that a wire with an electric current running through it acted like a magnet, making the needle move on a compass lying nearby.

Investigating this further, Faraday found that when he charged a coil of wire with electricity, an electric current also flowed in another, separate coil nearby. He reasoned that this second current must have been generated by the magnetic effect of the first one.

Faraday argued that if electricity flowing in a wire could produce a magnetic effect, then the opposite

might also be true - a magnetic effect should produce an electric current. He found that when he moved a magnet in and out of a coil of wire, the wire became charged with electricity. This showed that magnets alone could produce an electric current. Faraday had created the first dynamo (a machine that uses mechanical energy to generate electrical energy).

These discoveries had all kinds of far-reaching practical results. Faraday's work led to the invention of the electric motor, and to the development of large-scale systems to generate electricity. This eventually led to the introduction of a public electricity supply.

Faraday produced an electric current from a moving magnet, using this device called a disc dynamo.

The fight against disease

During the Renaissance in Europe much progress was made in the understanding of the human body (see page 64). But doctors were still unable to cure a number of diseases, including smallpox and the plague, which killed millions all over the world. Many of these illnesses were caused by viruses (microscopic particles that live off the body's cells). Another problem was that while surgical techniques had improved, many people still died from infections they caught during surgery. From the mid-18th century scientists began to find ways to beat these forms of disease.

This engraving of 1656 shows an Italian doctor wearing special clothing to protect him against the plague.

Early vaccination

Edward Jenner was born in Gloucestershire, England. From the age of 13 he went to work as an apprentice to a surgeon, and then became a medical student at St George's Hospital, London. After two years Jenner returned to his home town and set up a medical practice. At this time smallpox was one of the most serious viral diseases. Jenner had heard that people who had caught a mild disease called cowpox did not catch smallpox. The cowpox had immunized (protected) them against smallpox. In 1796 Jenner scratched some cowpox into the skin of a healthy boy. Two months later he did the same with smallpox. The experiment was a complete success: the boy did not develop smallpox and had therefore become immune to it. Jenner named the process vaccination, from *vacca*, the Latin word for cow. His work was one of the most important advances in medical science ever made. By 1980 there were no more reported cases of smallpox.

Edward Jenner (1749-1823)

The birth of bacteriology

Louis Pasteur was born near Dijon in eastern France. In 1843 he went to Paris to study chemistry, and in 1854 he was appointed professor of chemistry at the University of Lille. In Lille, Pasteur was asked to find out why alcohols such as wine and beer sometimes turn sour. He discovered that this was caused by germs called bacteria, and that heating the liquid to a certain temperature killed the bacteria but left the liquid unchanged. This process is now known as "pasteurization" and is used to treat milk. Pasteur also showed that the bacteria which cause liquids to go sour and meat to rot exist invisibly all around us.

Louis Pasteur (1822-95)

Pasteur's most famous work was on rabies, one of the most horrific diseases that can affect a human being. It causes paralysis and eventually kills the victim. In 1885 he injected a weak solution of rabies germs into a boy who had been bitten and infected by a rabid (rabies-infected) dog. After a series of these injections the boy recovered completely.

A statue of Joseph Meister, the boy Pasteur vaccinated against rabies

Normally the rabies germs would have become active a few weeks after the bite, but this did not happen. The injections, prepared from weakened germs, caused a very mild attack of rabies. This stimulated the boy's resistance, making him immune to the germs from the bite. This is the principle behind all vaccination.

Glass flask and microscope used by Pasteur

Robert Koch (1843-1910) was, with Pasteur, the founder of the science of bacteriology. Here Koch is inoculating a patient against tuberculosis.

Jenner used these points to scratch vaccine into the skin.

A 19th-century cartoon showing Jenner's patients turning into cows

Antiseptic operations

Joseph Lister was born in Essex, England, the son of a wine merchant and amateur scientist. In 1848 he enrolled at University College, London to study medicine. He qualified in 1852 and, because his work was so outstanding, he was made a Fellow of the Royal College of Surgeons the same year. In 1853 he moved to Edinburgh to take up the post of assistant to James Syme, a leading surgeon. In 1861 Lister was appointed surgeon at the Glasgow Royal Infirmary.

Joseph Lister
(1827-1912)

In those days, many patients died after surgical operations. Wounds rarely healed cleanly and usually became septic (badly infected). This often led to blood poisoning and other fatal diseases. In 1865 Pasteur published his theory of germ disease, which claimed that bacteria can cause disease and that fermentation and rotting are caused by bacteria which live in the air. When Lister read this, he thought that the rotting of meat and sepsis of wounds might

These machines sterilize instruments by steam-heating them.

Some modern sterilizing units use ultra-violet light and ultrasound to destroy germs.

be caused by the same thing. Shortly after the publication of Pasteur's paper, Lister performed his first operation in which he took care to clean everything that came into contact with the patient's wound with carbolic acid. This method is known as antisepsis and it destroys germs already present.

As a result of these precautions, the wounds in this and other similar operations healed properly, and the rate of infection fell dramatically. Lister received many awards for his work. His introduction of anti-sepsis to hospitals was one of the major advances in medicine in the 19th century. It changed general surgery from being highly dangerous into something that saves lives.

Lister's antiseptic carbolic spray

This illustration shows Lister directing an antiseptic surgical operation.

Antibiotic drugs

Alexander Fleming was born in Ayrshire, Scotland. From 1901 he studied medicine at St Mary's Hospital, London. Much later, in 1928, when he was studying the bacteria responsible for blood poisoning, he noticed that a dish of the bacteria had become infected with a growth called *Penicillium notatum*. The bacteria in the area infected by the growth had been killed. The chemical that had caused this is now known as "penicillin".

Alexander Fleming
(1881-1955)

Some years later two scientists called Howard Florey (1898-1968) and Ernst Chain (1906-79) produced the first large quantities of purified penicillin. This was the first of a group of drugs called antibiotics which attack and kill bacteria. Because of the development of antibiotics in the 20th century, bacterial illnesses are no longer a major cause of death.

A dish of *Penicillium notatum*, from which penicillin is made

More obstacles

Though smallpox and other diseases have been eradicated, many more fatal diseases still remain. Scientists are still seeking cures for viral and other diseases. Two of the major ones facing doctors today are cancer and the AIDS virus.

Waves and radiation

People have always been interested in nature and the world about them. From the earliest times they asked questions about why things get hot, how light works and sounds are made. Some of these questions were answered by scholars in the ancient world, but in the 19th century scientists began to study problems like these in more detail. They started to describe light, electricity, and magnetism as the products of different kinds of energy.

Developing Faraday's work

James Maxwell was born and brought up near Edinburgh, Scotland. He was a mathematician and physicist whose most important work was on electricity and magnetism. In 1820 Hans Oersted (see page 81) had shown that an electric current had a magnetic effect on a compass needle. An effect like this is now said to be "electromagnetic". Later, Michael Faraday (see page 81) suggested that electric and magnetic forces spread out in "fields" from their sources.

Lines of force in a magnetic field

In 1855 Maxwell developed Faraday's ideas to give a mathematical explanation for the transmission of electromagnetic forces. He devised mathematical equations which showed that the magnetic field generated by an electric current spreads outward from its source at a constant speed. He calculated that this speed was roughly the same as the speed of light. He suggested that light must therefore be some kind of electromagnetic wave and that the light we can see may be only one of many types of electromagnetic radiation. (Radiation is the emission of rays from a source.)

James Maxwell (1831-79), with a page of his calculations

Radio waves

Heinrich Hertz was born in Hamburg, Germany. He orginally trained to be an engineer but then began studying physics. His experiments showed that electro-magnetic waves emitted by an electrical spark on one side of his laboratory could be detected by a loop of wire some distance away. This proved the existence of radio waves, another form of electromagnetic radiation. It was later shown that, like light, radio waves could be focused and reflected. Hertz's work therefore proved Maxwell's earlier theory that electromagnetic waves behave in the same way as light waves.

Heinrich Hertz (1857-94)

More electromagnetic waves

Wilhelm Röntgen was born in a small village in Germany and studied at Zürich Polytechnic. He became professor of physics at the University of Würzburg where he experimented with gases and expanded Maxwell's work on electromagnetism.

In 1895 Röntgen was researching cathode rays, which are produced when an electric current is passed through a glass tube containing a near-vacuum. The tube glows whenever the rays hit the glass. In order to examine this more closely, Röntgen surrounded the tube with a piece of black paper. He was mystified when some cardboard on the other side of the room started to glow. It was coated with a chemical, known as a fluorescent, which glows when exposed to light.

Wilhelm Röntgen (1845-1923)

Röntgen found that the cardboard still glowed even when he moved it into the next room. It appeared that the tube was emitting another form of radiation which was able to pass through all sorts of materials. He named the new rays X-rays, because of their unknown origin.

Later Röntgen found that by directing X-rays at a person's hand he could take photographs which showed the bones inside it. The X-rays were stopped by the bones, but passed through the flesh, allowing a photographic image to form.

An early cathode ray tube

A 19th-century cartoon of the X-ray effect

STRAND-JDYLL Á LA

An early X-ray machine

Two X-ray photographs: A modern X-ray of the human head, generated in colour by a computer; and one of the first X-rays, taken by Röntgen of his wife's hand

Confirmation of radioactivity

Marya Sklodowska (later Marie Curie) was born in Warsaw, Poland. She left to study chemistry at the Sorbonne in Paris. In 1894 she married another chemist, Pierre Curie (1859-1906).

In their own research into radiation, the Curies discovered that pitchblende, a mineral that contains uranium, is four times as radioactive as pure uranium. They thought that it must therefore contain some other, unknown, radioactive element. The Curies spent several years purifying huge quantities of pitchblende, which became increasingly radioactive. By 1902 they had gathered 0.1 gram of the unknown element, which they gave the name "radium".

Caricature of the Curies

This revolutionized the medical world, particularly the diagnosis and treatment of broken bones.

The beginning of the atomic era

Antoine Becquerel was born into a scientific family and brought up in Paris. He was a physicist who specialized in the study of fluorescence. When he heard of Röntgen's discovery, he wanted to devise an experiment to find out whether fluorescent chemicals, as well as emitting ordinary light rays, would emit X-rays.

At that time Becquerel was studying a fluorescent compound that included an element called uranium. He wrapped some of it in metal foil, then placed the parcel on a photographic plate. He reasoned that any ordinary light emitted by the fluorescence in the

Antoine Becquerel (1852-1908)

substance would not be able to pass through the foil and register on the plate, but that X-rays might. When he developed the plate, it had indeed been blackened, so he was able to confirm that the substance was giving out some type of ray. He later discovered that this only happened with uranium compounds, not with other types of fluorescent chemical.

Becquerel realized that the substance was giving out an extremely strong form of radiation. At first he thought he had found a new form of electromagnetism. But further experiments showed that there were two distinct types of radiation, now known as alpha and beta radiation. These consisted of electrically-charged particles. Later a third type, gamma radiation, was discovered, which was proved to be a form of electromagnetic radiation. These discoveries implied that atoms of radioactive substances were themselves the source of energy. They led scientists to conclude that atoms must therefore have some kind of internal structure that was able to generate this energy. This realization was a very important step, because it marked the beginning of the modern understanding of the atom.

In 1903 the Curies received the Nobel Prize for physics. When Pierre was killed in a car crash three years later, Marie took over as professor in Paris, the first woman to hold such a position. In 1911 she was awarded the Nobel Prize for chemistry, the first person to receive two Nobel prizes.

Radium, used in small doses, became very important in the treatment of cancer. But years of exposure to it damaged Curie's own health, and she died of a blood cancer called leukemia.

A medal of Marie Curie (1867-1934), issued on the centenary of her birth

NTGEN

The science of life

Although by the end of the 19th century Darwin's theory of evolution was accepted by many scientists, there were a few who disagreed with it. They claimed that it did not explain how changes originated in plants and animals, or how characteristics were passed on from one generation to the next. People began to investigate these questions. Their studies led to the foundation of genetics, the science of heredity (how characteristics in plants and animals are inherited).

The birth of genetics

Gregor Mendel grew up in Heinzendorf in Austria. He became a priest at the monastery in Brno in 1847, and was elected abbot there eleven years later.

Mendel was interested in how plants pass on particular features such as height and shape to their offspring. He bred pea plants to find out how this worked, and noticed that characteristics like the shape of their flowers were passed on to the next generation. He also found that some features were more likely to be inherited than others. Those that had a three in four chance of being inherited he called "dominant". Those that only had a one in four chance of being inherited he called "recessive".

Mendel suggested that each characteristic was controlled by a pair of units (now called genes), one from each parent. This is known as Mendel's First

Mendel performed most of his experiments on pea plants.

Gregor Mendel (1822-84)

Law. His discoveries and theories revealed the secret of heredity and formed the basis of modern studies in genetics. However, though he published his work in 1866, its true significance remained unrecognized for nearly forty years.

Experiments with fruit flies

Thomas Morgan (1866-1945) was born in Kentucky, USA. He founded the department of biology at the California Institute of Technology in 1928, and ran it for the rest of his life. At first Morgan was one of the fiercest critics of Mendel's theory of heredity, but he later became its strongest supporter. He wanted to find out whether the kind of changes Mendel had noticed in plants also occurred in animals. In 1908 he began studying fruit flies; this work was very important in establishing Mendel's theories.

Fruit flies normally have red eyes, but Morgan found a white-eyed male in one of the breeding jars. When he bred this male with other members of the same generation, some white-eyed flies appeared again in

Fruit flies (Drosophila melanogaster)

the next generation. They were mostly male, but when one of these white-eyed males mated with females of the first generation, half the males and half the females of their offspring had white eyes. Morgan used Mendel's theory to explain this result by showing that the dominant feature of white eyes was passed on by the male parent's units.

Mapping chromosomes

All organisms (living things) are made up of cells, the basic units of life. Inside each cell is a tiny ball called a nucleus, which in turn contains thread-like forms called chromosomes.

Morgan and his research team discovered that the units suggested by Mendel were indeed actual physical units, placed at definite positions along each chromosome. They named the units "genes", after the Greek word for birth. Using this discovery, they were able to work out the first "chromosome map". This showed the position of the genes on a chromosome. By 1922 they had worked out a map

Magnified human chromosomes

showing the positions of more than 2000 genes on the chromosomes of fruit flies. This enabled them to identify the gene responsible for the white eyes in the flies. In this way they confirmed that Mendel's theories were correct, and provided the evidence to explain them.

Molecular biology

Genes provide a chemical code of instructions to control the way plants and animals look and how their bodies work. A "copy" of these instructions is passed from parents to their offspring. The study of how this happens is part of an important area of scientific research known as molecular biology, which is concerned with the structure of the molecules that make up living animals and plants.

Cross-section of an animal cell, magnified many times

Cell membrane (outer skin)

Nucleus

By the early 20th century scientists knew that plant and animal cells contained a chemical called deoxyribonucleic acid (DNA). By 1950, they thought that DNA molecules acted as the chemical code of instructions responsible for heredity, but they did not know what they looked like or how they worked. A number of scientists were using a variety of approaches to solve the problem.

Building the DNA model

Francis Crick was brought up in London. He studied physics at the University of London and then biology at Cambridge University.

With an American scientist called James Watson (b.1928), he carried out research into the structure of DNA. They also used the results of the work of other scientists, in particular Maurice Wilkins (b.1916) and Rosalind Franklin. Wilkins and Franklin studied DNA using X-ray photographs. Their work was crucial in the eventual discovery of the structure of DNA and how it transmits genetic information from one generation to the following one.

Francis Crick (b.1916)

In 1953, Crick and Watson built a scale model of the DNA molecule from pieces of wire and plastic balls. Its shape was that of a double helix, which looks like a twisted rope ladder. It showed how the DNA molecule divides to form two identical copies of itself.

When plants and animals reproduce, each of the cells they are made up from divides into two copies. Every time a new cell is

Rosalind Franklin (1920-58)

made, the DNA is also copied, so that when the cell divides, each of the two new cells has its own copy of the instructions responsible for heredity. In this way the characteristics are passed from parents to their offspring.

Many scientists regard this as one of the most important discoveries of the 20th century. In 1962 Crick, Watson and Wilkins were awarded the Nobel Prize for Medicine. Had she not died very young from cancer, Rosalind Franklin would have shared the prize with them.

This is a computer-generated illustration showing the structure of the DNA molecule.

1. DNA consists of two strands shaped in a double helix, like a twisted rope ladder.

2. The steps in the ladder are made up of four chemical building blocks, called bases, which are linked in pairs.

3. The two DNA strands separate

4. Spare bases join their matching pairs on the separated strands.

5. Two new identical strands are formed

Opening up the atom

At the end of the 19th century, many physicists believed they were close to explaining the construction of the universe. They described matter in terms of the movement of tiny, indivisible particles called atoms. However, new discoveries threatened their confidence. It became apparent that atoms themselves were composed of even smaller particles, and that the way in which they behaved could not be explained by Newton's laws of force and motion (see page 70).

The birth of quantum physics

Max Planck was born in Kiel, now in Germany. He studied physics at Munich University, where he later became a professor. In 1900 he published an article introducing the idea of "quantizing energy". On the basis of Planck's work, Einstein suggested that electromagnetic radiation (see page 84), instead of being made up of waves, is in fact discontinuous and is composed of tiny particles, or "quanta", of energy.

$$E = h\nu$$

This equation, formulated by Einstein, includes Planck's constant (h). This relates the mechanical properties of matter to its wave properties.

Max Planck (1858-1947)

Although Planck's idea was not seen as revolutionary at the time, it led to the development of quantum mechanics, a new set of laws describing how atomic particles behaved. Unlike Newton's laws, quantum mechanics is based on the idea that matter can behave either as waves or as particles.

From clerk to professor

Albert Einstein is one of the 20th century's most famous scientists. But he was a shy man whose work was very abstract and theoretical. He is best known for his relativity theories and for establishing the idea of the quantization of energy, both of which are important for describing how atoms and atomic particles move and interact.

Einstein was born in Ulm, Germany. His family moved to Switzerland and he studied physics at Zürich Polytechnic. After failing to secure an academic position, he became a clerk in Berne.

Albert Einstein (1879-1955)

In 1905, Einstein worked in his spare time to produce three papers which re-examined some of the most fundamental ideas in science. His theories were so revolutionary that they were not immediately accepted, but his ability was quickly recognized. In 1909 he became a professor at Zürich University, and then in 1914 moved to the University of Berlin.

The University of Berlin

The relativity theories

The first paper on relativity (known as the Special Theory of Relativity) overturned Newton's view of fixed measurements of time and motion. Einstein showed that all movement is relative; that all we can measure is how fast we are moving in relation to something else. There is a relation between the mass and energy of moving objects, which he expressed in the equation $E=mc^2$. This means that the energy (E) contained in any particle of matter is equal to its mass (m) multiplied by the square of the speed of light (c^2). This formula is at the heart of all methods of obtaining nuclear energy.

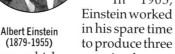

A sheet of Einstein's calculations

In 1915 Einstein published a second paper on relativity (the General Theory of Relativity), which dealt with what happens when an object is speeding up or slowing down. It included the idea that light has mass and is therefore affected by gravity. This theory was confirmed when the bending of light by gravity was detected by photographing the light from two stars during a solar eclipse in 1919. Einstein's discoveries caused a sensation and made him internationally famous.

A computer image of a solar eclipse

The heart of the atom

Ernest Rutherford is important for his brilliant experimental and theoretical work on the nucleus (core) of the atom, and for his laboratory skills. The son of a New Zealand farmer, Rutherford studied at Christchurch College where he carried out research based on Hertz's study of radio waves (see page 84). He won a scholarship to Cambridge University, England and worked at the Cavendish Laboratory on the recently discovered X-rays and uranium radiation (see page 85).

Ernest
Rutherford
(1871-1937)

Autunite, an ore from which uranium can be extracted

Rutherford was appointed a professor at McGill University in Montreal, and later returned to Britain as director of the Manchester physics laboratory. He and his team carried out important experiments into the structure of the atom, using particles called

Apparatus used by Rutherford for scattering alpha particles

alpha particles, which are emitted by radioactive substances.

From his experiments, Rutherford built up a detailed picture of the atom. He concluded that most atomic matter was concentrated into a tiny nucleus in the middle, with much lighter particles called electrons orbiting it, like planets around the sun. In 1908 Rutherford was awarded the Nobel Prize for Chemistry, and in 1919 he was appointed director of the Cavendish Laboratory, where he inspired much further research into atomic structure.

A new model of the atom

Niels Bohr grew up in Copenhagen, Denmark, the son of a professor of physiology. He was awarded a doctorate from Copenhagen University and in 1911 moved to Manchester to work with Rutherford. By 1913 he had devised a radical new model of the structure of the atom. It combined Rutherford's ideas with those of quantum mechanics. Bohr's model has now been superseded, but it is still a useful aid to understanding

the way atoms behaved.

In 1913 Bohr returned to Copenhagen as professor of physics and helped develop new theories of quantum mechanics. He drew up models of the structure of the nucleus and discussed the energy changes involved in nuclear fission. He won the Nobel Prize for Physics in 1922.

Niels Bohr
(1885-1962)

Bohr was a committed anti-fascist and, when the Germans invaded Denmark in 1940, he refused to participate in atomic research for the Nazis. In 1943, in danger of arrest, he escaped by boat to Sweden and then on to the United States.

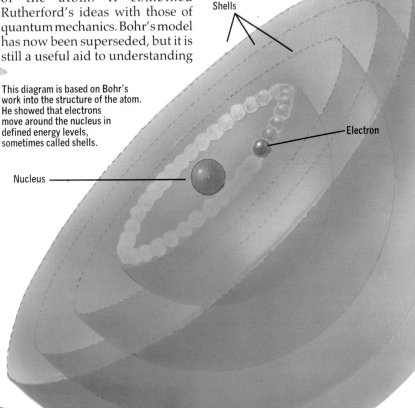

This diagram is based on Bohr's work into the structure of the atom. He showed that electrons move around the nucleus in defined energy levels, sometimes called shells.

Shells

Electron

Nucleus

The origin of the universe

For thousands of years people have been seeking answers to questions about the origin of the universe. For a long time many people thought that the universe had always existed in its present form, and that it would always remain the same. But ideas on the nature of the universe have altered as scientific understanding has increased. Evidence gathered over the centuries has shown that, rather than staying the same, the universe is always changing. The science of the universe is called cosmology. Cosmologists study the entire universe to find out how it began and how it has evolved.

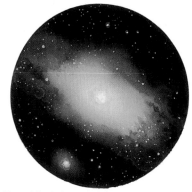
View of the Andromeda Spiral

This bronze plate depicts the Chinese idea of the creation of the universe.

Galaxies beyond our own

Edwin Hubble was born and brought up in the USA and studied law at the University of Chicago. He first worked as a lawyer but then turned to astronomy. For the rest of his life he worked at Mount Wilson Observatory in California.

In 1923 Hubble examined a galaxy (a giant group of stars) called the Andromeda Spiral. At that time, most astronomers thought that our galaxy, known as the Milky Way, made up the entire universe. They believed that the spiral forms we now know to be other galaxies were only clouds of gases. But Hubble saw stars on the edge of the Andromeda Spiral and estimated that they lay well beyond the Milky Way. His work proved that the Andromeda Spiral was another galaxy and therefore that other galaxies existed apart from our own. Gradually he and others began to identify more galaxies.

This picture shows Edwin Hubble (1889-1953) at the controls of the Mount Wilson telescope.

The Mount Wilson Observatory

The age of the universe

When examined closely, the light spectrum (see page 70) not only consists of the range of different shades, but also a series of lines. Astronomers noticed that when they examined light from stars, the shades and lines had moved toward the red end of the spectrum. This effect is known as "red shift". The reason for this is that when a source of light moves away from an observer, its wavelength increases. The greater the speed at which the light source is moving away, the greater the red shift. Hubble realized that in order to produce the shift effect, the stars must be moving away from us. He also noticed that the fainter the galaxies were, the greater the red shift. This implied that the more distant the galaxies

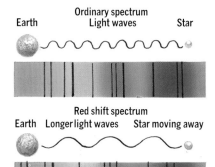

were, the faster they were moving. By 1929 he was able to measure the degree of red shift to calculate the speed of the galaxies and their distance from the earth. He found that the speed increases in proportion to the distance. This is known as Hubble's Law. His work provided the first evidence that the universe is expanding. This is the key to the Big Bang theory (see below). In addition, once astronomers were able to measure the speed at which galaxies are moving outward, they could calculate when the universe began. They now believe this happened between six and fifteen million years ago.

Creation from explosion

Georges Lemaître was born in Belgium. He studied astronomy at the University of Louvain in Belgium and then trained as a priest. He moved to Cambridge University in England and was later appointed professor of astronomy at Louvain where he remained for the rest of his career.

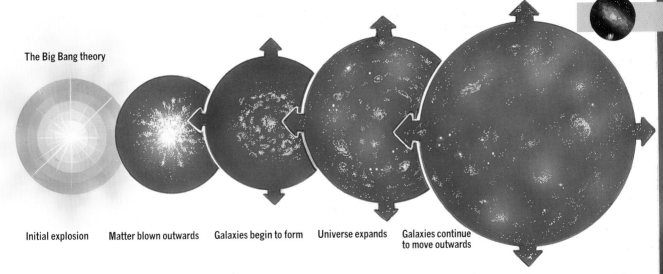

The Big Bang theory

Initial explosion   Matter blown outwards   Galaxies begin to form   Universe expands   Galaxies continue to move outwards

In 1927, using Einstein's General Theory of Relativity (see page 88), Lemaître proposed that the universe was still expanding. He claimed that at one time it must have been compressed into a tiny atom of energy and matter. He went on to suggest that the atom blew apart in a huge explosion, scattering hot gases in all directions This idea has become known as the Big Bang theory. At the time its true importance was not fully appreciated, but most scientists now see it as the best explanation of the origin of the universe.

Georges Lemaître (1894-1966)

As new discoveries in space have been made, the Big Bang theory has been refined and modified. In 1970 Roger Penrose (b.1931) and Stephen Hawking (b.1942) proved that if Einstein's General Theory of Relativity is correct, then it is possible that there was a definite beginning to the universe. At this point, called a singularity, space and time as we know them would not have existed. Moments after the explosion, the universe would have been an incredibly hot fireball. It expanded and cooled until, millions of years later, hydrogen and then other elements formed. Eventually, gravity drew atoms together and galaxies began to develop.

Another modification of the Big Bang theory, called the Oscillating Universe theory, states that the universe is alternately expanding and contracting. If this is true, when the limit of expansion is reached, the growth will stop and gravity will pull everything back together

The Oscillating Universe theory

Big Bang

Galaxies begin to form

Galaxies reach the limit of expansion

Galaxies fall back towards each other again

Big Bang

once more. The galaxies will be squeezed together so tightly that another cosmic explosion will set the whole process off again.

Staying the same

Hermann Bondi grew up in Vienna, Austria. He moved to England and studied at Cambridge University. In 1954 he became professor of mathematics at King's College,' London.

In 1948 Bondi proposed the Steady State theory, which says that new galaxies form at the middle of the expanding universe to replace those moving outward. As a result, he claimed, the universe would always look the same. However, later findings contradict this. For example, in 1964 two astronomers called Robert Wilson and Arno Penzias picked up faint radio noise from space. This is now thought to be the echo of the Big Bang.

Hermann Bondi (b.1919)

Wilson (b.1936) and Penzias (b.1933)

Women in science

Although many women throughout history have been involved in the development of science, their work has gained little recognition. For a number of reasons their achievements have often been ignored and their names left out of books. Women were unable to attend universities and were excluded from scientific societies and laboratories. Because they had little scientific education, many women could only serve as assistants to male scientists. The situation has improved slowly, but there are still far fewer women working in the sciences than there are men.

Early women scientists

Although there were women doctors in Ancient Egypt and Greece, there were very few opportunities for women to work in medicine and science in the ancient world. Accounts of the lives of successful women were invariably written by men who dismissed women scientists as immoral and dangerous. The first such scientist whose life is well-documented is Hypatia. Most of her writings have been lost, but there are a number of references to them by other scientists. Hypatia was born in Alexandria in Egypt, where she taught mathematics and philosophy. Her most important work was in algebra and geometry, but she was also interested in mechanics and technology. In

Tombstone of a woman doctor from the 1st century A.D.

Hypatia of Alexandria (A.D.370-415), based on a classical statue

addition she designed several scientific instruments, including a plane astrolabe. This was used for measuring the positions of the stars, planets and the sun.

Abbess and physician

Hildegard of Bingen was the abbess of a convent in Germany. She was educated in a wide range of subjects, including music and medicine. She wrote many books on religion as well as a natural history encyclopaedia called *Liber simplicis medicinae* which described animals and minerals and as many as 230 plants and 60 trees.

Hildegard devised a number of maps of the universe. In her first plan (shown below) of the universe, the earth lies in the middle surrounded by the stars and planets.

Hildegard of Bingen (1098-1179)

Hildegard's first plan of the universe

EAST

Fixed stars

Outer planets

Inner planets

NORTH

SOUTH

Earth

Hail and lightning

WEST

A forgotten mathematician

Anne, Countess of Conway (1631-79), a mathematician and philosopher, was born in London. Her brother, who acted as her tutor, supplied her with books and introduced her to the ideas of Descartes (see page 67). Her country house became a well-known meeting-place for scholars.

Ragley Hall, Lady Anne Conway's country house

Anne Conway's book, *The Principles of the most Ancient and Modern Philosophy*, was published eleven years after her death by a Dutch chemist called Francis van Helmont. It contained many of her scientific ideas and had a great influence on a German mathematician called Gottfried Leibniz (1646-1716). Although Leibniz acknowledged her importance, Conway's work was attributed to van Helmont and her name was soon forgotten.

A self-taught astronomer

Caroline Herschel (1750-1848) was born into a family of German musicians. In 1772 she moved to England to join her brother William, an astronomer. After teaching herself astronomy and mathematics with his help, she became his assistant. Later, in 1787, she became the first woman to be appointed assistant to the Court Astronomer.

This giant telescope, designed by Caroline's brother William, was built about 1780s.

Finding new comets

Herschel became recognized throughout Europe as a great astronomer. As well as her important collaborations with her brother, independently she discovered many new comets. She won a number of awards for her work, including the Gold Medal of the Royal Astronomical Society in 1828. Her success helped to open up astronomy to other women of her time.

Spreading scientific ideas

Mary Somerville made important contributions to science education. Born in Scotland, she became known as "the Queen of 19th-century science". Her first scientific paper, *On the Magnetizing Power of the More Refrangible Solar Rays*, had to be submitted to the Royal Society by her husband because women were banned from the organization. In 1831 she published *Mechanism of the Heavens*. As well as being her interpretation of the work of a French scientist called Pierre de Laplace (1749-1827), the book contained many original ideas of her own. For the rest of the century it was a standard text in the study of advanced mathematics.

Mary Somerville (1780-1872) and the title page of *Mechanism of the Heavens*

The first computer programmer

Ada, Countess of Lovelace, daughter of the poet Lord Byron, studied astronomy, Latin, music and mathematics. She worked with an English mathematician called Charles Babbage (1792-1871), as the designer of arithmetical operations for his calculating machines. As these machines are now often seen as the forerunners of computers, in a sense Lovelace was the first computer programmer. Her work for the machines and her ideas on their uses were published in 1843. But as it was considered unsuitable at that time for women to publish under their own names, she only signed the work with her initials. As a result, her work as a mathematician, like those of many other women scientists, has been largely forgotten.

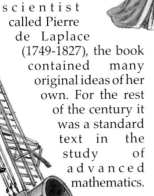

Countess of Lovelace (1815-52)

Academic frustration

Sophia Krukovsky was a Russian mathematician who gained the very highest awards for her work but was continually blocked in her efforts to make a career in mathematics. After her marriage to a law student called Vladimir Kovalevsky, she moved with him to Heidelberg in Germany. As a woman, Krukovsky was not allowed to join the university there and had to study privately. In 1874 she was awarded a doctorate in mathematics from Göttingen University, but was unable to find an academic post.

Sophia Krukovsky (1850-91) and some of her mathematical calculations

In 1884 Krukovsky became the first woman professor at the new University of Stockholm, Sweden. In 1888 she was awarded the Prix Bordin, the highest prize of the French Académie des Sciences (part of the Institute de France; see page 69) for her work in mathematics. But still she was unable to secure a job in France. She decided to resign her post at Stockholm and to devote her time to research, but she became ill and died soon after.

The letter announcing Krukovsky's award of the Prix Bordin.

Key dates in scientific discovery

Dates B.C.

4241B.C. The first year in which events can be precisely dated. This is made possible by the Egyptian calendar.

c.2630B.C. Imhotep becomes medical adviser to Djoser, Pharaoh of Egypt.

c.1000B.C. First records of Chinese knowledge of astronomy.

c.700B.C. Original compilation of the *Ayurveda*, an ancient Indian medical text.

c.600B.C. Thales of Miletus tries to find rational explanations for natural phenomena.

551B.C. Birth of the Chinese philosopher Confucius.

c.500B.C. Pythagoras discusses the mystical importance of numbers and harmony in the universe.

c.450B.C. Birth of Hippocrates, later an influential doctor on the island of Cos.

399B.C. Death of Socrates, one of the most important Greek philosophers.

387B.C. The philosopher Plato establishes the Academy in Athens.

c.335B.C. Aristotle writes important scientific books on natural history and the structure of the universe.

287B.C. Birth of Archimedes, mathematician and inventor.

Dates A.D.

150 Ptolemy writes the *Almagest*, about the movements of the stars and planets.

161 Greek anatomist Galen moves to Rome, where he becomes a famous doctor.

c.600 Mayan civilization flourishes in Central America.

813 The school of astronomy is founded in Baghdad.

c.854 Birth of al-Razi (Rhazes), the greatest Arabic alchemist.

965 Birth of ibn al-Haytham (Alhazen), an Islamic physicist famous for his work on optics.

1253 Death of Robert Grosseteste, teacher of mathematics and science.

1264 Thomas Aquinas reconciles Christian thought with Aristotle's teachings.

1267 Roger Bacon challenges the authority of traditional Christian education.

1452 Birth of Leonardo da Vinci, inventor and artist.

1527 Paracelsus becomes professor of medicine at the university of Basle.

1543 Copernicus publishes his theory that the planets move around the sun, not round the earth.

Andreas Vesalius produces a new guide to human anatomy.

1551 Konrad von Gesner starts to publish his extensive study of the animal kingdom.

1574 Tycho Brahe sets up an astronomical observatory on the island of Hven.

1596 Birth of René Descartes, mathematician and philosopher.

1610 Galileo Galilei publishes *The Starry Messenger*, about his astronomical discoveries made with the use of the telescope.

1616 William Harvey lectures on the circulation of blood.

1618 Johannes Kepler publishes laws describing the planets' elliptical orbits round the sun.

1627 Publication of Francis Bacon's *New Atlantis*, with its influential ideas about the role of science in society.

1632 Galileo publishes *Dialogue Concerning the Two Chief World Systems*, which describes the earth's movement around the sun.

1642 Galileo dies.
Isaac Newton is born.

1644 Publication of Descartes' most important scientific work, *Principles of Philosophy*.

1661 Robert Boyle proposes that matter is made up of tiny corpuscles, in his book *The Sceptical Chymist*.

1662 The Royal Society is founded in London.

1665 Publication of Robert Hooke's *Micrographia*, which contains detailed drawings made with the assistance of microscopes.

1666 The Académie Royale des Sciences is founded in Paris.

1682 Edmond Halley charts and describes the orbit of a comet, which is later named after him.

1687 Publication of Isaac Newton's book *Principia*, in which he formulates his laws of universal gravity.

1703 Newton becomes president of the Royal Society, and retains this post until his death in 1727.

1704 Newton publishes his book *Opticks*, about lenses and light.
John Ray completes his classification of 17,000 plants.

1705 Francis Hauksbee produces flashes of electricity by rubbing a globe containing a vacuum.

1729 Stephen Gray conducts electricity over long distances.

1745 Invention of the Leiden jar, an instrument that stores electricity.

1748 Georges de Buffon completes his 36-volume survey of natural history.

1752 Benjamin Franklin shows that lightning is caused by electricity.

1753 Carl Linnaeus publishes his new binomial system for classifying plants.

1756 Joseph Black finds "fixed air" (carbon dioxide) can be produced by heating chemicals.

1774 Joseph Priestley isolates the gas we now know as oxygen, calling it "dephlogisticated air".

1775 Abraham Werner founds a mining school at Freiberg, and gradually develops the "Neptunist" theory of geological change.

1779 Antoine Lavoisier confirms the existence of "dephlogisticated air", and renames it oxygen.

1787 Caroline Herschel receives royal recognition for her contributions to astronomy.

1789 Publication of Lavoisier's *Methods of Chemical Nomenclature*, which lists 33 elements, and introduces the modern system of naming them.

1791 Luigi Galvani publishes the results of his electrical experiments on frogs.

1795 James Hutton's book *The Theory of the Earth* questions the biblical account of the creation. It suggests instead that geological change has taken place over millions of years.

1796 Edward Jenner vaccinates a child against smallpox.

1799 Alessandro Volta builds the first electric battery.

1808 John Dalton's book *A New System of Chemical Philosophy* contains important new ideas about atomic theory.

1809 Jean de Lamarck publishes his explanation of change in living beings, including his idea that acquired characteristics can be inherited.

1820 Hans Oersted shows that an electric current has a magnetic effect on a compass needle.

1824 Justus von Liebig sets up his research laboratory in Giessen, Germany.

1831 Charles Lyell is appointed professor of geology at King's College, London.
Charles Darwin embarks on his voyage on HMS *Beagle*.
Michael Faraday produces an electric current from a moving magnet.

1843 Ada Lovelace publishes her mathematical work.

1858 Darwin receives Alfred Wallace's manuscript about natural selection.

1859 Darwin publishes *On the Origin of the Species by Natural Selection*, which contains his theories of evolution.

1867 Joseph Lister describes his success in reducing infections by using antiseptics.

1868 Gregor Mendel finishes his research into pea plants, which forms the basis of modern genetic theory.

1869 Dmitri Mendeleev devises the Periodic Table of the Elements.

1871 Darwin publishes his second book on evolution, *The Descent of Man*.

1872 James Maxwell uses algebraic equations to quantify Faraday's electrical theories.

1882 Robert Koch discovers the cholera virus.

1885 Using vaccinations, Louis Pasteur saves the life of a boy bitten by a rabid dog.

1886 Heinrich Hertz begins research that demonstrates the existence of radio waves.

1888 Sophia Krukovsky wins the Prix Bordin.

1895 Wilhelm Röntgen discovers X-rays.

1896 Antoine Becquerel discovers that uranium is radioactive.

1900 Max Planck introduces the idea of "quantizing energy".

1905 Albert Einstein publishes three scientific papers, including the Special Theory of Relativity.

1910 Thomas Morgan's experiments with fruit flies confirm Mendel's ideas about heredity.

1911 Marie Curie receives the Nobel Prize for her work on radioactivity, becoming the first person to win the prize twice.
Ernest Rutherford shows that atoms have a central nucleus.

1913 Niels Bohr proposes a new model of the hydrogen atom.

1915 Alfred Wegener publishes his theory of continental drift.

1919 Einstein publishes his paper on General Relativity.

1923 Edwin Hubble proves the existence of galaxies beside our own.

1927 Georges Lemaître proposes that the universe is continually expanding.

1928 Alexander Fleming notices that a growth, now called penicillin, kills bacteria.

1929 Hubble shows that the galaxies are moving away from each other. This forms the basis of the Big Bang theory.

1948 Hermann Bondi and Thomas Gold propose the Steady State theory of the universe.

1953 Francis Crick and James Watson discover the structure of the DNA molecule.

1963 Geological experiments confirm Wegener's ideas, and establish the theory of plate tectonics.

1964 Robert Wilson and Arno Penzias detect radio noise from space. This is thought to be the echo of the Big Bang.

The *Scientists* quiz

The answers to all the following questions can be found between pages 51 and 93 of this book. You will also find the answers upside down at the bottom of this page.

1. How did the Ancient Egyptians calculate when the River Nile would flood each year?
2. From what did the Mayans believe the world to be made?
3. Which Ancient Greek god was thought to cause earthquakes?
4. Name the two forces which Confucius believed were central to harmony in the Universe.
5. Name one of the two influential medical books written by Ibn Sina.
6. Name the four most important universities founded during the 12th-13th centuries.
7. What part of Tycho Brahe's body was cut off in a duel?
8. What two methods did Vesalius use to obtain specimens for his study of anatomy?
9. Identify these three scientists.

a)   b)   c)

10. Vesalius wrote one of the greatest scientific books ever published. What was its title?
11. What is the name given to the tiny blood vessels that connect veins and arteries?
12. Galileo was threatened with torture unless he denied which claim?
13. Name one of the founding members of the Royal Society.
14. What incident is said to have been the starting point for Isaac Newton's theory of gravitation?
15. Linaeus developed a method of classifying plants called "binomial nomenclature". What does it mean?
16. Can you identify the devices below and name their creators?

a)   b)   c)

17. Which book proposed that species had developed over long periods of time?
18. Name the two different theories concerning the structure of the earth preferred by Werner and Hutton.
19. What is the name given to the supercontinent by Wegener?
20. What was the name of the ship on which Charles Darwin sailed to South America?
21. What is the modern name for the gas that Joseph Priestley called "dephlogisticated gas" ?
22. What is the name given to Mendeleev's grouping of elements?
23. What is the name of the device Ewald von Kleist designed for storing static electricity?
24. What apparatus did Benjamin Franklin use to prove that lightning is a form of electricity?
25. Which measurement of electricity is named after an 18th century scientist?
26. Which process, discovered by Edward Jenner, is considered to be one of the most important advances ever made in medical science?
27. What is the name given to the process in which heat kills bacteria?
28. Who was the first person to receive two Nobel prizes?
29. On which plant did Mendel perform most of his experiments?
30. What was the equation Einstein used to express the relation between the mass and energy of moving objects?
31. Why did Niels Bohr go to live in the USA in 1943?
32. In 1927, Georges Lemaître proposed an idea that explained the origins of the Universe. What did this idea become known as?
33. Can you identify these scientific devices from the close-ups below?

a)   b)   c)

34. Who was the first woman to be appointed assistant to the Court Astronomer in 1787?
35. Why was Mary Somerville's first scientific paper submitted to the Royal Society by her husband?

Answers

1. They studied the position of the moon and the stars.
2. They believed that the world was made from the back of a giant crocodile lying in a pond.
3. Poseidon
4. Yin and Yang
5. *The Canon* and *The Cure*
6. Bologna, Oxford, Cambridge and Paris
7. His nose
8. Grave robbing and taking bodies from the gallows
9. a) Thales of Miletus; b) Alfred Wegener; c) Mary Somerville
10. *The Fabric of the Human Body*
11. Capillaries
12. The Earth moved around the Sun
13. Christopher Wren, Samuel Pepys
14. He saw an apple fall from a tree
15. It means that each plant has two names. One indicates its genus, the other its species.
16. a) A device use by Newton to illustrate his third law; b) Alessandro Volta's battery, know as a Voltaic pile; c) Lister's antiseptic carbolic spray.
17. *The Natural History* by Georges de Buffon
18. The "Neptunist" theory and the "Plutonist" theory
19. Pangaea
20. HMS Beagle
21. Oxygen
22. The Periodic Table
23. The Leiden jar
24. A kite fitted with a metal key
25. The volt, after Alessandro Volta
26. Vaccination
27. Pasteurization
28. Marie Curie
29. The pea plant
30. $E=mc^2$
31. To escape the Nazis
32. The Big Bang Theory
33. a) An early X-ray machine; b) Haukshee's static electricity generator; c) Joseph Priestley's microscope
34. Caroline Herschel
35. At that time women were banned from the organization

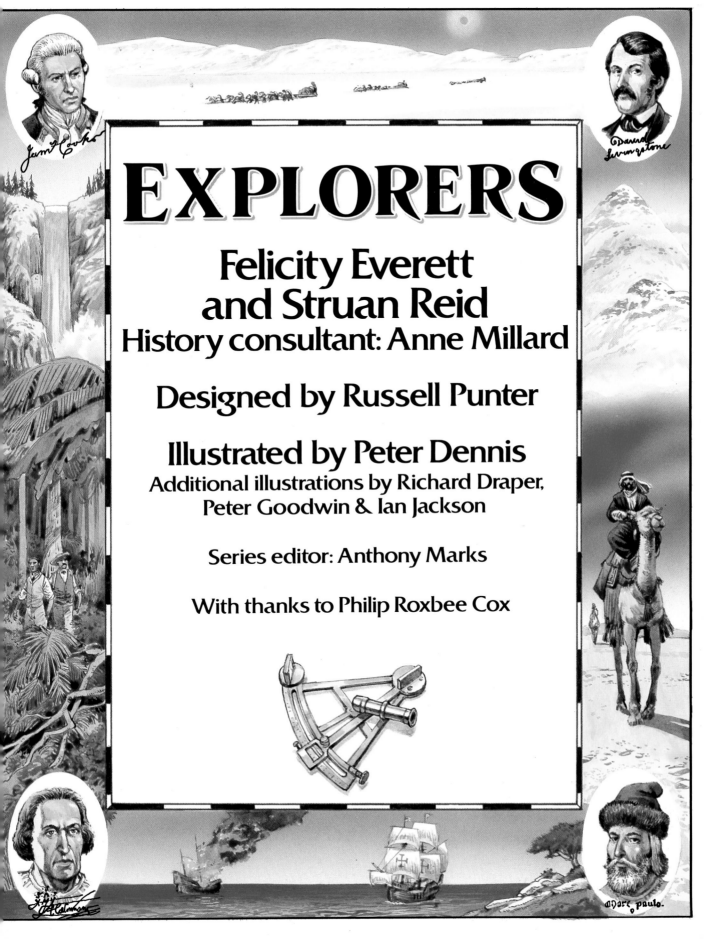

EXPLORERS

Felicity Everett and Struan Reid
History consultant: Anne Millard

Designed by Russell Punter

Illustrated by Peter Dennis
Additional illustrations by Richard Draper, Peter Goodwin & Ian Jackson

Series editor: Anthony Marks

With thanks to Philip Roxbee Cox

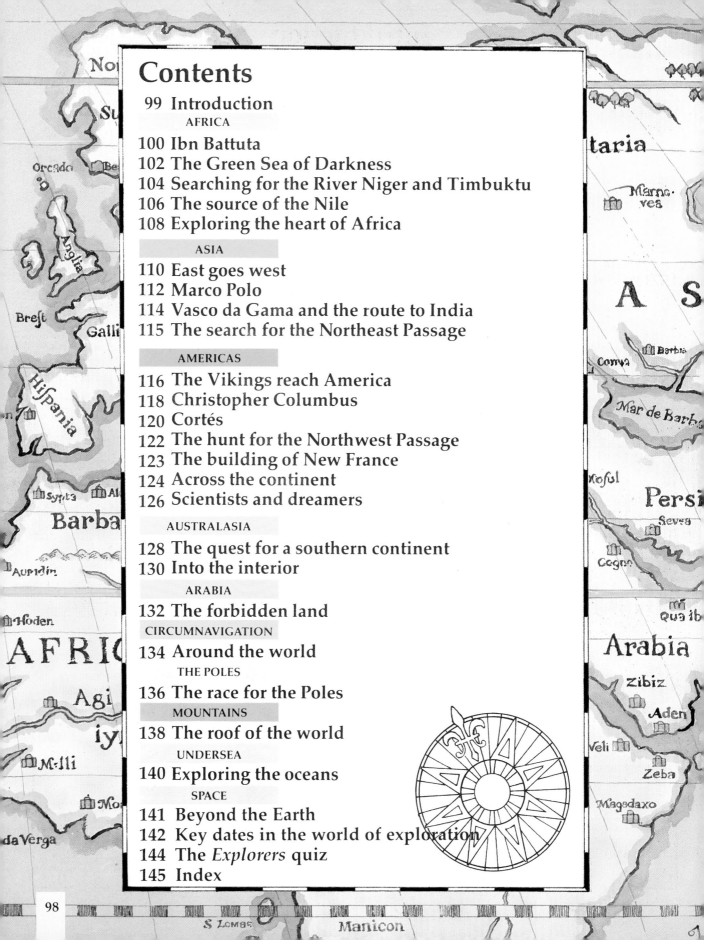

Contents

Introduction

This section of the book tells the stories of the lives of some of the world's greatest explorers. It is not a comprehensive history of exploration, but describes in detail the voyages of discovery that have had the most impact on the world.

What is an explorer?

Many of the explorers in this section of the book were not the first people to set foot in the lands they visisted, as the local inhabitants had been there for thousands of years. But they are thought of as explorers because they all changed the way people thought about the world. For example, Europeans returned from the Far East or America with important geographical information. Darwin's findings on the Galapagos Islands led him to challenge our basic ideas about the evolution of the planet.

Exploration is a way of learning about the world. As early travellers went further afield, they unravelled the mysteries of unknown continents. And even today, there are aspects of the Earth, and of space, that are still not fully understood. Each time scientists probe the frontiers of space, and when divers examine the sea bed, they continue to expand our knowledge with their explorations.

Why people explore

Throughout history, people have had an insatiable appetite for knowledge and adventure. But there have also been more specific reasons for exploration.

The competition for food forced our earliest ancestors in all directions in search of new places to live. Huge and powerful empires were built up through trade and

Mosaic of a Roman merchant ship.

conquest by the early civilizations - the Minoans, the Egyptians, the Phoenicians, the Greeks and the Romans.

Religion has always played an important part in the exploration of new lands. As early as the 5th century, Irish monks set out to convert the people of Wales, Cornwall and France to Christianity. But some later expeditions, though carried out

A 6th-century stone cross.

in the name of religion, were in fact accompanied by appalling savagery and destruction.

There were amateur explorers with a desire to see new places, like Ibn Battuta, Hsuan-tsang and Richard Burton. Others, such as Alexander Humboldt and Charles Darwin, led scientific expeditions which set out to learn as much as possible about the new lands.

How we know about exploration

Explorers, whether on land or on sea, have always kept records of the new lands and peoples they encountered, and some have used these to write books. The Greek explorer Diogenes' account of his journey inland from the east coast of Africa in the 1st century AD helped Ptolemy to draw his map of the world in the next century. In the 14th century, Ibn Battuta wrote down all he saw on his travels. Europeans

Medieval map

soon developed a taste for the accounts of mystery and adventure. Mungo Park wrote a book about his travels in Africa which was a best-seller, and Stanley's latest reports from Africa were eagerly awaited.

Geographical arrangement

This section of the book is arranged into groups, according to region: Africa, Asia, the Americas, and Australasia. There are also individual pages on Arabia, the Poles, Mountains, Circumnavigation, Undersea and Space.

Each chapter is introduced with a small map showing the areas covered, and a chart giving the most important dates in the exploration of that region. There is also a more detailed date chart on pages 142-143 that shows all the events in this section of the book in one list.

Dates

Many of the dates are from the period before the birth of Christ. They are indicated by the letters BC. Early dates in the period after Christ's birth are indicated by the letters AD. Some of the dates begin with the abbreviation "c". This stands for *circa*, the Latin for "about" and is used when historians are unsure exactly when an event took place.

Maps

There are detailed maps on many pages. These show the routes taken by the explorers, and also many of the places they visited.

Ibn Battuta

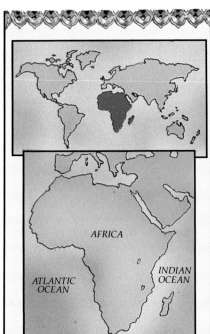

AFRICA

ATLANTIC OCEAN

INDIAN OCEAN

Key dates in African exploration

- **c.600BC** Pharaoh Necho II of Egypt sends out an expedition to explore the coasts of Africa.
- **c.AD150** Ptolemy draws his map of the world.
- **632** Death of the prophet Mohammed, founder of Islam.
- **c.860** Chinese reach Somali.
- **c.1060** Chinese reach Malindi.
- **c.1187** Chinese reach Zanzibar and Madagascar.
- **1304-77** Life of Ibn Battuta.
- **1394** Birth of Prince Henry the Navigator.
- **1405-33** Voyages of Cheng Ho.
- **c.1420** Chinese ships possibly round Cape of Good Hope.
- **1434** Gil Eannes rounds Cape Bojador.
- **1487** Bartolemeu Dias rounds the Cape of Good Hope.
- **1487** Pedro da Covilhã and Alfonso de Paiva set out.
- **1497** Vasco da Gama sails round Africa on his way to India.
- **1795** Mungo Park sails to Africa.
- **1805** Park leaves on his second trip to Africa.
- **1824** René Caillié sets out from France for Timbuktu.
- **1851** David Livingstone, his family and Cotton Oswell cross the Kalahari Desert.
- **1852-56** Livingstone becomes the first European to walk right across Africa.
- **1856** Richard Burton and John Speke leave England in search of the source of the Nile.
- **1858** Speke claims to have discovered the source of the Nile.
- **1858** Livingstone sets out to explore Zambezi River.
- **1860** Speke and James Grant leave on second journey to Africa.
- **1871** Henry Stanley and Livingstone meet at Ujiji.
- **1872** Livingstone starts out on his last journey, round the southern shores of Lake Tanganyika.
- **1874** Stanley returns to Africa to map lakes Victoria and Tanganyika.
- **1876-77** Stanley sails down the Lualaba and Congo rivers to the Atlantic.
- **1887** Stanley goes in search of Emin Pasha in the Sudan.

In the seventh century AD, the prophet Mohammed founded a new religion called Islam in Mecca, Arabia. Within a century of his death in 632 his followers, known as Muslims, had conquered a huge empire in the Middle East and North Africa.

Ibn Battuta was a rich Moroccan Muslim who in 1325 set out on a pilgrimage to Mecca. His adventures inspired him to travel further. He made daring journeys through parts of Africa, the Middle East and the Far East that before then were largely unknown to Europeans.

Ibn Battuta wrote detailed accounts of his travels. He used Arabic script, and probably had writing materials like these.

Through the Middle East

Ibn Battuta crossed Egypt to the Red Sea, hoping to sail to Jeddah. Because of a tribal war, however, he had to abandon his plans and go back to Cairo. He travelled on to Jerusalem and Damascus, then made his way by land through Arabia to Mecca.

From Mecca he travelled north to Baghdad, and was horrified that the city had been destroyed by the Mongols (fierce Asian warriors). He visited Anatolia (now part of Turkey), then went back to Mecca where he studied law. His new profession enabled him to pay for more travelling, and he soon set off again.

Around the coast of Africa

Ibn Battuta next crossed the Red Sea to Aden. There he boarded a dhow (a type of ship) which was heading for Zaila in Somalia. In his journal, he described Zaila as the dirtiest place he had ever visited.

Dhows are still quite common on the coast of East Africa.

From Zaila Ibn Battuta sailed on down the coast to Mombasa and Kilwa. He was impressed by the fine wooden houses there, and intrigued by the dark skins of the Africans.

Further afield

To get back to Mecca Ibn Battuta sailed along the south coast of Arabia and into the Persian Gulf, then crossed the Arabian Peninsula. Before long, however, his curiosity made him impatient to travel again.

The Caucasus Mountains

This time he headed north to Syria, Kaffa (the Crimea), and the Caucasus Mountains. He later crossed Central Asia, through Afghanistan, to India. From India he travelled by sea to Canton in China, then began the return journey to Morocco (via Malaysia and India). He eventually reached Fez in 1349.

A caravan crossing the Sahara desert

Across the Sahara

In 1352 Ibn Battuta set out again, this time to explore Africa. In many ways this was his most important expedition, for he was able to write about parts of the world that were unrecorded by other travellers at that time.

He crossed the Sahara Desert, heading for Mali. Conditions were harsh and bandits roamed the desert, so for protection he joined a caravan (a procession of traders and other travellers who used camels for transport).

First the caravan stopped in Taghaza, where Ibn Battuta noted that all the buildings were made of salt and camel skins. The travellers picked up supplies of water for the next ten days'

Timbuktu as it might have looked in Ibn Battuta's time.

journey to Tasarahla.

Then came the trek to Walata, which was made very dangerous because of shifting sands. Progress was slow, and there was the risk the water would run out.

Into unknown territory

Despite these dangers Ibn Battuta crossed the Sahara safely. He reached Mali, then continued as far as the River Niger. This was very daring, as few travellers had

ventured that far into the African interior before. The territory was so forbidding (see pages 104-109) that it was not further explored for another 400 years.

For the return journey, he chose an equally challenging route. This time he visited Timbuktu, an ancient city famed for its wealth and splendour.

These are some of the items traders used as currency in Timbuktu.

Iron chain

Copper ingot

Cowrie shells

Metal currency used like coins

The legacy of Ibn Battuta

Ibn Battuta's memoirs are vivid accounts of the places he visited, the people he met and the things he saw. Many people did not believe the strange stories he brought back from his travels.

This map shows the routes of Ibn Battuta's journeys in Africa. These, combined with his travels in Asia and the Far East, covered an amazing 120,700km (75,000 miles). This is more than many of today's travellers manage, even with all the benefits of modern methods of transport.

Exploring the Muslim world

Ibn Battuta
----- 1325
—— 1352

The Green Sea of Darkness

The first known journey round Africa took place about 600BC. Pharaoh Necho II of Egypt sent a sea captain to explore the coasts of Africa. The voyage was not repeated for almost two thousand years.

An Egyptian boat on a trading mission.

Europeans became interested in Africa during the Middle Ages. They acquired a taste for luxuries from the East such as spices, silks, sugar, pearls and precious stones. But the overland trade routes to the East were controlled by the Turks, who were at war with the Europeans. This made these goods very rare and expensive and the Europeans wanted to obtain them more cheaply. They became determined to find a sea route round Africa, avoiding the Turks, so that they could trade directly with India, China and the Spice Islands (now the Moluccas) in the Pacific Ocean.

The explorer who stayed at home

Prince Henry of Portugal was born in 1394 and later devoted his life to discovery. He was lured by the riches of the East and inspired by the stories of the Christian priest-king known as Prester John who was believed to live somewhere in Africa.

Henry the Navigator (1394-1460) Although the area opened up by his sailors was comparatively small, they took the first and most difficult steps into unknown lands.

In 1419 Henry was appointed Governor of the Algarve, in southern Portugal. On the windswept, rocky coast at Sagres, near the most southwesterly point of Europe (called by Europeans "the end of the world"), he built a palace, a church, a school to train navigators and pilots, an observatory and a shipyard. He recruited scholars, geographers, astronomers and mariners. He bullied and inspired his courtiers to lead expeditions that would open up new trade routes.

A barrier of fear

Henry sent out 14 expeditions over 12 years, but each one turned back at Cape Bojador on the west coast of Africa near the Canary Islands. This was as far south as the sailors dared go. They believed that at the Equator, in an area known as the "Green Sea of Darkness", the sun was so close to the Earth that people's skins were burned black, the sea boiled and there were whirlpools and thick green fogs where monsters lurked waiting to devour them.

The great breakthrough

Then, in 1434, one of Henry's courtiers called Gil Eannes managed to persuade his crew to carry on beyond the dreaded Cape. They survived to tell the tale, and from then on other Portuguese expeditions ventured further and further south.

None of Henry's ships had managed to sail round the southern tip of Africa by the time he died in 1460. But his inspiration paved

St Mary's rose, picked by Eannes from beyond Bojador.

the way for the journeys that would open up the world. Although he himself never sailed on any of the voyages he planned, he is always known as Henry the Navigator.

This Portuguese ship was called a caravel. It was very sturdy and could travel long distances.

102

Round the Cape

In August 1487 King John II of Portugal sent out an expedition of three ships from Lisbon. It was led by Bartolemeu Dias, who was instructed to open the sea route round Africa's southern tip. King John believed that the way east would be clear once the Indian Ocean was reached.

John II
(reigned 1481-95)

Off Cape Volta the ships were caught in a terrible storm which lasted nearly two weeks. The terrified sailors were blown round the southern tip of Africa and into the Indian Ocean. They sailed north to the Great Fish River and then turned round for home.

On their way back to Portugal, Dias and his crew saw the Cape and realized their achievement.

A Portuguese ship rounding the Cape of Good Hope.

Dias named it "Cabo Tormentoso", the Cape of Storms. King John renamed it the Cape of Good Hope, for a sea route to the East had been found.

Two spies set out

Pedro da Covilhã was one of the King of Portugal's courtiers and an experienced spy. In May 1487, he and Alfonso de Paiva set out on a secret mission. Covilhã was to find out all he could about the route to India, while Paiva was to seek out Prester John's kingdom in Africa. First they travelled to Rhodes where they disguised themselves as Arab traders and joined a party of merchants travelling to Egypt. They sailed to Cairo where they boarded a boat travelling down the Red Sea to Suakin in the Sudan. Here they parted company.

Paiva set off in search of Prester John, while Covilhã sailed for southwest India. He noted every detail of his voyages, of the geography along the way, and of the fabulous cargoes of cinnamon, cloves, pepper, silks, rugs and precious stones. At Goa, superb Arab horses were sold to the Indian rulers.

A new adventure

From India Covilhã sailed to the Persian Gulf, then on down the east coast of Africa. Returning to Cairo in 1490 he learned that Paiva had died without finding Prester John. Covilhã himself took up the search for the elusive monarch, whose kingdom was by this time thought to be Abyssinia (now Ethiopia). He sent a report of his travels to the King of Portugal, then set off south. First of all he visited the holy city of Mecca (see page 100) dressed as a Muslim pilgrim.

The happy captive

Although Abyssinia was a Christian country, Covilhã was surprised and disappointed to find that it was not the fabulously rich kingdom he expected. (Prester John was never found, but stories of his empire persisted well into the 16th century.)

Perhaps because he had seen too much, Covilhã was forbidden to leave Abyssinia and spent the remaining 30 years of his life there. He was treated well in his new homeland, eventually marrying a rich local woman. From time to time he entertained ambassadors from Europe and he encouraged trade between Abyssinia and Portugal.

The Cape and beyond

- – – – Eannes 1434
- ——— Dias 1487
- ——— Covilhã/de Paiva 1487
- ••••• Covilhã (c.1487-90)
- –••– Covilhã 1493

15th-century compass ▶

This is how 15th-century Europeans imagined Prester John.

Searching for the River Niger and Timbuktu

The Romans were the first Europeans to explore the interior of Africa. After their conquest of Egypt and the north African coast during the 1st century BC, they sent various expeditions over the Atlas Mountains and into the Sahara Desert, usually in pursuit of nomadic tribes who had attacked their soldiers and then disappeared.

Scientific explorers

Europeans set up trading stations along the coastline of Africa from the 15th century, but the traders ventured only a little way inland. During the 18th century, however, a new spirit of scientific enquiry grew up. In 1788 the Association for Promoting the Discovery of the Interior Parts of Africa was founded. It aimed to find and plot the course of the mysterious River Niger and to find the legendary trading city of Timbuktu, famed for its riches and palaces. But the first expeditions were failures, with the explorers dying from terrible diseases and heat.

The adventurous doctor

In 1794 a young Scottish doctor called Mungo Park was chosen to lead an expedition to the source of the River Niger to find out whether it flowed into the sea or into a lake. Park left England by ship in May 1795, and arrived at Pisania in the Gambia two months later. He stayed there for some months studying the local language and eventually set off into the African interior in December.

Mungo Park
(1771-1806)

Park would have carried a sextant similar to this, to calculate distances.

The Niger is sighted

At first all went well and Park was hospitably received. However, things started to go wrong when his guides became frightened and refused to go any further. Some of the local rulers robbed him of all his possessions until he had nothing left except the clothes he wore and his horse. Finally he was captured by horsemen and held prisoner.

Park was attacked and stripped of all his belongings.

Park was kept in terrible conditions in an isolated hut on the edge of the desert for four months. Late one night in June 1796 he managed to escape from his prison. But instead of heading back to the coast and safety he pressed on with his mission, travelling through the thick forests to avoid being seen. A month later he reached Segu and caught his first glimpse of the Niger. He was overjoyed and was able to confirm once and for all that the river flowed eastwards.

Park had managed to save the notes he had made throughout his adventures by carefully hiding them. After his return to Scotland, he used the notes to write a book called *Travels in the Interior Districts of Africa*. It quickly became a best-seller. But the lure of Africa proved too great and Park was eager to return and explore it further.

An illustration from Park's book, showing him knocking at the gates of a village to escape from a lion.

A doomed expedition

In January 1805 Park set sail for Pisania once more, this time to travel the whole length of the Niger. He went with a larger expedition of 30 soldiers and ten other Europeans. The expedition was doomed from the start. Park was impatient to leave, even though it was the rainy season. By the time they reached the Niger the river was swollen and 29 members of the team had died of exhaustion and disease.

Park was determined to carry on, for the river turned south towards the Atlantic. At Sansanding he found two old canoes and joined them together, intending to float down the Niger to the sea. But by now the party was reduced to just nine members. This exhausted group reached the rapids at Boussa, 805km (500 miles) from the mouth of the river. Here they were attacked by warriors of the local king. Park and his men drowned when their boat capsized.

Park and his team being attacked by African warriors.

Inspired by travel stories

At the beginning of the 1820's, the Geographical Society of Paris offered a prize of 10,000 francs to the first Frenchman to reach the city of Timbuktu and return. René Caillié, a young man from a poor family, heard of the competition and was determined to win the prize. He had wanted to become an explorer since reading *Robinson Crusoe* by Daniel Defoe. He began careful preparations for the journey and plotted his route. He worked hard

René Caillié
(1799-1838)

and saved enough money to pay for everything himself, including equipment and helpers. In 1824 Caillié left France and sailed to Senegal on the west coast of Africa and remained there for three years, learning the Arabic language and finding out about the Muslim faith.

In April 1827 Caillié and his team of ten Africans joined a caravan and set off for the Rio Nuñez between Sierra Leone and Senegal. In June they reached Kouroussa on the Niger. They set off on the next leg of the journey, but soon afterwards Caillié fell ill with malaria and scurvy. Five months

Caillié in Arabic dress.

Caillié travelling through the African jungle.

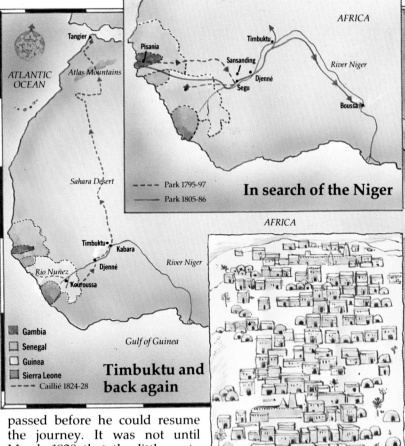

In search of the Niger

Timbuktu and back again

- Gambia
- Senegal
- Guinea
- Sierra Leone
- - - Caillié 1824-28

Caillié's sketch of Timbuktu. The city was a pale shadow of the rich place it had once been.

passed before he could resume the journey. It was not until March 1828 that the little party reached Djenné, having walked nearly the entire distance of 1,610km (1,000 miles). From there they were able to sail down the Niger another 805km (500 miles) to Kabara, the port near Timbuktu.

Excitement and disappointment

They finally reached Timbuktu in April. For Caillié this moment, which he had looked forward to for years, was an anticlimax. The fabled city looked poor, neglected and drab. The trade in gold from Guinea had ceased many years before and the great trade caravans no longer visited it.

However, Caillié was welcomed by the inhabitants and stayed for two weeks. Then he joined a 1,000-strong camel caravan taking slaves and other goods across the Sahara. This return journey was hard and long, and he experienced such thirst that he could think only of water. When he reached Tangier, the officials there could not believe someone of his humble background could have travelled to Timbuktu and back. It was not until he was back in France that a panel of judges awarded him the prize.

The source of the Nile

The valley of the River Nile in Egypt is one of the most fertile areas in the world. Crops have been grown there since ancient times and the river has been a source of life to millions of people, many of whom have worshipped it as a god. But the origin of its waters remained a mystery for thousands of years. In the 5th century BC the Greek historian Herodotus wrote: "Of the sources of the Nile no-one can give any account." He believed that the river began at a fountain at the foot of some high mountains.

Over the centuries many expeditions tried to follow the river from Egypt to its source. One of the first of these was led by two Roman soldiers sent out by the Emperor Nero. But they had to abandon their journey when they reached a huge, impenetrable swamp known today as the Sudd.

Later expeditions were defeated by the great distance, perilous swamps and stifling heat. In addition many explorers caught dreadful fevers.

In about AD150 a Greek geographer called Ptolemy drew a map of the world from various pieces of information. On it he showed two great lakes in Africa near a range of snow-capped mountains he called the Mountains of the Moon. He claimed that these lakes were the source of the Nile.

The Nile

Ptolemy's map

Some of the equipment carried by Speke and Burton.

The rivals

By the middle of the 19th century no more was known about the source than in Ptolemy's days. In the 1840s German missionaries reported seeing two mountains, their tops covered with snow.

Richard Burton (1821-90)

John Speke (1827-64)

These were Mount Kilimanjaro and Mount Kenya. They also heard of the existence of two great lakes lying further inland. They were sure that these were the mountains and lakes on Ptolemy's map.

Many explorers and geographers wanted to be first to solve the mystery. In 1856 the Royal Geographical Society of London appointed Richard Burton as leader of a new expedition, with John Speke as his deputy. They had travelled together before but they made an unusual pair. Burton was a flamboyant and brilliant scholar who spoke 29 languages and had written numerous books; Speke was a quiet and careful planner. But both men were ruthless and determined.

A view of the port at Zanzibar.

They sailed to Zanzibar, an important slave market off the east coast of Africa where they recruited the rest of their team. In June 1857 the expedition – consisting of about 130 porters, 30 donkeys and enough provisions to last two years – set off for the Sea of Ujiji (now called Lake Tanganyika). They believed this was one of Ptolemy's lakes and that it would prove to be the source of the Nile.

But after only two weeks both Burton and Speke were suffering from malaria. It took the expedition five months to make its way to Tabora, a large slave market lying between Zanzibar and the Sea of Ujiji. The two men were exhausted and had to rest for a month. Shortly after setting off again, however, they both became extremely ill. Burton's legs became paralyzed and Speke went deaf and blind. It was some time before they both recovered.

The expedition sets out for the Sea of Ujiji in 1857.

Ugandan tribespeople entertain Speke and Grant.

Discovery and disappointment

Eventually, on 13 February 1858, they reached the Sea of Ujiji and spent three and a half months

Part of the team exploring the Sea of Ujiji.

exploring the area. But their hopes were dashed when they questioned some local people and discovered that although there was a great river at the northern end, it flowed into the lake, not out of it. This indicated that it came from elsewhere and was not the Nile.

Although the discovery of the lake was important, Burton and Speke were very disappointed that they had not found the source of the Nile and they returned to Tabora. Burton was pleased to be among the Arab slave dealers again as he had travelled in Arabia (see page 133) and spoke Arabic. But Speke knew little Arabic and felt excluded. As he was impatient to leave, the two men parted. Burton stayed to rest while Speke left to try and locate another great lake to the north, Lake N'yanza, which he had heard about but which no European had yet seen.

The start of a feud

After an easy journey of just 16 days, Speke reached Mwanza on the southern shores of the lake. The pale blue waters stretched out endlessly before him. He was certain that he had at last found the

Speke on the shores of Lake N'yanza (Lake Victoria).

source of the Nile. But he did not explore it thoroughly enough to prove his theory. He renamed his discovery Lake Victoria after Britain's queen, then hurried back to Burton to tell him the news. Burton is believed to have been furious. He may have been jealous of Speke's discovery, or angry that his partner had relied on guesswork and not collected enough evidence to back up his claim.

The two men decided to return to England and travelled as far as Zanzibar. Burton became too sick to continue. He and Speke parted, agreeing not to break the news of their discoveries until both were back home. Speke, however, rushed back, and by the time Burton returned he had already reported the expedition's findings and taken most of the credit for them. A bitter feud then broke out between the two men when Speke, rather than Burton, was appointed to lead a new expedition to Lake Victoria.

The second expedition

Speke and his second-in-command, James Grant, left for Africa in the spring of 1860. It was not until the end of 1861 that they reached the unknown territory of Karagwe at the southern end of Lake Victoria. In January 1862 they became the first Europeans to enter Uganda,

James Grant (1827-92)

where they met the young King Mutesa. They remained there until July, when they moved on. Grant soon fell seriously ill but, rather than wait for him to recover, Speke travelled on alone. On 21 July 1862 he arrived at Urondogani, where he stood alone on the banks of a river flowing north out of Lake Victoria. He was now certain that he was looking at the beginnings of the Nile and that Lake Victoria was the source. But once again he failed to explore thoroughly enough to prove beyond doubt that the river became the Nile.

A mysterious death

Speke and Grant returned triumphant to England, but there was still uncertainty about Speke's findings. To settle the dispute, a final public discussion with Burton was arranged, to take place before a panel of scholars. But in September 1864, the day before the meeting was due to take place, Speke died in a shooting accident. There were rumours of suicide - perhaps he did not dare to face the brilliant Burton. It was many years before Lake Victoria was finally proved to be the main source of the Nile by the explorer and journalist H.M. Stanley (see page 109).

Memorial to Speke in Kensington Gardens, London.

IN MEMORY OF
SPEKE
VICTORIA NYANZA
AND THE NILE
1864

107

Exploring the heart of Africa

David Livingstone came from a very poor Scottish family, and at the age of ten went to work in a cotton mill. However he was determined to study, and while he was working in the mill he also taught himself Greek, Latin and mathematics. This enabled him to go to Glasgow University. At the age of 25 he qualified as a doctor and in 1840 he was ordained a Christian missionary and sent to Cape Town in South Africa to do religious and social work.

In 1843 Livingstone founded his own mission at Kolobeng, south of the Kalahari Desert. Apart from his religious work, he was also fired by the idea of the eradication of slavery. Throughout his travels in Africa he was to be constantly reminded of this cruel trade in human life. He set about opening up the unknown central regions of Africa, so other Christian missionaries and Europeans could follow. He believed that this would lead to the collapse of the slave trade.

A line of Africans being marched away to be sold into slavery.

David Livingstone (1813-73)

◀ The Victoria Falls

Livingstone's travels

His first success in exploration, after two earlier failures, was to cross the wilderness of the Kalahari Desert in 1851 and reach Lake Ngami on the northern edge of the desert. His wife Mary and their children also accompanied him, as well as his great friend Cotton Oswell. They all nearly died when their guide lost his way and they ran out of food and water. In 1852 Livingstone's family returned to England while he stayed behind to devote his energies to African exploration.

Over the years 1852-56 Livingstone became the first European to walk right across Africa. He was also the first European to see the great waterfalls known locally as "the smoke that thunders", which he renamed the Victoria Falls. The news of these great exploits quickly reached Britain and when he returned to England he was welcomed as a national hero and introduced to Queen Victoria.

In 1858 he organized an expedition to the Zambezi River, hoping that the presence of Europeans there would help to end the slave trade.

The *Ma-Robert* on the Zambezi.

But when his paddle steamer (the *Ma-Robert*) could not cross the rapids on the river, Livingstone abandoned the expedition and returned to England. He was back in Africa again in April 1866 and disappeared for three years. This time he was trying to find the source of the Nile (see page 106). Heading towards Lake Nyasa (Lake Malawi), he entered the heart of slaving country. He set up a base at Ujiji on the shores of Lake Tanganyika but the supplies he was expecting to find had been stolen and there was little to eat.

H.M. Stanley

John Rowlands was the real name of H.M. Stanley. He was born in Wales in 1841 and spent most of his unhappy childhood in an orphanage. As soon as he could he ran away and worked as a cabin boy on a ship bound for North America. There, at the age of 19, he was adopted by a cotton merchant from New Orleans. In gratitude he became an American citizen and took the name of his benefactor, Henry Morton Stanley.

Henry Stanley (1841-1904)

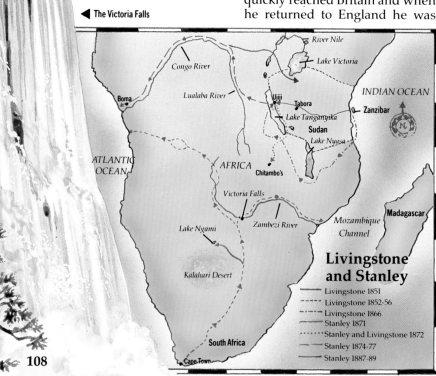

Livingstone and Stanley

- River Nile
- Congo River
- Lake Victoria
- Lualaba River
- INDIAN OCEAN
- Boma
- Ujiji
- Tabora
- Zanzibar
- Lake Tanganyika
- Sudan
- Lake Nyasa
- AFRICA
- Chitambo's
- ATLANTIC OCEAN
- Victoria Falls
- Lake Ngami
- Zambezi River
- Mozambique Channel
- Madagascar
- Kalahari Desert
- South Africa
- Cape Town

Livingstone and Stanley
— Livingstone 1851
--- Livingstone 1852-56
— Livingstone 1866
— Stanley 1871
···· Stanley and Livingstone 1872
— Stanley 1874-77
— Stanley 1887-89

Stanley's boat, the *Lady Alice*, could be taken apart and carried overland.

Travelling down the Lualaba River in the *Lady Alice*.

AFRICA

A new life in America

The young Stanley led an adventurous life in his adopted country. During the American Civil War of 1861-65, he fought first on one side and then the other. He later spent some time in the navy. Eventually he drifted into journalism and became a foreign correspondent for the *New York Herald*.

The search for Livingstone

In 1869 the owner of the newspaper commissioned Stanley to find out the fate of Livingstone, who had not been heard of since travelling into the interior of Africa three years earlier. At the beginning of 1871 Stanley arrived in Zanzibar. He immediately set about organizing one of the most expensive expeditions ever mounted with 192 of the best porters and the finest supplies.

During the exhausting journey west, Stanley fell ill with malaria, his two European assistants died and

Stanley's hat and boots

the team was caught up in bloody battles between slave traders and African villagers. On 10 November 1871 they entered Ujiji. Stanley was led through the village by an excited crowd and, to his surprise and relief, he was introduced to the sick and frail Livingstone. Food and medicine soon restored Livingstone's strength and he and Stanley spent three weeks together exploring the northern end of Lake Tanganyika. At Tabora they parted company and Stanley returned to Zanzibar.

Stanley's meeting with Livingstone at Ujiji.

Livingstone's final journey

Before Stanley left Zanzibar for England, he sent new supplies to Livingstone. On 25 August 1872, Livingstone set out on his final journey, this time round the southern shores of Lake Tanganyika. Once more he caught a terrible fever, but at last he managed to reach a village in Ulala called Chitambo's. There he grew weaker and weaker and died eight months later. His heart was cut out by his faithful

Livingstone is carried dying into Chitambo's.

companions Chuma and Susi and buried under a tree. They then embalmed his body and carried it to Zanzibar, an eight-month journey of 1,609km (1,000 miles). From there it was shipped back to London and buried in Westminster Abbey. Livingstone is the only explorer to have received this honour.

Stanley returns to Africa

Inspired by his travels with Livingstone, Stanley returned to Africa in 1874, leading a huge expedition to map Lake Victoria and Lake Tanganyika. While out in their boats they were attacked by tribesmen and hippopotamuses and drenched by storms. However, the journey did establish that Lake Victoria had only one major inlet and one major outlet – the Nile. Speke's guess (see page 107) had been proved correct.

In October 1876 the group left Lake Tanganyika on its most exciting journey. Stanley intended to travel down the Lualaba River, following it wherever it went. All the way they were attacked by warriors. They entered dark, forbidding rainforests, where cannibals lived among the damp, dripping trees. At one point they walked along a road flanked by 186 human skulls.

The Lualaba flows into the Congo River and they sailed on down it until they finally arrived at Boma on the Atlantic coast. The last of Africa's great rivers had been conquered. Of the original 356 members of the expedition only 114 remained. The rest had either died or deserted and all three of Stanley's English assistants had died along the way.

The last exploration

In 1887 Stanley travelled once more to Africa on his final journey through the continent. He went to southern Sudan to rescue a German explorer called Emin Pasha who had become cut off from the outside world. The team of 700 men had to hack through some of the world's densest jungle. This was the last major exploration in Africa. It was no longer the mysterious continent it had once been and already the European powers were beginning to divide it up into colonies.

Stanley attacked by tribesmen.

109

East goes west

The ancient civilization of China evolved in isolation from those in the West, protected behind the barrier of deserts and mountains of central Asia. It was not until the 2nd century BC that people from China ventured to make their first contacts with the kingdoms and empires of the West.

Chang Ch'ien

During the 1st century BC, China's long borders were under attack from the Huns, fierce nomadic tribesmen from central Asia. The Emperor Wu Ti of China hoped to make an alliance with the Yuechi, a tribe who had been forced westwards by the Huns, against this threat. For this mission he chose an official called Chang Ch'ien.

Chang Ch'ien set off in 138BC on what turned out to be a very long journey. Almost immediately he was captured by the Huns and held prisoner. After ten years he eventually managed to escape and struggled to Heyuchi, the Yuechi capital lying close to the Khyber Pass .

But the Yuechi were not interested and Chang Ch'ien failed to win their support, so he set off on his return journey to China. This time he chose a roundabout route through Tibet to try to

A Chinese official and his attendants.

avoid the Huns. However, he fell into their hands once more. But he managed to escape and arrived back at Ch'ang-an, then the capital of China, after 12 years away and with just two of his original party of 100 men.

The Silk Road

Although Chang Ch'ien had failed in his mission, he learned a lot about the people and places he had seen along the way. This knowledge was used to open up the Silk Road, a trade route between China and the West. From about 105BC, long caravans of camels set out from China laden with bales of silk, spices, rare woods and resins, tortoiseshell, precious stones and pearls. They travelled through Asia to Antioch and then by ship to Rome.

Key dates in Asian exploration

- **c.300BC** Great Wall of China started. Built to keep out invading tribes.
- **221BC** Emperor Shih Huang-ti unites China.
- **206BC-AD220** Rule of Han dynasty in China.
- **202BC** Chinese capital established at Ch'ang-an.
- **140-86BC** Reign of Emperor Wu Ti.
- **138BC** Chang Ch'ien leaves on journey to Yuechi.
- **126BC** Chang Ch'ien returns to China.
- **c.105BC** Opening of Silk Road.
- **AD220** End of Han dynasty. China breaks into three states.
- **245** Chinese ambassadors travel to Funan (Cambodia).
- **304** Hsiung-nu (Huns) invade China.
- **629** Hsuan-tsang leaves China for India.
- **645** Hsuan-tsang returns to China.
- **1162** Birth of Temujin (Genghis Khan), later ruler of Mongols.
- **1215** Genghis Khan captures Chung-tu (Beijing), capital of Chinese Chin empire, and establishes Mongol rule.
- **1227** Death of Genghis Khan.
- **1240** Mongols capture Kiev, Russia.
- **1246** Giovanni da Pian del Carpini reaches Mongol capital at Karakorum.
- **1253** William of Rubrouck sent to Karakorum.
- **1260** Kublai Khan proclaimed Great Khan.
- **1265** Niccolo and Maffeo Polo first reach new Mongol capital at Khanbalik (Beijing).
- **1269** Niccolo and Maffeo return to Venice.
- **1271** Niccolo, Maffeo and Marco Polo leave Venice for China.
- **1292** Polos leave China for home.
- **1295** Polos arrive back in Venice.
- **1368** Mongols driven out of China.
- **1405** Cheng Ho makes first of sea journeys in Indian Ocean.
- **1420** Chinese round Cape of Good Hope.
- **1497** Vasco da Gama sets sail from Portugal to India.
- **1498** Da Gama reaches Calicut, India.
- **1499** Da Gama returns to Portugal.
- **1597** Portuguese establish trading station at Macao, China.

Out of China

Antioch · Syria · Persian Gulf · Arabia · Red Sea · Arabian Sea · Hindu Kush · Khyber Pass · Kashmir · River Indus · Tibet · River Ganges · Allahabad · Assam · India · Gobi Desert · Beijing · Luoyang · Ch'ang-an · China · Bay of Bengal · Siam · Indochina · Maldives

- - - Chang Ch'ien
—— Hsuan-tsang
—— Silk Road

A caravan of camels on the Silk Road passes a statue of the Buddha at Luoyang, China.

Hsuan-tsang

One of the most adventurous travellers was a Buddhist monk called Hsuan-tsang. In AD629, against the emperor's strict instructions not to travel, he set out from China with the aim of learning more about his religion. His fortunes were to fluctuate from being honoured by kings to encounters with murderous brigands. His route to India, the birthplace of Buddhism, took him west through the Gobi Desert, along perilous roads and through dark gorges to Bactria, over the Hindu Kush and east into Kashmir. He remained studying for two years, visiting the libraries of monasteries in the Ganges valley.

Hsuan-tsang (c.602-664)

He visited Allahabad where he was captured by pirates and nearly sacrificed. In Assam he joined the procession of King Harsha, in the company of 20,000 elephants and 30,000 boats. While crossing the River Indus he lost many of his rare manuscripts and his entire collection of flower seeds. He set off north across the mountains, this time accompanied by an elephant with a huge appetite which ate 40 bundles of hay and hundreds of buns every day.

Despite all the perils, Hsuan-tsang finally arrived back in China after an absence of 16 years. He entered Ch'ang-an with a chariot drawn by 20 horses piled with 700 religious books, and statues and relics of the Buddha. His expedition was considered so important that, far from being reprimanded for disobeying the emperor's orders years before, he was showered with honours.

Cheng Ho

During the years following Hsuan-tsang's adventures, the Chinese established trade contacts with India. By the 8th century they had reached the Arabian peninsula and the east coast of Africa. Chinese coins and porcelain were exchanged for African gold, ivory, rhinoceros horns and precious woods and spices. In 1415 the Chinese emperor was delighted when ambassadors from Malindi presented him with a giraffe.

In 1368 the Mongols, who had ruled China for 150 years, were driven out. At the beginning of the 15th century the new Emperor Cheng Tsu planned a huge programme of exploration abroad. The man put in charge was a high-ranking courtier called Cheng Ho. He was in command of more than 27,000 men and a fleet of 317 ships.

Between 1405 and 1433, Cheng Ho made seven great voyages visiting, among other places, Indochina, Java, Sumatra, Siam (now Thailand), the Maldive Islands, Borneo, the Persian Gulf, Arabia and the east coast of Africa. Some of the ships were sent on surveying expeditions into the Pacific Ocean where they may even have reached the northern coast of Australia. Another group may also have rounded the Cape of Good Hope, for a Chinese map of about 1420 clearly shows part of Africa's west coast. This was 60 years before Bartolemeu Dias became the first European to round the Cape (see page 103).

Two years after Cheng Ho returned from his final expedition the last emperor of the Ming dynasty died. With him died the Chinese interest in exploration and a new foreign policy was adopted. They turned their backs on the outside world and stopped all exploration of the West.

15th-century Chinese map showing the Cape of Good Hope at the top.

The Chinese junk

15th-century Chinese ships, called junks, were huge compared with European ones of the same period. Some of Cheng Ho's ships weighed more than ten times as much as Vasco da Gama's (see page 114).

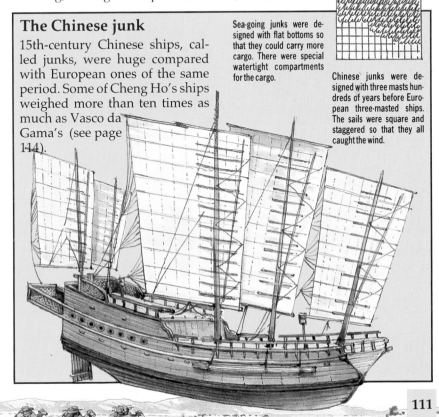

Sea-going junks were designed with flat bottoms so that they could carry more cargo. There were special watertight compartments for the cargo.

Chinese junks were designed with three masts hundreds of years before European three-masted ships. The sails were square and staggered so that they all caught the wind.

Marco Polo

In the 13th century, a warrior tribe from northeast Asia called the Mongols, led by Genghis Khan, conquered huge areas of land in China and the Middle East. They reached as far west as Poland and Hungary.

The Mongols were nomads (wandering people). They carried tents with them from place to place.

Hole for chimney

Felt covering

Wooden frame

At first, some European countries feared the Mongols would invade them too, leaving a trail of death and destruction. Once it became clear that this was not going to happen, however, Europe began to consider the Mongols as possible allies against their long-standing enemies, the Turks.

Ambassador priests

Several European countries sent ambassadors to the Mongol capital, Karakorum. In 1245 Pope Innocent IV sent a priest, Giovanni da Pian del Carpini, to meet the Great Khan (the Mongol leader). Later a monk, William of Rubrouck, made the same journey on behalf of the king of France. But both visits were diplomatic failures.

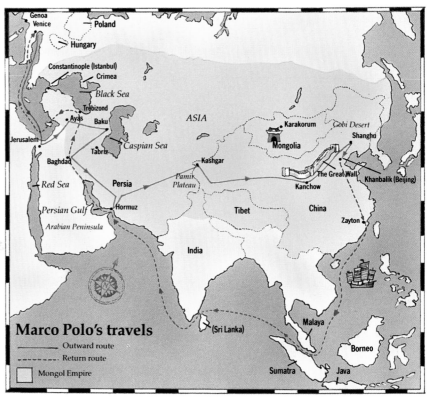

Marco Polo's travels

— Outward route
- - - Return route
☐ Mongol Empire

William of Rubrouck meeting the Great Khan

The triumph of trade

Carpini's route was later used by merchants. In the early 1260s the Venetian brothers Maffeo and Niccolo Polo, returning from a trade mission in the Crimea, found their way blocked by the Mongols. They made a lengthy detour, and on the way met a Mongol ambassador who invited them to China. They succeeded where the priests had not, and returned to Europe with a friendly letter for the Pope from Kublai Khan, the Mongol ruler in China.

Marco Polo's expedition

In 1271 the brothers set off for China again. This time they took with them Niccolo's son Marco, who was 15 years old. On the way they saw many amazing sights, such as a geyser pumping out hot oil, and large sheep with curly horns, each about 1.5m (4ft) in length. Marco noted many things, such as crafts and farming of the different areas, the people, and their religion and customs.

At Kublai Khan's court

Eventually, after three and a half years' travelling, the Polos reached Kublai Khan's court in Khanbalik (modern Beijing). They were again made welcome and Kublai Khan was particularly impressed by young Marco – so much so that he employed him as a representative of the imperial court. Marco went on many diplomatic missions, to such places as Malaya, Sumatra, Tibet and Sri Lanka, on behalf of Kublai Khan. He even recorded a journey to Burma and India.

Kublai Khan, the Mongol ruler of China, wearing Chinese imperial robes.

Chinese marvels

While working for the Khan, Marco came across marvels both natural and man-made. On the right are some of the commodities which attracted world-wide trade to the East. Below are some of the inventions and discoveries which enriched Chinese culture and allowed it to flourish, even in the grip of Mongol occupation. It was to be many centuries before some of these reached the West.

Plants and animals

Ginger, a hot-tasting spice, was highly prized in the 13th century.

Saffron is used to give colour and flavour to food and as a natural dye.

Silkworms produce long threads of silk which can be woven into very valuable fabrics.

Inventions and discoveries

Paper money was used in China centuries before it was used in Europe.

The Chinese printed books with stamps like this long before the process was developed in Europe.

The "crumbly earth" that Marco described was clay from which the Chinese made beautiful ceramic vessels.

Marco noted the Chinese burning a black stone. This must have been coal.

The Chinese invented gunpowder. This was used in war, but also for spectacular firework displays.

A final diplomatic mission

The Polos stayed in the service of Kublai Khan for 17 years. In 1292 they decided it was time to leave, but the Khan was reluctant to lose his loyal servants. A last diplomatic mission gave them an excuse: they were to return via Persia (now Iran), so that they could escort a Mongol princess to her husband-to-be, the Il-Khan Arghun. By the time they arrived, however, the Il-Khan had died. The Princess married his son instead.

The Polos sailed to Hormuz in Chinese boats called junks. From there they went by land to Trebizond and sailed back to Venice via

A Chinese town in the time of Marco Polo.

Constantinople. In all the journey took three years, and when they finally arrived back in Venice they had been away for 24 years. Marco was 39 when he returned. He married and became a merchant like his father and uncle.

Home to Venice

Settling in Venice again did not diminish Marco Polo's spirit of adventure. When Venice was at war with Genoa, he was taken prisoner while fighting for his city.

While in prison, Marco told his life story to his cell-mate, a writer called Rustichello. Rustichello later produced a book, *The Travels of Marco Polo*, which made his story famous all over the world.

Many of Marco's stories

seemed so far-fetched that people thought he had made them up. Some of his claims have never been verified. Although many merchants later followed the Polos' routes, they left no accounts of their travels to back up his claims. Marco's book inspired many later explorers, including Christopher Columbus (see page 118).

Marco Polo and Rustichello

The way east is closed

In 1368 the Chinese rebelled against the Mongols. They installed their own emperors who forbade visitors from Europe. Further west, some Mongols became Muslims and did not welcome Christians, so the land-route east from Europe was blocked again.

Vasco da Gama and the route to India

Having reached the Cape of Good Hope (see page 103), the Portuguese wanted to find a route around Africa to India. King Manuel I of Portugal chose a courtier called Vasco da Gama to lead an expedition to see if this route actually existed. Da Gama set sail in July 1497 with four ships and 170 men. Some of the men were convicts, recruited to do the most dangerous tasks. The king ordered da Gama to investigate any opportunities for trade along the way.

Vasco da Gama
(1460-1524)

Into the unknown

The man who had first rounded the Cape of Good Hope, Bartolemeu Dias, accompanied the new expedition in his own ship as far as the Cape Verde Islands. From here, da Gama and his fleet took four months to reach the Cape. They then sailed up the eastern coast of Africa. From time to time they landed to take food and water on board, to make repairs, and to trade.

Scurvy strikes

Many of the crew fell ill with scurvy, a disease caused by a deficiency of vitamin C. Victims grew weak, developing fever and blisters, and rarely survived the illness. So many of his men died that da Gama had to burn one of his ships because there were not enough sailors left to form a crew to operate it.

Rival traders

Further up the coast, da Gama reached the ports of Kilwa and Mombasa. But trade in this area was controlled by Arab merchants. They were hostile to da Gama, fearing he would disrupt their trade agreements with the Africans.

Da Gama's ship being attacked.

Some African rulers were unimpressed with da Gama's goods and refused to trade. Others were more aggressive. In Mombasa armed men tried to capture the Portuguese, who only just managed to escape.

Monsoon winds to Calicut

In nearby Malindi, the locals were more sympathetic. Da Gama hired an experienced guide to steer his ships cross the Indian Ocean. Driven by a seasonal wind called the monsoon, they made the crossing in just 23 days. They reached Calicut in India after a total of ten months at sea.

A long way home

Da Gama was welcomed by the Indian princes, but his goods did not compare with their magnificent wealth. He could only buy small amounts of spices. Again, Arab merchants in the area were hostile. After only three months da Gama and his men left India for Portugal. The voyage was three months longer than the outward journey.

Da Gama returns

When he reached home, da Gama received a hero's welcome. He had only acquired a few samples of goods, but these proved to the king that there were good trading opportunities in India. Da Gama's voyage opened up the route for many later traders from Portugal.

The Portuguese only had beads, cheap cloth and food to trade.

Da Gama's route to India

From India came pearls, rubies and spices.

East Africa was a source of grain, ivory and gold.

The search for the Northeast Passage

To compete with Portugal for eastern trade, northern European countries needed another sea route to the East. There were many attempts to find a Northeast Passage round northern Asia into the Pacific Ocean, and on to China and India.

Willem Barents

Barents, a Dutchman, made several voyages to find a way through to the East. In 1594 he sailed round the tip of Norway

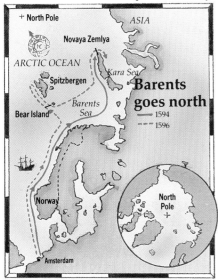

and reached the huge island of Novaya Zemlya. Here pack ice blocked his route and he had to turn back.

Trapped by ice

Barents sailed again in 1596. After reaching Spitzbergen he headed south and east to Novaya Zemlya once more. This time he sailed round its northernmost tip, but his ship became stuck in the ice. It was the beginning of the Arctic winter. Barents and his crew had no option but to build themselves a hut for shelter, and wait for warmer weather in the spring. Their ship was slowly crushed by the advancing ice, the timbers cracking.

A winter refuge

The hut was built from pieces of the wrecked ship. In 1871 a Norwegian fisherman found it, perfectly preserved by the ice.

Barents and his crew salvaged items which they could adapt for use on land. The crow's nest from the ship was put on top of the hut and used as a lookout tower.

The fisherman found books (including Barents' diary), a clock and cooking utensils.

A bath was adapted from a wooden barrel.

The ship's bunks were taken ashore and used as beds.

The front and side of the hut have been cut away in this picture to show the interior.

Surviving an Arctic winter

Barents and his men managed to survive the winter in their makeshift house. They killed bears and foxes for food, and burned polar bear fat and wood for light and heat. When the weather allowed, they played golf on the ice for exercise.

They suffered dreadfully from cold, hunger and scurvy. Even inside the hut the discomfort was hard to endure. The sheets froze on their beds and the smoke from the fire made it difficult to breathe.

When the Arctic spring came, and the ice began to melt, the expedition headed for home in the ship's two open boats. But for Barents, who was weakened by the rigours of the winter, the return journey proved too much. He had also fallen ill with scurvy and was so sickly he was unable to keep command of the boats. He grew weaker and weaker and died just five days after setting out for home, on Bear Island in the sea that is now named after him.

Polar bears often attacked the shelter.

Was there a way through?

Barents made great advances in Arctic exploration, but the Northeast Passage remained a mystery for centuries. Its existence was not proved until 1741, when a Dane, Vitus Bering, sailed through the narrow straits between Alaska and Asia which are now named after him. However the passage was far too dangerous and remote to be a good trade route.

The Vikings reach America

The Vikings were seafarers and warriors who had lived in Norway, Sweden and Denmark since ancient times. They began sailing west in the 9th century, searching for new territory. By about 860 some of them had reached Iceland and settled there. During their frequent journeys west, they became the first Europeans to discover America.

The Vikings were excellent metalworkers and used elaborately decorated swords like these.

Around 900, a ship commanded by a man called Gunnbjorn was sailing to Iceland from Norway. His ship was blown off course, and he saw a new land which he described to the settlers when he finally got to Iceland. His story inspired other Vikings to go in search of the new country.

Eric the Red

Eric the Red was a Norwegian who was banished from his country for three years for murder. He decided to use his period of exile to search for new lands to colonize, and set his sights in particular on the place that Gunnbjorn had spotted. After a hazardous voyage he arrived there but found that it had a hostile climate and landscape.

Eric the Red wanted other Vikings to follow him there. He called the new country Greenland – not a very appropriate name for such unforgiving territory. By 986 he had convinced a group of colonists to settle there.

After a gruelling journey the expedition arrived in Greenland. It was summer, and conditions were favourable enough to establish farms. Settlements soon grew up, and the colonists were able to begin trading with Scandinavia.

Bjarni Herjolfsson

Soon another Norwegian, called Bjarni Herjolfsson, set out for Greenland, but went astray in fog and gales. He realized he had lost his way when land finally loomed out of the fog at him. It was not the harsh territory he had been told to expect when he reached Greenland. Instead it proved to be hilly and wooded.

In fact, the storms had blown Herjolfsson's ship far to the southwest of Greenland. We now know that the shoreline he saw was the northeastern coast of America. Instead of landing there, however, he turned back. When he finally reached Greenland, he reported his findings to the Viking colonists there.

A Viking warrior

The Vikings' exploits were later recorded in long tales called sagas. This is a page from the saga about Eric the Red's discovery of Greenland.

Key dates in American exploration

- **c.860** Vikings settle in Iceland.
- **c.986** Viking colony established in Greenland under Eric the Red.
- **c.1000** Leif Ericsson lands on the east coast of North America.
- **1002** Thorwald, brother of Leif, establishes colony on the east coast.
- **1492** Christopher Columbus leaves Spain for the East. He reaches and explores the Indies.
- **1519** Hernándo Cortés sails from Cuba to Mexico.
- **1521** Siege of Tenochtitlán. Collapse of Aztec empire.
- **1534** Jacques Cartier leaves France for North America.
- **1535** Cartier founds Montreal.
- **1576** Martin Frobisher leaves England on the first of three voyages to find the Northwest Passage.
- **1585-87** John Davis makes three voyages to find the Northwest Passage.
- **1608** Samuel de Champlain founds Quebec.
- **1609-10** Henry Hudson makes two journeys in search of the Northwest Passage.
- **1678-82** Robert de La Salle travels across North America.
- **1799** Alexander von Humboldt and Aimé Bonpland leave Europe for South America.
- **1804** Meriwether Lewis and William Clark lead expedition across the United States of America.
- **1831** Charles Darwin leaves for South America on the *Beagle*.
- **1925** Percy Fawcett sets off across Brazil.

A Viking ship

Rudder

Tiller

Seamen's chests

Mast →

Supports for spars

Jug for water or wine

← Square sail

Rigging

Spar

Barrel

This type of ship, called a *knorr*, was used by the Vikings for trading expeditions. It had plenty of storage space, but was not built for comfort.

Each plank of the hull overlapped the next. Any gaps were plugged with rope to keep water out.

Oar hole

Oar

Leif Ericsson

The first European actually to set foot on American soil was Eric the Red's son, Leif Ericsson. Around the year 1000 he and his men left Greenland and sailed southwest. They landed at three places on the eastern coast of America. Leif gave these names: Markland ("forest land"; now the region of Labrador); Heluland ("slab-land", after the rocky landscape; now Baffin Island); and Vinland ("vine-land"; experts are unsure, but Vinland was probably where either New England or Newfoundland is now).

According to the saga of his voyage, Ericsson found wild grapes on the American coast, and the biggest fish he had ever seen.

Defeated by the Skraelings

Ericsson's men spent the winter in Vinland, then returned to Greenland with the news of their discovery. Although Leif himself never returned to the new lands, his brother Thorwald set out in 1002 to set up a colony there. He and his men found Vinland, but they were not prepared for the hostility of the native American Indians (known by the

Vikings as Skraelings). Thorwald was killed in a fight, and his companions returned to Greenland discouraged.

Eric the Red's descendants made two more attempts to colonize Vinland. The first expedition included his daughter-in-law Gudrid and her second husband. They settled there and started a family, and succeeded in trading successfully with the Skraelings. But later relations between settlers and natives deteriorated. The Vikings had to give up their home and return to Greenland. They finally settled in Iceland.

This is what a Skraeling warrior might have looked like.

A second expedition was led by Eric the Red's daughter Freydis, but she too failed to establish good relations with the Indians. She also caused chaos among her own people, and murdered several of her fellow colonists.

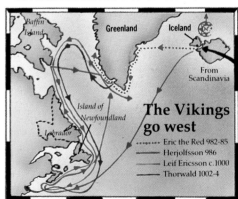

The Vikings go west

······· Eric the Red 982-85
——— Herjolfsson 986
——— Leif Ericsson c.1000
——— Thorwald 1002-4

Baffin Island

Greenland

Iceland

From Scandinavia

Island of Newfoundland

Labrador

The evidence

The theory that the Vikings had reached America was quite common for many years, but until the mid-1960s there was no reliable evidence. Doubts also arose when a map of the northeast coast, said to date from Viking times, turned out to be a fake. But in 1968 the remains of a Viking settlement were discovered in Newfoundland, proving that the Vikings had managed to reach America.

Fragments of Viking woodwork found at Newfoundland.

117

Christopher Columbus

Christopher Columbus is probably the most famous explorer of all. However his greatest discovery, the continent of America, was made by mistake.

Columbus (c.1451-1506) was given his own coat of arms in 1493, in honour of his discoveries.

Born in 1451 in Genoa, Italy, Columbus first went to sea as a young boy. He settled in Lisbon in 1479 and married the daughter of a Portuguese nobleman. From Lisbon he made various sea voyages, acquiring excellent skills as a navigator.

"Gold, God and Cathay"

Columbus's ambition was to sail to the Far East. His reasons are often summed up in the phrase "Gold, God and Cathay". The gold he had in mind was the fortune to be made bringing spices and silk home from China and Japan.

"God" refers to Columbus's wish to spread Christianity to non-Christian countries and to claim new lands in the name of God. This was a common motive among Europeans at that time. It was considered a worthy aim in itself, but

This Spanish gold cross symbolizes Columbus's motives for sailing to the Far East: spreading Christianity and making money.

Columbus hoped to find precious spices like cinnamon (left), nutmeg and peppercorns (below).

many explorers also saw another benefit. They thought that foreign trade would be easier with Christian countries.

"Cathay" was an ancient name for China. Columbus was obsessed with the Far East, and wanted to lead an expedition there.

Testing a theory

In the 15th century most people believed that the Earth was flat. Columbus, however, thought it was round. He hoped to prove this by sailing west to get to the Far East (see globe opposite), instead of taking the usual route from Europe, east round Africa.

Columbus took years to find money for his scheme, as few people believed it would work. Eventually, in 1492, Queen Isabella and King Ferdinand of Spain gave him the money he needed.

The voyage begins

Columbus left Spain on 3 August 1492 with three ships (see box). On 6 September they sailed from the Canary Islands out into open seas. At that time it was unusual to travel out of sight of the coast, and as days went by without a glimpse of land the crewmen became anxious. By the time they reached the strange, weed-infested Sargasso Sea, many of the men were desperate to turn back.

Many of Columbus's crew believed they were sailing into seas that were full of huge monsters.

Columbus persuaded them to go on by promising to give up if they did not sight land within a few days. But in his diary he recorded his intention to continue regardless of his men's desires.

Columbus's ships

These are the three ships that Spain provided for Columbus's voyage.

The Santa Maria

The *Santa Maria* was the fleet's largest ship, captained by Columbus himself.

The *Niña*

The *Niña* was smaller than the *Santa Maria*. The captain was Martín Alonzo Pinzón.

The *Pinta*

The *Pinta* was similar to the *Niña*. Pinzón's brother, Vicente Yanez Pinzón, was its captain.

Between them the ships carried 104 men and vast quantities of supplies, including live pigs and chickens, salted meat, flour, rice, wine and water. There was also equipment for repairing the ships.

Land ahoy!

On 12 October, the lookout on the *Pinta* saw land. It was what is now called Watling Island in the Bahamas, off the coast of America. Columbus, however, was convinced he had reached Cathay. As he had wildly under-estimated how long it would take him to reach the Far East, he was not at all surprised to find land when he did. He would not accept his mistake as long as he lived, and never realized the significance of his discovery.

Columbus's route would have worked if America had not been in his path.

------- Intended route

------- Actual route

Columbus named the island San Salvador. The inhabitants were friendly, and eager to trade. Columbus found little evidence of the riches of the East, but he was still certain that he was near his goal. Guided by the local people, he led the fleet onward in search of Cathay and its treasures.

He visited Cuba, then an island which he named La Española (now Hispaniola). He was then impatient to return to Spain to report his findings.

This woodcut, from the 1493 edition of Columbus's journals, shows some of the islands he visited.

The Allegory of Discovery

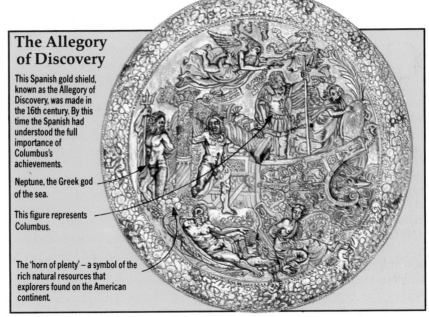

This Spanish gold shield, known as the Allegory of Discovery, was made in the 16th century. By this time the Spanish had understood the full importance of Columbus's achievements.

Neptune, the Greek god of the sea.

This figure represents Columbus.

The 'horn of plenty' – a symbol of the rich natural resources that explorers found on the American continent.

Disaster and triumph

On Christmas Day 1492, the *Santa Maria* was wrecked at La Española when it hit a reef. Columbus had to leave 43 men behind, as there was no room on the other ships. He was welcomed as a hero when he reached Spain. The islands he had found became known as "the Indies", as people thought they were off the coast of Asia in the Indian Ocean.

A second expedition

In 1493 Columbus led a new fleet to the Indies, but his visit was not a success. Firstly he found at La Española that the men he had left behind had been killed by the islanders. Then he formed a new settlement, but governed it badly, brutally mistreating the natives and Spaniards alike.

Columbus disgraced

News of Columbus's behaviour had reached Spain when he returned in 1496. Although the king and queen were angry, they let him go back to the Indies in 1498. But further unrest there alarmed Ferdinand and Isabella, and they appointed a new governor.

When Columbus reached Cuba having failed to calm a revolt on La Española, he was arrested by the governor and sent back to Spain in chains. Isabella later forgave him, but his pride was badly wounded. He claimed he had been misunderstood, and asked to be buried with the chains as a reminder of the way he had been treated.

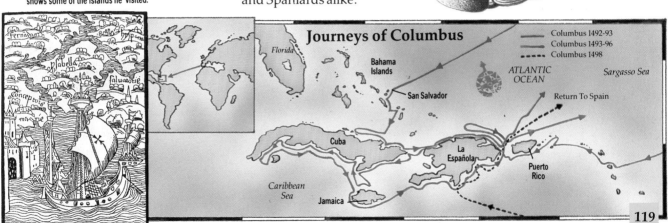

Journeys of Columbus

Florida

Bahama Islands

San Salvador

ATLANTIC OCEAN

Sargasso Sea

Return To Spain

Cuba

La Española

Puerto Rico

Caribbean Sea

Jamaica

——— Columbus 1492-93
——— Columbus 1493-96
----- Columbus 1498

Cortés

Columbus's death marks a turning point in the history of European exploration. Before that most explorers were professional navigators and seamen employed by monarchs. Though they wanted personal profit from their voyages, they had other, more long-term aims. These included finding trade routes for their patrons and taking Christianity to non-Christian countries. In the 16th century, new, more ruthless explorers became common. They are known as conquistadors, after the Spanish word for "conquerors".

The conquistadors

At the turn of the century an Italian explorer, Amerigo Vespucci, sailed to the land Columbus had found and established that it was an entirely new continent. In 1507 this "New World", as it was known, was named America, after Vespucci.

The conquistadors were Spanish adventurers and soldiers. They believed America and its resources were there to be taken regardless of who lived there. In conquering the new lands many of them remorselessly wiped out whole civilizations.

Cortés sails to the New World

Hernándo Cortés was born in 1485 to a distinguished but poor Spanish family. He first studied law, but soon found he was more attracted to the excitement of a soldier's life. His first major expedition was with Diego Velazquez, a conquistador who set out in 1511 to seize Cuba. When Velazquez succeeded, Cortés did well out of the conquest. He was soon a rich and important man, and for a time he was even Mayor of Cuba's capital Santiago. Soon, however, rumours of an empire rich in gold on the American mainland aroused his curiosity, and he set off in search of it.

Cortés
1485-1547

The Aztec empire

The Aztecs were American Indians who lived in what is now Mexico. Their civilization began in about 1325, when they arrived in the area from further north and began building their capital city Tenochtitlán. Aztec culture was highly sophisticated in many areas, especially science, art, architecture and agriculture. The Aztecs had their own mode of picture writing and a great many laws and elaborate religious rites and ceremonies. They were also highly skilled jewellers and weavers.

Sacrificial knives like this were used at the ceremonies.

Human sacrifices

One of the most shocking Aztec customs was the ritual of human sacrifice. The Aztecs believed their sun god, Huitzilpochtli, died each night, and would only be reborn the next day if he was nourished with a constant supply of human blood. Thousands of victims were brutally sacrificed each year. They were often slaves or prisoners of war, but sometimes Atzecs themselves. Many had their hearts cut out while they were still living.

The heads of victims were kept on skull racks like this.

Towards Tenochtitlán

In 1519 Cortés left Santiago, intending to make his fortune by conquering the Aztecs. He sailed for the American mainland with

Shrine to the sun god

Sacrificial altar

This is what an Aztec temple might have looked like.

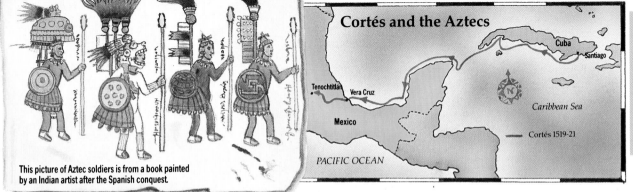

Cortés and the Aztecs

Cuba
Santiago
Tenochtitlán
Vera Cruz
Caribbean Sea
Mexico
—— Cortés 1519-21
PACIFIC OCEAN

This picture of Aztec soldiers is from a book painted by an Indian artist after the Spanish conquest.

600 men, 16 horses and several cannons. After founding the city of Vera Cruz on the coast, he continued inland towards Tenochtitlán.

The Aztecs had recently conquered several rival tribes in the area and had made many enemies. Malinche, the daughter of one tribal chief, fell in love with Cortés and offered to accompany him on his journey as a guide and interpreter. (The Spaniards named her Dona Mariña.) Her services were crucial in gaining support from the other Indian tribes for his invasion of the Aztecs.

Mask of Quetzalcoatl (see below).

Warrior gods

The Aztecs were terrified by Cortés's cannons and horses. Some thought his arrival was the god Quetzalcoatl returning to Earth, as predicted in an Aztec myth. But their emperor Montezuma thought otherwise. Astrologers had spoken of an invasion and the downfall of the Aztec Empire, and he worried that the predictions were coming true. To put the Spaniards off their guard,

he treated them like the gods his people took them for, kissing the ground before their feet and giving them precious gifts.

Montezuma's downfall

Montezuma's attempt to pacify the Spaniards did him no good. Cortés took him prisoner and demanded a huge ransom of gold. The gold was paid, but Cortés cheated the Aztecs and kept Montezuma captive.

Gold jewellery like this whetted Cortés's appetite.

Serpent
Monkey
Puma
Owl

Then news reached Cortés that a rival in Vera Cruz had challenged his authority. He rushed to the coast to deal with the problem, and returned to find that one of his men had staged an unprovoked attack on an Aztec religious meeting and killed many of the participants.

The Aztecs were in uproar, so Cortés produced Montezuma, hoping to calm the rioters. But the former ruler had never been popular, and the sight of him enraged the crowds even more. They stoned him to death then turned on the Spaniards.

Cortés's men suffered heavy losses in the fighting and withdrew to

Serpent-shaped
Aztec pendant inlaid with turquoise

the protection of friendly tribes nearby. Then in August 1521, Cortés besieged Tenochtitlán. Food and water were cut off for nearly three months. Countless Aztecs died. Some starved, but many caught smallpox which the Spanish had unknowingly brought with them from Europe.

An empire destroyed

After the fall of Tenochtitlán, the Aztec Empire was rapidly destroyed. The Indians had no immunity to European diseases, so millions of them died. In addition many conquistadors were brutal rulers. Within a few years of Montezuma's death, little of the Aztec world remained.

Aztec armour

The Aztecs had weapons and armour that terrified the Spanish.

Wooden club edged with sharpened flint. ▶

Cane shield covered ▶ with painted animal hide.

◀ Padded cotton suit

The hunt for the Northwest Passage

Like the Spanish, the British and French were also keen to reach the riches of the East by sailing west. Rather than following the Spanish routes round South America (see pages 134-135), they sought a new route round North America. They were sure that they would find a channel through which their ships could sail. This was known as the Northwest Passage.

Frobisher meets the challenge

An English expedition to find the Northwest Passage was organized by the navigator Sir Humphrey Gilbert. Three ships set sail from London in 1576 under the command of a captain called Martin Frobisher.

Martin Frobisher (1535-94)

The coast of Greenland was blocked by ice and Frobisher's ship lost its mast in a gale. But he repaired the damage and continued with his journey. Believing he had found the approach to the Northwest Passage, he named it Frobisher's Strait, without realizing it was only an inlet (now Frobisher Bay) that led nowhere.

Encounter with the Inuit

While he was exploring the inlet, Frobisher was met by Inuit (the local inhabitants). They skimmed across the water in one-man canoes called kayaks and surrounded Frobisher's ship.

Kayaks are made from wooden frames covered with sealskins.

Wooden frame

Sealskin covering

Paddle

When Frobisher first saw a kayak from a distance, he thought it was a seal or a large fish.

Kidnap

The Inuit seemed friendly and traded food and furs. But five of the crew were kidnapped when they left their ship. Frobisher captured an Inuit as a hostage against the return of his sailors, but they were never seen again. The Inuit was taken back to England, where he died of pneumonia.

The search for gold

One of the crew went ashore and brought back some black rocks streaked with glittering gold veins. When Frobisher returned to London experts declared that the rocks contained gold. On his next two voyages to the region in 1577 and 1578, Frobisher collected huge quantities of the rocks. When he returned home after the final journey, he was told that the rocks he had collected were worthless. They had been identified as iron pyrites, also known as "fool's gold".

Iron pyrites or "fool's gold".

The quest continues

The failure to find the elusive Northwest Passage did not discourage others from making the attempt. John Davis, who discovered the Davis Strait, made three voyages between 1585 and 1587.

In 1610 Henry Hudson sailed along the north coast of Canada in a ship called the *Discovery*. But his crew, convinced he had a secret hoard of food, cast him adrift with his son and a few loyal sailors. Hudson was lost forever in the bay that now bears his name.

In 1616 William Baffin and Robert Bylot sailed up the Davis Strait as far as Smith Sound, which would have taken them through to open sea, but the icy weather forced them to turn back. The Northwest Passage remained uncharted for centuries. It was finally navigated by Roald Amundsen (see pages 136-137).

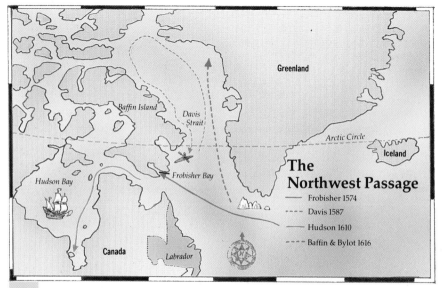

Greenland

Baffin Island

Davis Strait

Arctic Circle

Iceland

The Northwest Passage

— Frobisher 1574
---- Davis 1587
— Hudson 1610
---- Baffin & Bylot 1616

Hudson Bay

Frobisher Bay

Canada

Labrador

An Inuit hunting bow made out of walrus-tusk ivory.

Carvings of hunting scenes

The building of New France

W hile the English were enduring the miseries of the freezing Arctic waters, the French were also trying to find a route through to the East. In 1534 King François I commissioned a sailor from St Malo called Jacques Cartier to find a way west to the Pacific and claim new lands for France.

Jacques Cartier
(1491-1557)

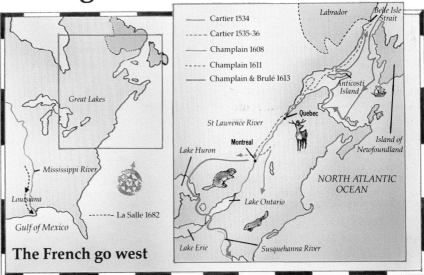

The French go west

Missed opportunities

Cartier's expedition set out in two ships from St Malo in 1534. He headed for Newfoundland and then sailed through the Belle Isle Strait, noting that the rocky shores would be of no use to settlers. Rounding Anticosti Island, he sighted the mouth of the St Lawrence River. Mistaking it for a bay, he failed to investigate it and returned to France.

Help from the Indians

Cartier left on a second voyage in May 1535 and reached Belle Isle Strait at the end of July. He acquired two guides from the Huron tribe who led his party up the St Lawrence River. They passed the small native village of Stadacona (later Quebec), then pressed on upstream through the rapids to a town called Hochelaga where they met the Huron chief, Donnaconna. Cartier named a nearby hill Mont Réal (Mount Royal), which later became the site of the city of Montreal.

Cartier and his men spent a terrible winter at Stadacona, suffering from scurvy and extreme cold. On 6 May 1536 they finally sailed for home. On the way they kidnapped Donnaconna to try to get him to reveal the whereabouts of gold mines. He was taken back to France, where he later died.

In the wake of Cartier

With wars raging in Europe, French kings lost interest in the New World for a time. However small groups of Frenchmen continued to follow Cartier's route up the St Lawrence and spread out along the many waterways. They learned how to survive in the wilderness, build birch-bark canoes and trap beavers and other animals for their fur. They established a trade network with the American Indians, which flourished rapidly. At the same time they were gradually building up an empire for France.

The French empire grows

Samuel de Champlain, the French Royal Geographer, founded Quebec in 1608 and Montreal in 1611, strengthening France's hold in North America. In 1613 he was joined by Etienne Brulé who later reached the Susquehanna River.

In 1678 King Louis XIV sent an explorer called Robert de La Salle to build a chain of trading forts across the continent. La Salle followed the Mississippi River, reaching the Gulf of Mexico in 1682. He named the lands he passed through Louisiana after the king.

Cartier travelled by canoe with Indian guides up the St Lawrence River.

French explorers encountered many animals which they trapped for their fur and hide. ►

Across the continent

By the mid-18th century there were so many new immigrants entering North America from Europe that the original colonies in the Northeast were overcrowded. Expansion was difficult as the settlers were afraid to venture west into the unknown lands over the Appalachian Mountains.

In 1803 the United States government bought the state of Louisiana from France. This prompted Thomas Jefferson, the American president, to plan an expedition to explore the lands beyond the Mississippi. This was mainly to assess opportunities for trade with American Indians and Mexicans, but also to find a route to the Pacific Ocean.

The team departs

The leaders of the expedition were Captain Meriwether Lewis, the president's private secretary, and Lieutenant William Clark. Lewis chose all the equipment needed, while Clark recruited

William Clark (1770-1838)

Meriwether Lewis (1774-1809)

and trained the men. The team of 30 men was known as the Corps of Discovery and left St Louis in a blaze of publicity on 14 May 1804, sailing up the River Missouri. As well as the usual equipment such as rifles, medicines and food supplies, they carried with them many trinkets as presents for the Indians.

An air-gun used on the expedition

Clark's pocket compass

Entering new lands

The two leaders made many notes on the profusion of plants and animals they saw along the way. Lewis complained of the terrible weather and the swarms of mosquitoes that plagued them throughout the night and day.

Prairie dog
Lewis's woodpecker
Mountain flower

After eleven weeks they encountered the Oto, Missouri and Omaha tribes of Indians. They exchanged gifts and made peace and trade treaties with them. Then, moving deeper into the plains, they met about a thousand members of the Teton Sioux who made the team take part in a peace-pipe ceremony before allowing them to cross their lands.

Moving on

They reached an area now part of North Dakota where they set up camp and built a log fort. They spent the bitter winter there among the Mandan tribe. The team resumed its journey in the

A barge similar to the one used by Lewis and Clark

spring, travelling by barge up the Missouri. Gradually the currents ran stronger and the journey became more difficult, but by the end of May they were in sight of the majestic, snow-covered Rocky Mountains. Here they came across grizzly bears and were surprised by the power and ferocity of these huge animals that frequently attacked the party.

The explorers were often powerless when attacked by bears.

A way through the Rockies

Next, they had to find a way round the Great Falls on the Missouri as they could go no further. The task of moving the equipment round the falls took nearly a month and exhausted the men. By August they entered the lands of the Shoshoni Indians and here they encountered more difficulties, for they had underestimated the height of the Rockies. But they were helped by Sacagewea, the Shoshoni Indian wife of a Canadian interpreter in the party. She showed them the Lemhi Pass and guided them towards the Columbia River. They made contact with Sacagewea's people and were given new horses to continue their journey.

Sacagewea

Ocean in view!

The western face of the Rockies was very steep, criss-crossed by roaring waterfalls and slippery precipices. The going was tough,

Crossing the Rockies

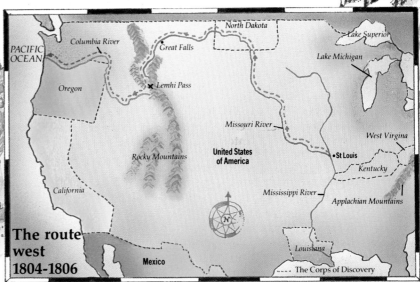

The route west 1804-1806

The Corps of Discovery

food was in short supply and the nights were bitterly cold. They passed through the lands of the Chinook, the Clatsops and the majestic Nez Percé tribe, and finally reached the Columbia River. They paddled towards the coast, and on 7 November heard the roar of the Pacific breakers and smelled the sea-salt in the air. They climbed to the top of the final hill and saw the ocean spread before them. At last they had reached their goal.

The journey home

Winter was now closing in, so they built a camp which they named Fort Clatsop. From there they could watch the Pacific to hail any passing ship that might carry them back east. But nothing appeared on the horizon, so the team packed up and on 23 March set off on their six-month return journey to St Louis. Although they now knew the way, it was as

exhausting as the outward trek. Also, conflict with the Blackfoot Indians caused difficulties which were to plague pioneers for many years. On 20 September 1806 they reached a French settlement where they saw the first Europeans for over two years.

A triumphant return

On 23 September 1806 they finally arrived back at St Louis after a journey of over 12,000km (7,456 miles) and an absence of two-and-a-half years. They had been gone for so long that many thought they must be dead. But Lewis and Clark had accomplished all they had set out to do. Most importantly, they had discovered a way to the West which gave access to the rest of the continent and the Pacific. They had also established good relations with many of the Indian tribes and opened up new trade routes.

A member of the party being attacked by Blackfoot Indians.

The rush West

This mammoth expedition by the Corps of Discovery was followed by a new wave of explorers, mainly fur trappers known as "mountain men" who spilled over the mountains to make their fortunes. Further south, the Santa Fe, the Old Spanish, the Oregon and the Californian trade routes were established between the United States and Mexico.

Farmers and gold prospectors

Where the traders went, the farmers followed. In 1843 a group of settlers travelled west to Oregon in a thousand-strong wagon-train. When gold was discovered in California in 1849, a huge rush to the West began. Thousands of people left the East for the new lands, braving incredible hardship and the growing hostility of the Indians who realized that the settlers threatened their territory and way of life.

Mountain man in search of furs.

Gold nuggets from California.

125

Scientists and dreamers

The first Europeans to explore and colonize South America in the 16th and 17th centuries were treasure hunters and missionaries. But during the 18th century many of the explorers were scientists. They were more interested in mapping the continent and in studying its geology and plant and animal life. The first such scientific expedition travelled to Peru in 1735.

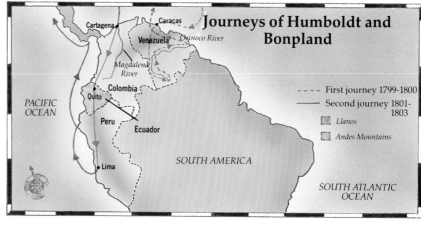

Journeys of Humboldt and Bonpland

- - - First journey 1799-1800
—— Second journey 1801-1803
Llanos
Andes Mountains

Cartagena • Caracas
Venezuela • Orinoco River
Magdalena River
Colombia
Quito
Peru
Ecuador
Lima
PACIFIC OCEAN
SOUTH AMERICA
SOUTH ATLANTIC OCEAN

Alexander von Humboldt

One of the greatest scientific explorers was a German called Alexander von Humboldt. As well as being a brilliant naturalist, he was an astronomer, biologist and geologist and also an expert linguist. In June 1797 Humboldt left his home in Berlin for Paris. In June 1799 he and a French doctor called Aimé Bonpland sailed from Europe to South America, reaching the north east coast near Caracas in present-day Venezuela the following month.

Alexander von Humboldt (1769-1859)

Aimé Bonpland (1773-1858)

One of their first projects was to explore the Orinoco River. But in order to reach it, they first had to cross the dry, baking and dusty plains called the *llanos* stretching to the south.

◀ The Incas were very skilled stonemasons. They cut the stones so accurately that they fitted perfectly.

All along the way they made detailed records of the many plants, animals and birds they saw and the country through which they passed – scorching deserts that parched their throats and dried up their skin. They travelled along winding rivers through hot steamy jungles, the silence pierced by the shrieks of parrots and monkeys, where they were plagued by swarms of blood-sucking insects.

Up mountains, down south

They made a second journey to South America in 1801 and reached Quito (one of the highest cities in the world) in January 1802, after an exhausting voyage along rivers and over mountains. Outside the city they climbed 5,878m (19,285ft) almost to the top of a volcanic peak called Chimborazo. Then they travelled south through lush forests and across the chilly slopes of the Andes Mountains until they reached Lima, Peru. Here they studied the archaeological remains of the Inca civilization. (The Incas flourished in Peru from the 13th century, but were wiped out by Spanish conquistadors (see page 120) in the 1530s.)

Humboldt also recorded the steady, cold current which flows along the Peruvian coast and is rich in stocks of fish. It was later named the Humboldt Current (now known as the Peru Current).

Back in Europe

Great crowds turned out to welcome the two explorers on their return to France in 1804. They had travelled 64,000km (40,000 miles) in South America and collected 30 chests of specimens and 60,000 plants, many of which were unknown before. Humboldt returned to Germany and spent the next 23 years preparing all their work for publication which eventually filled 29 volumes.

Bonpland identified thousands of plants for the first time.

Humboldt and Bonpland at the foot of Mount Chimborazo. ▼

Charles Darwin

Charles Darwin was an English naturalist and explorer. He joined a ship called the *Beagle* in December 1831 on a five-year expedition to map the coast of Chile. He made copious notes on all he saw, and although there was little room on the ship he built up a huge collection of rocks, fossils, plants, birds, animals and shells. The sights he saw and the observations he made would later lead him to challenge the traditional beliefs about how life on Earth began and evolved.

Charles Darwin (1809-82)

The land of giants

The expedition reached Bahia in Brazil in the spring of 1832. Darwin was amazed by the number and dazzling colours of the flowers and birds he saw. The Beagle sailed south along the coast of Patagonia where the crew discovered the fossil remains of several extinct animals, including a giant sloth and armadillo.

This is how the giant sloth and the armadillo might have looked.

They travelled to the bleak and wind-swept lands of Tierra del Fuego, at the very tip of South America. Darwin made a journey inland to the plains of Argentina known as the *pampas*, living among the *gauchos* (cowboys).

Darwin on a plant-hunting expedition.

A world apart

In September 1835 the expedition reached the strange, remote Galapagos Islands, lying 965km (600 miles) off the coast of Ecuador in the Pacific Ocean. There Darwin saw birds, animals and plants that are found nowhere else on Earth. Cut off from the mainland they had developed in isolation from their relations in America. They were to play an important part in Darwin's theories on how animals and humans evolve (see below).

These animals are only found on the Galapagos Islands.

The Bible is questioned

The *Beagle* reached England in October 1836 and Darwin spent over 20 years writing up his findings. In 1859 he published *The Origin of Species*, which set out his theories on evolution. These turned the teachings of the Church upside down. One of Darwin's most revolutionary theories was that all living things had evolved over many millions of years. This caused uproar, because it questioned the biblical idea that the world was created in six days and had remained unchanged since then.

Giant tortoise

Marine iguana

Galapagos finch

Percy Fawcett

Percy Fawcett was an army officer and surveyor with 20 years' experience of travel in South America. Inspired by the legend of El Dorado, "the golden man", he believed that somewhere deep in the Brazilian jungle lay the remains of a fabulous civilization. Near Salvador (Bahia) in 1921 he found remains which encouraged him and he intended to prove his theory by finding one of the lost cities, which he called "Z".

Percy Fawcett (1867-1925)

An unsolved mystery

On 20 April 1925, Fawcett set off with his eldest son Jack and a school friend of Jack's called Raleigh Rimell. They followed piranha-infested rivers into the Mato Grosso region of Brazil, and were never seen again. Over the following years rumours of what had happened to them came out of the jungle. They were probably killed by Indians, but nothing could be proved and their disappearance remains as much a mystery as Fawcett's fabled city.

SOUTH AMERICA
Ecuador
Brazil
Galapagos Islands
Bahia (Salvador)
Mato Grosso
PACIFIC OCEAN
Chile
Argentina
SOUTH ATLANTIC OCEAN
Pampas
Darwin and Fawcett
Darwin 1831-1835
Fawcett 1925
Patagonia
Tierra del Fuego   Cape Horn

The quest for a southern continent

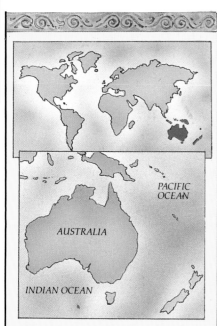

Key dates in Australasian exploration

- **1565** Andres de Urdaneta crosses the Pacific Ocean.
- **1606** Pedro Fernandes de Quiros reaches the New Hebrides Islands.
- **1606** Willem Jantszoon becomes the first European to reach Australia.
- **1642** Abel Tasman sights Tasmania, off the southern coast of Australia.
- **1642** Abel Tasman sights an island off the southern coast of Australia, and names it Van Diemen's Land. Guinea.
- **1721** Jakob Roggeveen discovers Easter Island, on Easter Sunday.
- **1769** James Cook sails in the *Endeavour* to Tahiti and makes observations of Venus. He sails on to New Zealand where he discovers the east coast.
- **1770** Cook lands in Botany Bay, Australia.
- **1772** Cook's second voyage leaves Plymouth.
- **1774** Cook crosses Latitude 70° and the Antarctic Circle.
- **1776** Cook sets sail on his third voyage. Its main purpose was to find a route through the Northwest Passage (see page 26) from west to east.
- **1778** Cook sails to the Society Islands (Hawaiian Islands) where he is killed.
- **1785** François de la Pérouse leaves France in search of Solomon Islands.
- **1788** Pérouse lands at Port Jackson, New South Wales, Australia.
- **1795** Mathew Flinders and George Bass make the first inland expedition from the east coast of Australia.
- **1801-2** Flinders carries out survey of nearly all the Australian coastline.
- **1828** Charles Sturt and Hamilton Hume cross the Blue Mountains, Australia.
- **1860** Robert Burke leads expedition from Melbourne to cross Australia from south to north.
- **1861** John Stuart leads second, rival expedition north across Australia from Adelaide.
- **1861** Death of Charles Gray, William Wills and Burke.
- **1862** Stuart returns south, having completed his crossing of Australia.

In 1565 a Spanish monk called Andres de Urdaneta made the first crossing of the Pacific. His account of the journey led many people to believe that a great southern continent lay somewhere to the west of the tip of South America. In 1606 Pedro Fernandes de Quiros, a Portuguese captain working for Spain, reached land he believed to be that continent. He named it "Austrialia" (after the King of Spain who was also Archduke of Austria), but it was in fact one of the islands now called the New Hebrides.

Discovery of a new continent

By the end of the 16th century, the Dutch were a powerful trading nation. In 1606 a Dutch captain from Amsterdam, Willem Jantszoon, became the first European to reach Australia. He sailed into the Gulf of Carpentaria on the northern coast. In 1642, another Dutchman, Abel Tasman, sighted the island that is now called Tasmania. He named it Van Diemen's Land after the governor of his employers, the Dutch East India Company. Tasman went on to discover New Zealand, then stopped at Tonga and Fiji. After this, Dutch interest in exploration dwindled. It was more than a hundred years before Australia was further explored.

Captain Cook

James Cook was born in Yorkshire, England. The son of a farm labourer, he received a very limited education at the local school. He began work when he was 12, first in a shop, then with a shipping comany. In 1756 he joined the navy as a sailor.

Cook was a very tall man, with a strong character and great intelligence. He was a gifted navigator and astronomer and in 1768 was appointed a lieutenant and given command of his first ship, the *Endeavour*.

James Cook (1728-79)

The fight against disease

In the 18th century an average of 60 out of every 100 seamen died on long voyages, 50 of them from disease. Cook tried to reduce illness by introducing rigid rules. The men had to bathe every day. Their clothing and bedding were aired twice a week and the ship was regularly fumigated.

Cook took large quantities of fresh fruit on board ship. This was to prevent scurvy, a disease caused by a lack of vitamin C and one of the main causes of death among sailors. He also ensured that fresh meat and vegetables were obtained wherever possible. These measures improved the health of the sailors.

The *Endeavour* was built in Whitby, Yorkshire. It was originally designed to deliver coal to ports along the British coast.

Officer's cabin.

The great cabin was where the captain and his officers met to talk and eat.

The captain's private cabin, where he slept and worked.

Surgeon's cabin. Throughout the journey, sailors suffered from various illnesses and injuries.

Storerooms. The supplies of food for the long journey were kept here.

The men and the mission

In keeping with the scientific spirit of the times, Cook's first mission was to take his ship to Tahiti to observe the planet Venus as it passed between the Earth and the sun in 1769. Travelling with him on this voyage were a naturalist, a botanist and two artists. Cook carried with him a sealed envelope, to be opened after the observations had been recorded. It contained secret orders to seek out the fifth continent, to allow the scientists to study the plants, animals and native peoples, and to claim the land for Britain.

The expedition reached the island of Tahiti in April 1769. The scientists made their observations of Venus on 3 June and set sail again ten days later. Two of the islanders went with them as guides to help the expedition explore smaller islands nearby.

Australasian pioneers
······· De Quiros 1606
······· Jantszoon 1605-6
– – – Tasman 1642-43
——— Cook 1768-71
——— Cook 1772-75
······· Cook 1776-79

A Maori warrior

Sword used by the Maoris

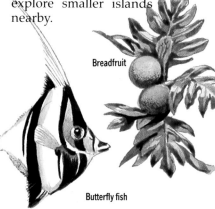

Breadfruit

Butterfly fish

The ships moved on to New Zealand, where they had a hostile reception from the Maoris. Fighting broke out and at one point the *Endeavour* was chased by about a hundred warriors in canoes.

Run aground

In April 1770 Cook landed at an inlet on the east coast of Australia. He named it Botany Bay after the many botanical specimens found there. Following the coast north, the ship was damaged when it ran into coral on the Great Barrier Reef. Once repairs were complete they set sail again and finally reached home in July 1771.

Cook's last voyages

Cook led two more expeditions, making further discoveries. The first set sail in two ships from Plymouth in July 1772. In January 1774 Cook and his crew crossed the Latitude 70°, the furthest south yet reached by Europeans, and visited Easter Island.

In 1778 Cook travelled to the Society Islands (now the Hawaiian Islands). At first the Hawaiians treated him like a god, but they soon grew tired of their visitors. Cook set sail but returned six days later when his ship, the *Resolution*, suffered storm damage. A fight broke out and Cook was stabbed to death.

Settlement of the continent

In January 1788, a French expedition under the command of a captain called Jean François de la Pérouse arrived in Australia. Pérouse intended to claim the country for the French, but he was too late. Only the day before, the British had established a colony there.

On Easter Island in the South Pacific Ocean there are giant stone heads, some 12m (40ft) tall.

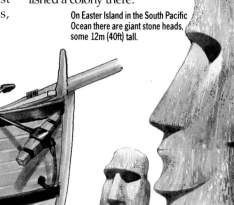

Locker room. Sails were stored here, carefully folded.

Boatswain's quarters. Ropes, tackle, pulleys and various other pieces of equipment were kept here.

Storerooms. Powder and ammunition for the guns.

Into the interior

Australia's coastline was well-mapped by the end of the 18th century. For many years, however, the interior remained a mystery to all except the local inhabitants, the Aborigines. There were many theories about what lay on the other side of the Blue Mountains. Some believed the land there was rich, and fertile, but others thought it was desert or marshland.

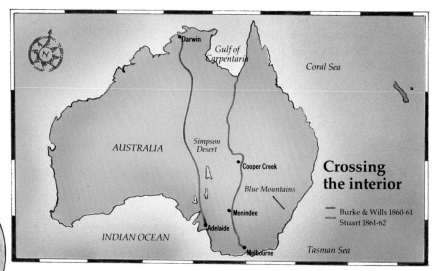

Crossing the interior

— Burke & Wills 1860-61
— Stuart 1861-62

Robert Burke (1820-61)

William Wills (1834-61)

Besides the glory of being first to cross the continent, there was a need to set up a telegraph line to link Australia to the rest of the world. The men who first ventured into the interior suffered dreadful hardships and some even lost their lives. The journey of Robert Burke and William Wills best illustrates the bravery, misery, bad judgement and terrible luck experienced by so many of these explorers.

In 1859 the government of South Australia offered a prize to the first person to cross the continent from south to north. Burke and Wills were appointed leader and surveyor of one of the most expensively equipped expeditions in Australia's history. But there was one fatal flaw. Neither Burke nor Wills had any knowledge of the outback or much experience of exploration.

Burke leading the expedition

The expedition sets out

The expedition left Melbourne in August 1860, cheered on its way by an enthusiastic crowd. Burke went first, followed by the other 15 members of his team and a long line consisting of 25 camels, 23 horses and wagons. After two months they had reached Menindee where they set up camp, but quarrels broke out among the men and Burke dismissed several of them. The expedition had now become very dispersed because of the varying speeds of parts of the team, with the wagons travelling long distances apart.

Hearing of a second, rival expedition, Burke became very impatient to move on. In scorching temperatures he, Wills and seven others set off for Cooper Creek, 645km (400 miles) northwest. The expedition was now divided into scattered groups. Once they arrived at Cooper Creek, Burke left one of the party, William Brahe, in charge of the remaining animals and provisions. Brahe was instructed to wait three months or until supplies ran out. Meanwhile Burke, Wills, Charles Gray and John King carried on to try and reach the Gulf of Carpentaria on the north coast.

Wildlife of the outback

The interior region of Australia is known as the outback. It contains many extraordinary plants and animals that are unknown elsewhere.

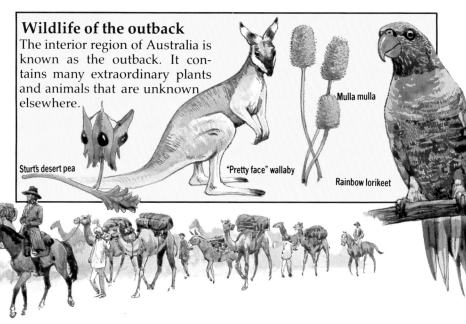

Sturt's desert pea

"Pretty face" wallaby

Mulla mulla

Rainbow lorikeet

An Aboriginal bark painting

Instructions carved into a tree by Brahe.

Food and a message buried by Brahe.

Dead end

The weather suddenly changed and it rained endlessly for days. The ground became too waterlogged for the camels to move, so Burke and Wills went ahead on foot. By mid-February 1861 they were within sight of the shores of the gulf and could smell the sea. But their path was blocked by swamps of trees called mangroves and they decided to turn back.

The return journey

The journey south turned into a nightmare. Reunited with Gray and King, Burke and Wills headed back to Cooper Creek once more. Heavy rains fell for days on end, the men were soaked through to the skin and they became extremely feverish. The land turned into a quagmire of mud and slush. Food supplies were running so low that, one after another, the camels had to be shot for food and their baggage abandoned. Finally Gray, who seemed the strongest in the group, collapsed and died.

Aborigine

The deserted camp

Four days later, on 21 April, the three exhausted survivors staggered into Cooper Creek, hoping to find Brahe and the supplies waiting for them there. But instead they were horrified to find that the camp was deserted. They searched the place from top to bottom looking for supplies and eventually found a message left behind by Brahe. Believing they were dead, he had departed with the remaining animals for Menindee just seven hours before.

Lost in the desert

Instead of trying to catch up with Brahe – unknown to them, he was only 23km (14 miles) away – Burke decided that they should return south by a shorter route towards Adelaide. They wandered in giant circles in the baking desert for weeks and ate the last of their camels. They were only saved from death because they were fed by some Aborigines who had been following them. The three exhausted men eventually found their way back to Cooper Creek.

To the Aborigines, the outback was a source of foods unknown to the explorers.

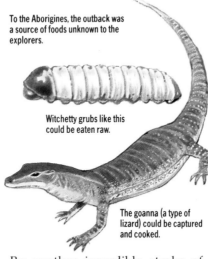

Witchetty grubs like this could be eaten raw.

The goanna (a type of lizard) could be captured and cooked.

By another incredible stroke of bad luck they had just missed Brahe once again. He had returned to Cooper Creek with a rescue party to look for them. But, seeing no sign that they had been anywhere near the camp, he moved on once more and headed back to Melbourne.

A tragic ending

Burke, Wills and King were only a few kilometres away, near to death. Their food had now completely run out and they began to slowly starve, growing weaker and weaker by the hour. King was the strongest and looked after the other two, doing as much as he could to help them. Wills was the first to die, followed by Burke some days later. King was now the only one left alive. Very weak himself, he staggered into the desert where he was looked after by some Aborigines living nearby. He was eventually found three months later by another search party from Melbourne. He was thin and burnt by the sun. Without the help of the Aborigines he would certainly have died. The remains of Burke and Wills were recovered and taken back to Melbourne for a state funeral.

Stuart wins the prize

Burke and Wills were the first to reach the north coast of Australia. But the first person to reach the coast and return alive was John McDouall Stuart. He was the leader of the rival expedition which left Adelaide in January 1861 in the race for the prize. This expedition arrived at the north coast seven months later. Burke, Wills and Stuart had proved that though much of the Australian interior was desert it was possible to travel across it.

John Stuart (1815-66)

Burke, close to death, is looked after by King.

The forbidden land

The Arabian Peninsula is surrounded on three sides by sea: the Persian Gulf, the Indian Ocean and the Red Sea. This made it a very important staging post on the trade routes from the Middle East, Africa, India and the Far East. Precious cargoes wound their way along the routes that criss-crossed the desert. Arabia also had valuable goods of its own to sell – incense, spices, drugs and perfumes, gold and precious stones. Because it was such a rich region, the Romans called it *Arabia Felix*, "Happy Arabia".

In contrast to the thin fertile strip along the south coast where rich kingdoms once flourished, further north the land rises steeply to a dry, barren region. Here nomadic tribes called Bedouin move flocks and herds between oases. In the centre of the peninsula are two fearsome deserts of shifting sand: to the north lies the Nefud while to the south lies the desolate Rub' al-Khali, the Empty Quarter.

A Bedouin encampment with tents made of goats' hair. ▼

An early adventurer

After the rise of Islam in the 7th century AD (see page 100), very few non-Muslims travelled in Arabia and the holy cities of Mecca and Medina were closed to all but Muslims. The first European to travel there after Covilhã's journey to Mecca in 1492 (see page 103) was a Venetian called Ludovico di Varthema. He arrived in Damascus in 1503 and set off disguised as a Muslim soldier in the pilgrim caravan to Mecca. He was the first non-Muslim to enter the Great Mosque and had many adventures before travelling on to India. He stayed there for some months before returning to Venice.

The rose-red city rediscovered

Johann Burckhardt was a Swiss scholar who had joined the Association for Promoting the Discovery of the Interior Parts of Africa (see page 104). He left for Africa via Syria, which he reached in 1809. He stayed in Aleppo for three years, learning Arabic and Islamic law.

The Khaznet Firaun (Pharaoh's Treasury) at the ▶ entrance into Petra.

On his way to Cairo in 1812, Burckhardt travelled through deserts and mountains to the remains of the fabulously rich city of Petra. This had been the capital of the merchant kingdom of the Nabataeans, who flourished from the 3rd to 1st centuries BC. Burckhardt was the first European to visit the city for over 1,500 years. He gazed on the Khaznet, a fantastic building carved from the pink-gold rock. Spellbound, he walked through the winding valley between elaborate tombs, temples and chapels, carved into the mountainsides and piled one above the other.

Johann Burckhardt (1784-1817)

Burckhardt reached Cairo and then travelled down the Nile Valley, stopping at the huge temple cut into the rock at Abu Simbel. He crossed the Red Sea to Jeddah and then visited Mecca, journeyed north through Arabia and arrived back in Cairo in 1815. Here he started to write up a report of his journeys. However, he died there two years later before he could continue his journey down into Africa.

El Haj Abdullah

In 1853 Richard Burton (see page 106) set sail from Suez in a pilgrim ship bound for Yenbo on the Red Sea coast. He went disguised as an Afghan doctor called El Haj Abdullah. The journey was chaotic, with fights breaking out among the pilgrims because of the lack of space. At the end of January they reached Medina where Burton stayed until August, writing an account of the city and its holy shrines.

Moving on, by the end of September he had arrived at the gates of Mecca. He prepared himself for entry into the city, shaving his head and donning the special white cotton pilgrim's robe. Inside the city, he took part in the holy ceremonies with hundreds of other pilgrims.

Burton had originally planned to cross the Arabian Peninsula from the west to the east coast. But, exhausted by the heat, he finally left Mecca at the end of the month and set sail for India.

Burton disguised as an Arab doctor.

A traveller's masterpiece

Although Charles Doughty spent less than two years in just a small part of Arabia, he is now regarded as one of the greatest explorers of the region. During his travels he made no attempt to disguise the fact that he was a Christian European, even though it was still dangerous for non-Muslims to travel in Arabia.

Charles Doughty (1843-1926)

Desert travels

- —— Di Varthema 1502-3
- --- Burckhardt 1812
- —— Burckhardt 1813-15
- ···· Burton 1853-54
- Doughty 1875
- —— Doughty 1876-78
- --- Thomas 1930-31
- —— Philby 1932

Damascus · Palestine · Syria · Suez · Petra · Cairo · Egypt · Nefud · Meda 'in Salih · Khaybar · Medina · Yenbo · Hejaz · River Nile · AFRICA · Jeddah · Mecca · As Sulayyil · Arabian Peninsula · Hofuf · Persian Gulf · Rub'al-Khali (Empty Quarter) · Red Sea · INDIAN OCEAN

Sketch made by Doughty of some of the inscriptions at Meda'in Salih.

In 1875 he sailed to Palestine and by November 1876 he was in northern Arabia, studying the monuments at Meda'in Salih. Like those at Petra, they were cut into the mountains and decorated with ancient inscriptions. He travelled along the edges of the Nefud Desert with his Bedouin companions, making careful observations of their customs and the countryside they crossed.

At times Doughty was thrown out of towns because he was a Christian, but on other occasions he was warmly welcomed. In 1878 he returned to England and spent the following ten years writing one of the greatest works of travel literature, entitled *Travels in Arabia Deserta*.

Crossing the Empty Quarter

There remained one last little-known area of Arabia, the treacherous Rub' al-Khali Desert or Empty Quarter. This desert is so vast and forbidding that even the Bedouin called it "the abode of death". They preferred to avoid it and very few had ever ventured inside the baking wilderness.

This great sea of sand was finally conquered in the winter of 1930-31 when Bertram Thomas, an Englishman who was acting as adviser to the Sultan of Muscat, crossed the desert from south to north. The following year another Englishman called Harry St John Philby crossed the desert from east to west, travelling 3,000km (1,864 miles) over the burning sand in just 90 days.

Philby in Arabic dress.

Philby and his travelling companions in the Empty Quarter.

Around the world

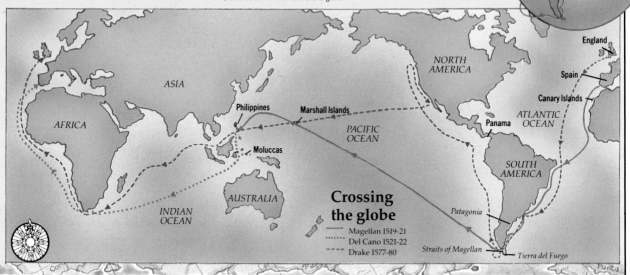

People still sail round the world as a test of skill and endurance. But the first people to circumnavigate the globe had very practical reasons for their travels: trade and colonization.

Key dates in circumnavigation

- **Sept. 1519** Magellan leaves Spain.
- **Oct. 1520** Magellan travels through Straits of Magellan.
- **March 1521** Death of Magellan.
- **Sept. 1522** Remaining crew return to Spain.
- **Dec. 1577** Drake sets sail round the world.
- **Nov. 1580** Drake returns to England.

Western Europe and West Africa are shown twice on the map below. This is so that the routes around the world described on these pages can be shown clearly.

Crossing the globe
— Magellan 1519-21
····· Del Cano 1521-22
--- Drake 1577-80

The first circumnavigation of the globe was led by a Portuguese aristocrat called Ferdinand Magellan. He had already made several journeys to find trade routes for the Portuguese, but he quarrelled with the king and went to sea for the Spanish instead.

The Spanish wanted to establish trade routes to the East and claim territory there, particularly the Moluccas (Spice Islands). Magellan believed he could reach the Moluccas by sailing west round the southern tip of America, instead of following the Portuguese sea routes to the East around Africa (see page 114). Only two months after Magellan's arrival at the Spanish court, the young King Charles of Spain (later Emperor Charles V) agreed to finance the scheme.

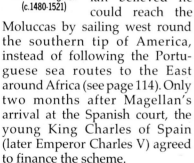

Ferdinand Magellan (c.1480-1521)

The fleet sets sail

In September 1519 Magellan left Spain with 260 men and five ships: the *Trinidad*, the *Vittoria*, the *Santiago*, the *Concepción*, and the *San Antonio*. They were carrying plenty of trading goods, but Magellan had underestimated the length of the voyage and did not take enough food and supplies. The fleet crossed the Atlantic, briefly stopping at the Canary Islands first. Then they sailed to Brazil and down the east coast of South America.

A mutiny and a shipwreck

Magellan encountered many problems. The weather was so bad that he decided to land for the winter on the coast of what is now

The *Vittoria*

Patagonia. Some of his men rebelled because of short rations and bitter cold, and he had to suppress the mutiny by executing the leaders. Later, the Santiago was shipwrecked.

The remaining ships finally found a route to the Pacific through a narrow sea passage now called the Straits of Magellan. From the ships, the crew saw fires that the natives had lit on the shore, so they named the area Tierra del Fuego ("land of fire"). Magellan's discovery of the straits named after him proved that there was another way to the East: to the south of the Americas.

Tierra del Fuego as it might have looked from the sea.

Disease, starvation, death

By this time conditions were worse. The *San Antonio's* crew deserted, sailing away with most of the fleet's food. Twenty men on the other ships starved to death as they crossed the Pacific.

After loading up with supplies at the Marshall Islands, the fleet continued to the Philippines. Here tragedy struck. Magellan became involved in a quarrel between local chiefs. He and 40 of his men were killed.

Magellan's successor

A captain called Sebastian del Cano took command of the 115 survivors. Without enough men to crew three ships, he abandoned the *Concepción*. The other ships sailed on, reached the

The starving sailors ate rats, animal hide and mouldy biscuits.

Moluccas in November 1521, and bought the spices they set out for.

To improve the chance of getting at least some of the cargo home, the ships took two different routes back to Spain. The *Trinidad* went east towards the Spanish territory of Panama, but was seized by the Portuguese. Few of its crew survived.

A single ship returns

The *Vittoria* went westwards. It crossed Portuguese trade routes in the Indian Ocean and rounded the southern cape of Africa. It managed to avoid being captured, and reached Spain in 1522, having sailed round the globe in three years.

Francis Drake

The second great voyage of circumnavigation was led by an Englishman called Francis Drake. His voyage lasted from 1577 to 1580. At that time many people believed that Tierra del Fuego was part of a huge southern continent which they called Terra Australis. Others said the area was an island. Elizabeth I, the Queen of England, sent Drake to sail down the Straits of Magellan to find out which of these beliefs was true.

Francis Drake
(c.1545-1596)

She also secretly expected him to bring back a good haul of treasure and spices. Both of them knew, however, that this would involve piracy and could damage relations between England and Spain. The expedition set sail in five ships: the *Pelican*, the *Marigold*, the *Elizabeth*, the *Swan* and the *Christopher*.

Drake plundered gold, silver, pearls and emeralds from Spanish ships.

Like Magellan, Drake suffered many hardships on his voyage. Storms, starvation and sickness provoked mutinies among his crew, but he pressed on through the straits. He did not find Terra Australis, but he did establish that Tierra del Fuego was an island. Drake returned to England on 3 November 1580. Queen Elizabeth visited him on board ship and knighted him.

Pigafetta's chronicle

One survivor of the voyage was an Italian sailor called Antonio Pigafetta. Most of our information about the journeys of Magellan and del Cano comes from his journal, which was published two years after his return. His account gives us many fascinating details of things he saw on his travels. These include man-eating sharks in the South Atlantic and a natural electrical phenomenon known as St Elmo's Fire. He recorded the terrible conditions the men endured, the cold and storms. He described the poor food and the stinking water they had to drink. He also wrote about the different people they encountered.

Two pages from Antonio Pigafetta's account of Magellan's voyage.

This sand shark is probably the type Pigafetta saw.

St Elmo's Fire made the ship's mast look as if it was burning.

The race for the Poles

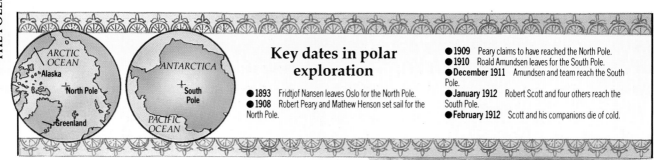

Key dates in polar exploration

- **1893** Fridtjof Nansen leaves Oslo for the North Pole.
- **1908** Robert Peary and Mathew Henson set sail for the North Pole.

- **1909** Peary claims to have reached the North Pole.
- **1910** Roald Amundsen leaves for the South Pole.
- **December 1911** Amundsen and team reach the South Pole.
- **January 1912** Robert Scott and four others reach the South Pole.
- **February 1912** Scott and his companions die of cold.

The North Pole lies in the Arctic Ocean and the South Pole in the continent of Antarctica. They are the most hostile extremities of the Earth. By the end of the 19th century much of the world had been explored but the frozen polar wastes remained largely unknown. A number of determined explorers, however, set their sights on becoming the first to reach the Poles. It was a dangerous race and many people died in the attempt to win it.

The great Norwegian

One of the greatest of the Arctic explorers was a Norwegian called Fridtjof Nansen. For his journey to the North Pole, Nansen planned to use the drift of the ice in the Arctic Ocean to carry his ship along, rather than try and force a way through it. He designed a ship called the *Fram* ("Forward") that could withstand the pressure of the ice and drift with it until the spring thaw.

Fridtjof Nansen (1861-1930)

Nansen and his crew of 13 set sail for the North Pole from Oslo in June 1893. In September the *Fram* became locked into the Arctic ice. From then on the boat had to go wherever it was carried.

The movement of the ice was terribly slow. They drifted for months, but instead of being drawn across the North Pole they began to move west. So Nansen and one other team member set off for the Pole with dogs, sledges and two kayaks (canoes). 386km (240 miles) from the Pole they turned back as the ice was beginning to break up with the onset of spring.

By pure luck they were later discovered by an English team on Franz Josef Land and travelled back with them by ship to Norway. The *Fram* arrived safely back with the others a week later.

Peary's claim

In 1886, Robert Peary of the United States Navy made the first of many expeditions to the Arctic. On this and five later journeys he travelled to Greenland, each time edging closer to the North Pole.

In July 1908 Peary and his assistant Mathew Henson set sail for their goal in the *Roosevelt*. At Etah in Greenland they recruited 50 Inuit (the local inhabitants) and gathered 250 dogs. In February 1909 the expedition moved off, with teams of Inuit setting up bases, and Peary, Henson and the dogs following.

Peary and his team struggling over the ice and snow.

Gradually each team was sent back until only Peary, Henson and four Inuit, five sledges and 40 dogs were left. With the North Pole 214km (133 miles) away, this group set off on the final leg of the journey. It battled through blizzards, over ice ridges and perilous stretches of water.

On 5 April 1909 Peary recorded in his diary "The Pole at last!" believing he had finally reached his goal. However, experts raised doubts about whether he could have covered the distance so quickly. Despite recent attempts to prove that Peary did indeed reach the North Pole, the evidence remains questionable.

Seals at the North Pole.

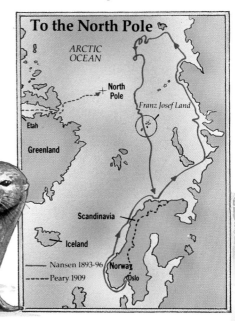

To the North Pole

ARCTIC OCEAN
North Pole
Franz Josef Land
Etah
Greenland
Scandinavia
Iceland
Norway
Oslo

— Nansen 1893-96
- - - Peary 1909

The Fram in the ice.

The triumph

In August 1910 a Norwegian explorer called Roald Amundsen set sail from Norway with eight others in Nansen's boat, the *Fram*. He originally planned to head for the North Pole, but hearing that Peary had reached it he decided to aim for the South Pole instead.

He was now entering a race against a British team that had already left for the South Pole led by Robert Scott, a captain in the Royal Navy. He sent Scott a telegram warning him that he now had competition. Although he had to contend with the same appalling conditions as Scott did, Amundsen's expedition was much more efficient. It had fewer men so it could travel faster. Amundsen's men also wore lighter but warmer Inuit-style clothing.

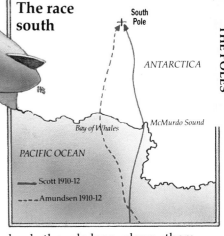

The *Norge*

They arrived at the Bay of Whales in January 1911 and set up camp at a point on the coast 97km (60 miles) nearer the Pole than Scott's camp. They struggled through blizzards with their dog sledges, and reached the South Pole on 14 December 1911. After remaining there for three days they headed back to their base camp, which they reached on 25 January 1912.

Amundsen and his team were able to travel more quickly because they were using light, fast husky dogs rather than heavy horses.

Roald Amundsen dressed in his special Antarctic clothing.

Later, in 1926, Amundsen became the first person to reach both Poles. He was a passenger on the airship *Norge* when it flew over the North Pole.

The tragedy

Two months before Amundsen, on 1 June 1910, Robert Scott set sail for the South Pole in the *Terra Nova* with a team of 53 men. The expedition was carefully planned and lavishly equipped, but the choice of equipment was to lead to a tragic ending: scientific machinery was to slow the team down; their clothes would prove inadequate against the bitter cold; horses were brought along to pull the sledges, rather than the lighter and faster husky dogs used by Amundsen, which were better suited to the terrible environment.

After a slow journey through the pack ice, their ship finally reached McMurdo Sound where they established their base camp.

Adélie penguins at the South Pole.

In January 1912 Scott set out on the last stretch with Lawrence Oates, Edward Wilson, Edgar Evans and Henry "Birdie" Bowers. The progress of this smaller team became slower and slower and eventually the horses had to be shot because they got stuck in the snow. The men now had to haul the sledges along themselves. On 18 January the exhausted team finally reached the South Pole, only to find the Norwegian flag flying there already.

Scott's team at the South Pole.

Disheartened, the men began the return journey to McMurdo Sound. But they were exhausted and frostbitten. With 692km (430 miles) to go, Evans collapsed and died. They eventually reached one of their depots, to find that the stored fuel oil had leaked away. There was now nothing to burn to keep them warm.

One night Oates, believing that he was holding up the team because he was so ill, walked out of their tent into the blizzard and was never seen again. His sacrifice was in vain for within two weeks the three remaining members were also dead. Their frozen bodies were found by a search party eight months later.

The race south

ANTARCTICA

South Pole

PACIFIC OCEAN

Bay of Whales

McMurdo Sound

—— Scott 1910-12

- - - Amundsen 1910-12

The roof of the world

Key dates in mountain conquest

This chart lists the world's ten highest mountains, in order of the date each one was first climbed. Each entry gives: the mountain's name and location; its height; the year of the expedition; the name and nationality of the expedition leader. The location of each peak is shown on the maps above.

1. Chimborazo, Ecuador; 6,267m (20,561ft). 1880, Whymper of Britain.
2. Aconcagua, Argentina; 6,960m (22,834ft). 1897, Zurbriggen of Switzerland.
3. Huascaran, Peru; 6,768m (22,205ft). 1908, Annie Peck of USA.
4. Lenin Peak, USSR; 7,134m (23,405ft). 1928, Soviet-German team led by Rickmers.
5. Communism Peak, USSR; 7,495m (24,590ft). 1933, Abalakov of USSR.
6. Annapurna, Nepal; 8,078m (26,504ft). 1950, French party led by Herzog.
7. Mount Everest, Nepal/Tibet; 8,848m (29,028ft). 1953, British party led by Hunt.
8. Nanga Parbat, Pakistan; 8,126m (26,660ft). 1953, Austro-German party led by Herrligkoffer.
9. K2 (Mount Godwin Austen), India; 8,611m (28,251ft). 1954, Desio, Lacedelli and Campagnoni of Italy.
10. Kangchenjunga, Nepal/Sikkim; 8,598m (28,208ft). 1955, Brown, Band, Streather and Hardie of Britain.

S ince the very earliest times mountains have been regarded with awe and wonder. The peaks and summits were once believed to be the homes of gods and the cracks and crevasses the dwelling places of imps and demons. Howling winds echoed the eerie calls of the spirits and crashing avalanches warned people to keep away. Mountains such as Popocatepetl in Mexico and Mount Olympus in Greece have been worshipped as sacred places.

The earliest known climbs

For thousands of years people have feared mountains. It is only in the last 200 years that they have begun climbing them. Only a few genuine climbs are known to have been made in ancient times. In 350BC King Philip of Macedon climbed a mountain in the Balkans, and in about AD120 the Roman emperor Hadrian climbed Mount Etna to watch the sunrise.

Emperor Hadrian (AD76-138)

At the start of the Renaissance in Europe in the 14th century, people began to take a more scientific approach to their surroundings. Mountains were looked at in a different way, as places of interest rather than fear. The first known climb in the Alps took place on 26 April 1336 when the Italian poet Petrarch climbed Mont Ventoux (1,909m/6,263ft).

Petrarch (1304-74)

At first climbing was dangerous, for proper equipment was virtually non-existent. People simply wore warmer versions of everyday clothes. It was not possible to climb the highest peaks until suitable oxygen apparatus became available, because the higher a climber gets, the less oxygen there is in the air. This makes breathing very difficult. But as the years passed and experience increased, techniques were perfected and the equipment was improved. Mountaineers became able to climb higher and higher.

Modern mountaineering

Mountaineering as we know it today was developed by a Swiss scientist called Horace de Saussure. He was fascinated by the plants and rocks of the Alps, and in 1773 he made the first of many trips to the region. Gradually he became obsessed with the idea of climbing Mont Blanc, Europe's highest mountain at 4,807m (15,771ft), and offered a reward to the first person who could find a route to the top.

A plant from the Alps, Pygmy Ranunculus.

Early climbers caught in
an avalanche.

Many attempts were made but
they were repeatedly driven back
by avalanches, steep walls of ice
and deep crevasses. One local
doctor called Michel Paccard tried
a number of times. On 7 August
1786 he set out once more, with a
deer-hunter called Jacques Balmat
acting as his guide. They reached
the top of the lower slopes and
spent the night there. The following morning they continued their
hazardous journey up slippery

Michel Paccard
Jacques Balmat

peaks, over jagged edges and
wading through waist-deep snow
drifts; they finally reached the
summit the same evening.

The following year, Saussure
himself fulfilled
his ambition by
climbing to the
top of Mont
Blanc. 18 others
went with him
and they opened
bottles of wine
at the top to
celebrate the achievement.

Saussure's climbing
shoes

A climbing
expedition in
the late 18th
century. Their
clothing was
unsuitable for
the terrain and
cold.

The highest of all

No other mountain chain com-
pares with the Himalayas. It
contains the highest peaks in the
world and stretches for
thousands of miles across the
length of northern India, and
covers much of Sikkim, Nepal,
Bhutan and southern Tibet.

In 1953 a British expedition led
by John Hunt set off to climb
Mount Everest, named after a
British surveyor-general of India
called Sir George Everest, but
known locally as Chomolungma
("Mother Goddess of the
World"). It is the world's highest
mountain at 8,848m (29,028ft).

The climb to the final summit
was made by the New Zealander
Edmund Hillary and Tenzing
Norgay of Nepal. On 29 May the
weather cleared and they set off at
6:30am. On the way up their
oxygen cylinders froze and there
was a danger that they would not
have enough oxygen. The going
was extremely slow and they
could only cover 0.3m (1ft) a
minute.

The final obstacle was a sheer
pinnacle of rock, 12m (40ft) high
and covered with ice. Their route
seemed to be blocked, but Hillary
eventually found a way over it
and edged himself up to the top.
He then threw down a rope to
Tenzing and at 11:30am on 29 May
1953, the two mountaineers stood
alone at the top of the world.

The highest mountain in the
world may have been conquered
but many challenges still remain,
including hundreds more peaks
in the Himalayas
and in other parts
of the world. The
urge to climb is
as great as ever,
spurred by the
challenge, the
thrill and glory
of conquest and
a deep respect for
the mountains
themselves.

Tenzing at
the top of
Everest

Hidden kingdoms of the Himalayas

After China broke off contacts
with the West (see page 111) it
once more became a land of
mystery. But if China was
remote, Tibet and Nepal, hidden
away in the mountain fortress
of the Himalayas, were even
more inaccessible. In 1661 two
Jesuit missionaries called John
Grueber and Albert d'Orville
became the first Europeans to
reach Lhasa, the capital of Tibet.
In 1811 a British official called
Thomas Manning travelled in
disguise to Lhasa, where he was
received by the seven-year-old
Dalai Lama (religious ruler) in the
Potala Palace.

Potala Palace,
Lhasa

In the 1860s a French priest called
Père (Father) David travelled extensively in Asia and China. He
brought three animals to the
attention of naturalists in the
West: an unusual deer later
named after him, a monkey
named Roxellana's snub-nosed
langur, and the giant panda.

Giant panda

Snub-nosed
langur

Père David's
deer

Exploring the oceans

Key dates in undersea exploration

- **1690** Edmund Halley invents a method of pumping air down to diving machines.
- **1872** HMS *Challenger* starts its journey of exploration.
- **1930** William Beebe designs the bathysphere.
- **1943** Jacques Cousteau and Emile Gagnan design the aqualung.
- **1948** Auguste Piccard designs the bathyscape, *FNRS3*.
- **1950** *Challenger II* starts its journey of exploration.
- **1960** Jacques Piccard descends in the *Trieste*.

Nearly three quarters of the surface of the Earth is covered by water. For centuries people have been diving for precious underwater products such as pearls and natural sponges. But until the 20th century very little exploration had been made beneath the seas. This was because breathing apparatus was not available. Without it, divers could only stay below the water for as long as they could hold their breath.

Early diving devices

It is thought that in the 4th century BC Alexander the Great was lowered to the sea bed in a glass container to make observations. But he would probably have had to remain in shallow water because of the lack of air. It was not until 1690 that a method of pumping air down a pipe was invented, by an Englishman called Edmund Halley.

Halley's diving bell.

Going deeper

The deeper a diver goes in the sea, the greater the pressure of the water. In 1930 a North American called William Beebe designed the bathysphere, a spherical diving machine. Water exerts equal force all around a sphere, so it is able to withstand pressure at deep levels.

A modern bathysphere

In 1948 a Swiss scientist called Auguste Piccard designed a diving ship called a bathyscape. Known as *FNRS3*, it could dive and surface without having to be lowered and pulled up by a ship. On its first dive it reached a depth of 3,140m (10,300ft).

In 1960 Auguste's son Jacques Piccard descended nearly 11.25km (7 miles) in a craft called the *Trieste*. He reached the bottom

The *Trieste*

of the Mariana Trench in the Pacific Ocean. The journey down to the sea-floor took five hours.

Extra lungs

In 1943 two Frenchmen, Jacques Cousteau and Emile Gagnan, designed the first aqualung.

The aqualung consists of air cylinders containing compressed air and a mouth-piece. A "demand regulator" feeds the diver with exactly the amount of compressed air needed.

This invention opened a new period of underwater exploration and with its help many exciting discoveries have been made. Divers became able to descend to depths of 60m (200ft) without having to wear heavy protective suits and air cables. They were free to swim around and study underwater archaeology. They could photograph marine life, and also search for deposits of oil, tin, diamonds and other minerals.

Jacques Cousteau (1910-)

A diver using an underwater "scooter".

The *Challenger* expeditions

In December 1872 a British ship, HMS *Challenger*, set sail under the command of George Nares. There were many leading scientists on board, led by a Scottish naturalist called Charles Thomson, and many cabins were converted into laboratories. It covered a distance of nearly 112,650km (70,000 miles) across the Atlantic, Indian and Pacific oceans. Measurements down to the sea bed were made to determine its contours, and currents and weather conditions were measured. The ship returned to England in May 1876, full of facts and figures and 4,417 species of fish and underwater plants.

In 1950 the *Challenger II* set out across the Atlantic, Indian and Pacific oceans and the Mediterranean Sea. The latest echo-sounding equipment was used to make accurate recordings of the ocean floors.

HMS *Challenger* setting out on its journey of three-and-a-half years.

Deep-sea red prawn

These types of fish are found at very deep levels.

Angler fish

Sabre-toothed viper fish

Beyond the Earth

Key dates in space exploration

- **1903** Konstantin Tsiolkovsky publishes theory of rocket propulsion, recommending the use of liquid fuels.
- **1926** Robert Goddard launches first liquid-fuel rocket.
- **1957** *Sputnik I* launched by the USSR.
- **1961** Yuri Gagarin becomes first person in space.
- **1969** Neil Armstrong and Edwin Aldrin become first people
- on the Moon.
- **1971** *Salyut I*, the first space station, launched.
- **1977** Space Shuttle *Enterprise* makes first test flight.

Since the very earliest times the sun, the moon and the stars have always been objects of wonder and worship. Comets were believed to be warnings from the gods. Astronomy, the observation of the stars, is one of the oldest sciences. The ancient Egyptians were observing the planets thousands of years ago, and some people believe that Stonehenge in England, built in about 2500BC, was used as a giant observatory.

Early rockets

In order to travel in space, a rocket has to be powerful enough to break out of the pull of the Earth's gravity. In the 19th century a Russian scientist called Konstantin Tsiolkovsky made many experiments using liquid fuel. The first liquid-fuel rocket was launched in 1926 by an American called Robert Goddard. The flight lasted only 2.5 seconds but the break away from the Earth's atmosphere had been made. In October 1957 the Russians launched the first satellite into space, called *Sputnik I*.

Gird X, an early Russian rocket.

The first person in space

On 12 April 1961 a Russian astronaut called Yuri Gagarin became the first person to travel in space. His space-ship, *Vostok I*,

Vostok I

Yuri Gagarin (1934-68)

travelled at a speed of 8km (5 miles) a second, 160km (100 miles) above the Earth. Through his porthole, Gagarin

Telescopes

The first telescopes were invented in the 17th century. They enabled people to look at the moon and stars in more detail. The Italian scientist Galileo Galilei designed a stronger telescope. He was using it in 1610 when he discovered Jupiter's satellites, sunspots and mountains and craters on the Moon. Today, radio telescopes are used to detect radio waves coming from stars millions of light years away in space. These machines have discovered distant galaxies and strange objects like pulsating stars and black holes.

Galileo's telescope

The space telescope is designed to detect objects seven times further away than anything which can be seen from earth.

could see the world's surface laid out below him. *Vostok I* sped once round the Earth and after 108 minutes Gagarin returned, the cabin section of the spacecraft floating down on a parachute.

Exploring the moon

Tragically, Gagarin was killed in an air crash in 1968, before he could achieve his aim of being the first person on the moon. But his pioneering flights paved the way for Neil Armstrong and Edwin "Buzz" Aldrin of the United States to step out of their *Apollo* lunar module on to the surface of the moon on 21 July 1969. They took samples of rock and set up scientific equipment before returning to Earth.

One more manned lunar landing took place in 1969, two in 1971 and two in 1972. In 1970 and 1973 the Russians sent two unmanned vehicles called *lunokhods* to explore the surface of the moon.

The Apollo 11 lunar module on the moon.

Space stations and probes

During the 1970s giant space stations, such as the Russian *Salyut* and American *Skylab*, were launched into space. They were laboratories orbiting round Earth and manned by crews who stayed aboard for a number of weeks on end without returning to Earth. One of the main purposes of these stations was to study the effect on people of long periods in space.

The US Skylab space station

Today space probes are sent to the more distant planets in the solar system. They carry cameras to take photographs and equipment to measure the temperature, magnetic fields and radiation of the planets. *Mariner 10* took about 4,300 close-up photographs of Mercury during three visits from 1974.

In the future

By the early 21st century people may be living in bases on the Moon. But we have only just started the exploration of space. So far only two other of our neighbouring planets in the solar system have been visited by unmanned spacecraft.

Key dates in world exploration

Dates BC

c.1492BC   Queen Hatshepsut of Egypt sends out a trading expedition to the land of Punt.

c.600BC   Pharaoh Necho II of Egypt sends out an expedition to explore the coasts of Africa.

c.450BC   Herodotus draws a map of the world.

327-23BC   Alexander the Great and his armies expand east from Persia.

c.300BC   Building of the Great Wall of China begins.

138BC   Chang Ch'ien leaves on a journey to Yuechi, China .

126BC   Chang Ch'ien returns to China.

c.105BC   Opening of the Silk Road, from China to the West.

Dates AD

AD150   Ptolemy draws his map of the world.

245   Chinese ambassadors travel to Funan (Cambodia).

304   Hsiung-nu (Huns) invade China.

629   Hsuan-tsang leaves China for India.

632   Death of the Prophet Mohammed, founder of Islam.

645   Hsuan-tsang returns to China.

c.860   Chinese reach Somali, Africa.
Vikings settle in Iceland.

c.900   Gunnbjorn sights Greenland.

c.986   Viking colony established on Greenland by Eric the Red. Bjarni Herjolfsson sights North America.

c.1000   Leif Ericsson lands on east coast of North America.

1002   Thorwald, brother of Leif, establishes a colony on the east coast.

1060   Chinese reach Malindi, Africa.

1162   Birth of Genghis Khan, later ruler of Mongols.

1187   Chinese reach Zanzibar and Madagascar, off the east coast of Africa.

1215   Genghis Khan captures Chung-tu (Beijing), capital of Chinese Chin empire, and establishes Mongol rule.

1240   Mongols capture Kiev, Russia.

1246   Giovanni da Pian del Carpini reaches the Mongol capital at Karakorum.

1253   William of Rubrouck sent to Karakorum.

1260   Kublai Khan proclaimed Great Khan.

1265   Niccolo and Maffeo Polo first reach the Chinese capital at Khanbalik (Beijing).

1269   Niccolo and Maffeo Polo return to Venice.

1271   Niccolo, Maffeo and Marco Polo leave Venice for China.

1292   The Polos leave China for home.

1325   Ibn Battuta travels to Arabia.

1368   The Mongols are driven out of China.

1394   Birth of Prince Henry of Portugal "the Navigator".

1405-33   Voyages of Cheng Ho in the Indian Ocean.

c.1420   The Chinese are believed to have rounded the Cape of Good Hope, Africa.

1434   Gil Eannes rounds Cape Bojador, West Africa.

1487   Bartolemeu Dias rounds the Cape of Good Hope. Pedro da Covilhã and Alfonso de Paiva set out from Portugal on their journeys East.

1492   Pedro da Covilhã visits Mecca.
Christopher Columbus leaves Spain for the East. He reaches and explores the "Indies".

1497   Vasco da Gama sails round Africa on his way to India.

1498   Da Gama visits Calicut.

1499   Da Gama returns to Portugal.

1503   Ludovico di Varthema visits Mecca.

1507   America is named after Amerigo Vespucci.

1511   Diego Velazquez and Hernándo Cortés sieze Cuba for Spain.

1519   Cortés sails to Mexico. Ferdinand Magellan begins his journey round the world.

1521   Siege of Tenochtitlán and fall of the Aztec empire.

1534   Jacques Cartier leaves France for North America.

1535   Cartier founds Montreal.

1569   Andres de Urdaneta crosses the Pacific.

1576   Martin Frobisher leaves England on his first voyage to find the Northwest Passage.

1577   Francis Drake sets sail round the world.

1585-87   John Davis makes three voyages to find the Northwest Passage.

1597   The Portuguese establish a trading station at Macao, China.

1606   Pedro Fernandes de Quiros reaches the New Hebrides Islands.
Willem Jantszoon becomes the first European to reach the shores of Australia.

1608   Samuel de Champlain founds Quebec.

1609   Henry Hudson sails along east coast of North America, in search of Northwest Passage.

1610   Hudson makes a second journey.

1642   Abel Tasman sights Van Diemen's Land (Tasmania). Tasman discovers the west coast of New Zealand.

1678-82   Robert de La Salle travels across North America.

1690   Edmund Halley invents a method of pumping air down to diving machines.

1700 William Dampier, an English pirate, discovers the north coast of New Guinea.

1721 Jakob Roggeveen discovers Easter Island.

1769 James Cook sails in the *Endeavour* to Tahiti and makes observations of Venus. Sails on to New Zealand.

1770 Cook lands in Botany Bay, Australia.

1772 Cook's second voyage leaves Plymouth.

1774 Cook crosses the Antarctic Circle.

1776 Cook sets sail on his third voyage, in search of the Northwest Passage.

1778 Cook sails to the Society Islands (Hawaiian Islands) where he is killed.

1785 François de la Pérouse leaves France in search of the Solomon Islands.

1788 Pérouse lands on the coast of New South Wales, Australia.

1795 Mungo Park sails to Africa.
Mathew Flinders and George Bass make the first inland expedition from the east coast of Australia.

1799 Alexander von Humboldt and Aimé Bonpland leave Europe for South America.

1801-2 Flinders carries out a survey of nearly all the coast of Australia.

1804 Meriwether Lewis and William Clark lead expedition across the United States.

1805 Park leaves on his second trip to Africa.

1810 Johann Burckhardt visits Palmyra, Syria.

1812 Burckhardt visits Petra, Palestine.

1813 Burckhardt rediscovers temple of Abu Simbel, Egypt.

1814 Burckhardt visits Mecca.

1817 Burckhardt dies in Cairo.

1824 René Caillié sets out from France for Timbuktu.

1828 Charles Sturt and Hamilton Hume cross the Blue Mountains, Australia.

1831 Charles Darwin leaves for South America in the *Beagle*.

1849 California Gold Rush.

1851 David Livingstone, his family and Cotton Oswell cross the Kalahari Desert, southern Africa.

1852-56 Livingstone becomes the first European to walk right across Africa.

1853 Richard Burton makes a pilgrimage to Mecca.

1856 Burton and John Speke leave England in search of the source of the Nile.

1858 Livingstone sets out to explore the Zambezi River.

1860 Robert Burke leads expedition from Melbourne to cross Australia from south to north.
Speke and James Grant leave on a second journey to Africa.

1861 John Stuart leads second, rival expedition to cross Australia, north from Adelaide. Death of Charles Gray, William Wills and Burke.

1862 Stuart returns south, having completed crossing of Australia.

1871 Henry Morton Stanley and Livingstone meet at the village of Ujiji, Africa.

1872 Livingstone starts out on his final African jouney, round the southern shores of Lake Tanganyika.
HMS *Challenger* starts out on its journey of exploration in the Atlantic, Pacific and Indian oceans.

1874 Stanley returns to Africa to map lakes Victoria and Tanganyika.

1875 Charles Doughty reaches Palestine.

1876 Doughty explores in the Nefud, northern Arabia.

1876-77 Stanley sails down the Lualaba and Congo rivers to the Atlantic.

1880 Edward Whymper climbs Mt Chimborazo, Ecuador.

1887 Stanley leads expedition to Sudan to find Emin Pasha.

1893 Fridtjof Nansen sets sail from Oslo for the North Pole.

1897 Mathias Zurbriggen climbs Mt Aconcagua, Argentina.

1908 Robert Peary and Matthew Henson sail for the North Pole. Annie Peck climbs to the top of Mt Huascaran, Peru.

1909 Peary claims to have reached the North Pole.

1910 Roald Amundsen and team leaves for the South Pole.

1911 Amundsen reaches the South Pole.

1912 Robert Scott and his team reach the South Pole. Scott and team die of cold.

1916 T.E. Lawrence (Lawrence of Arabia) explores the Hejaz region in northern Arabia.

1925 Percy Fawcett disappears in the Brazilian jungle.

1926 Robert Goddard launches the first liquid-fuel rocket.

1930 William Beebe designs the bathysphere.

1930-31 Bertram Thomas crosses the Empty Quarter of Arabia.

1932 Harry Philby crosses the Empty Quarter.

1943 Jacques Cousteau and Emile Gagnan design the first aqualung.

1948 Auguste Piccard designs the bathyscape, *FNRS3*.

1950 *Challenger II* starts its journey of exploration.

1953 Edmund Hillary and Tenzing Norgay climb Mt Everest, Nepal/Tibet.

1957 *Sputnik I* launched by the USSR.

1960 Jacques Piccard descends to the bottom of the Pacific Ocean in the *Trieste*.

1961 Yuri Gagarin becomes the first person in space.

1969 Armstrong and Aldrin land on the Moon.

The *Explorers* quiz

The answers to all the following questions can be found between pages 99 and 141 of this book. You will also find the answers upside down at the bottom of this page.

AFRICA

1. How did Ibn Battuta protect himself from bandits in the Sahara Desert?
2. What was the name of the Christian priest-king for whom many explorers searched, but never found?
3. What was the prize offered by the Geographical Society of Paris to the first Frenchman to reach Timbuktu and return?
4. What happened to Livingstone's heart on his death?
5. Which lake was proved to be the source of the Nile?
6. Can you identify these countries by their shapes?

a)   b)   c)

ASIA

7. What was the Silk Road?
8. How many elephants were there in the procession of King Harsha which was joined by Hsuan-tsang?
9. What causes scurvy, the disease which killed many early sailors?
10. How did Barents and his men exercise during the Arctic winter?
11. Who discovered the Northeast Passage?

THE AMERICAS

12. Why did Eric the Red choose the name Greenland for the country that he had discovered?
13. Who was the first European to set foot on American soil?
14. In the 15th century, what shape did most people believe the Earth to be?
15. Match the names of Columbus's three ships with the silhouettes below.

a)   b)   c)

16. Columbus reached America by mistake. Where was he originally heading on his journey?
17. After whom was America named?
18. How did the Aztec emperor Montezuma die?
19. What is another name for the iron pyrites rocks discovered by Frobisher?
20. What was the name given to the team of men led by Lewis and Clark?
21. What was the name given by Percy Fawcett to the lost city he hoped to find in the Brazilian jungle?

AUSTRALIA

22. What happened the day before a French expedition arrived in Australia to claim the country for France?
23. Where did Brahe leave his message for Burke and Wills?

ARABIA

24. The Romans called Arabia "Arabia Felix". What does it mean?
25. How did Richard Burton disguise himself on his journey from Suez to Mecca?

CIRCUMNAVIGATION

26. Name the five ships led by Magellan in his circumnavigation attempt.
27. What is the name of the natural electrical phenomenon recorded by Pigafetta?

THE POLES

28. What was the name of the ship used by both Nansen and Amundsen during their explorations?
29. Which member of Scott's team sacrificed his life because he believed he was holding up the expedition's progress?

MOUNTAINS

30. Can you identify these three explorers?

a)   b)   c)

31. What is the name of Europe's highest mountain?
32. Who were the first people to reach the summit of Mount Everest?

UNDER THE SEA

33. What is the name of the spherical diving machine designed by William Beebe?
34. Who designed the first aqualung?

SPACE

35. What was the name of the first satellite to be launched into space?
36. Who was the first person to travel in space?

Answers

1. He joined a caravan
2. Prester John
3. 10,000 francs
4. It was cut out and buried.
5. Lake Victoria
6. a) Egypt; b) Morocco; c) Mali
7. A trade route between China and the West
8. 20,000
9. A deficiency of Vitamin C.
10. They played golf on the ice.
11. Vitus Bering
12. He wanted other Vikings to follow him there and settle.
13. Leif Ericsson
14. Flat
15. a) *Niña*; b) *Santa Maria*; c) *Pinta*
16. The Far East
17. Amerigo Vespucci
18. He was stoned to death.
19. Fool's gold
20. The Corps of Discovery
21. Z
22. The British established a colony there.
23. In a bottle buried in the ground.
24. Happy Arabia
25. As an Afghan doctor
26. *Trinidad, Vittoria, Santiago, Concepción* and *San Antonio*
27. St. Elmo's fire
28. *Fram*
29. Lawrence Oates
30. a) Emperor Hadrian; b) Petrarch; c) Michel Paccard
31. Mount Blanc
32. Edmund Hillary and Tenzing Norgay
33. Bathysphere
34. Jacques Cousteau and Emile Gagnan
35. *Sputnik I*
36. Yuri Gagarin

Index

146

The publishers are grateful to the following organizations for permission to reproduce their material:
Inventors
CNRI/Science Photo library, p.39
Duckworth, p.44
Fox Talbot Museum, p.1, p.30
The Hulton Deutsch Collection, p.15, p.16, p.19, p.23, p.25, p.32, p.41
Library of Congress, front cover, p.31
Manchester University, p.43
The Mansell Collection, p.12
National Museum of Photography, Film and Television, p.31
Royal Geographical Society, p.7
Syndication International, p.17
Ullstein, Front Cover

Scientists and *Explorers*
Science Museum Library, London
The Royal Society
The Ann Ronan Picture Library
Popperfoto

Mary Evans Picture Library
Bibliothèque Nationale, Paris
Dover Publications Inc.
The Mansell Collection (London)

Elevator compartment illustration, p. 24 by Peter Dennis
The three pictures at the bottom of p.66 are based on drawings by Leonardo da Vinci in the Royal Collection, Windsor.

The *Inventors* picture quiz

This list reveals what the picture or cartoon beside the title of every chapter shows.

p. 4 A primitive irrigation machine from Egypt called a shadoof
p. 6 An Oriental clockmaker
p. 8 Galileo's method of measuring the height of mountains on the moon
p. 10 An idea for a steam turbine
p. 12 A steam carriage
p. 14 A railway policeman of 1844
p. 16 Alexander the Great in a glass barrel
p. 18 Icarus wearing wings
p. 20 A vacuum cleaner operated using a foot pedal
p. 22 Carlson's patent drawing for his photocopier
p. 24 A toilet designed by John Harington in 1596
p. 26 A woodcut of a printer preparing type
p. 28 Bell's first telephone
p. 30 A 15th century box camera obscura
p. 32 A portable radio set
p. 34 An illustration showing an Edison phonograph recording a piano (1880)
p. 36 An early fire fighters' tower
p. 38 A clockwork dental drill designed by Harrington
p. 40 A hand gun of c.1400
p. 42 A machine used to calculate the motion of the Sun and stars
p. 44 A design for an aerial cycling machine of 1888

First published in 1994 by Usborne Publishing Ltd, Usborne House, 83-85 Saffron Hill London EC1N 8RT, England.

First published in America in August 1994
Printed in Spain